W9-BDR-530

The Nuarn Rift

Book Three

F.T. Barbini

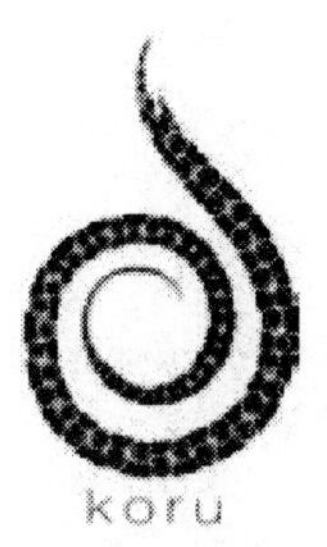

Second Edition
Second Printing, 2014
ISBN-10: 1940992125
ISBN-13: 978-1-940992-12-9

Koru Books is an imprint of Oloris Publishing.

Contact Oloris Publishing at info@olorispublishing.com. For more information please see: www.olorispublishing.com.

Acknowledgments

To Catriona Macrae, for her Spanish expertise.

And to Robert S. Malan. Third time lucky.

Contents

1. A BOLT FROM THE BLUE 1
2. 3 MIZKI APPRENTICE 12
3. THE AMBASSADOR 35
4. LONG LOST FRIENDS 61
5. THE CHALLENGE 76
6. ZED TOON 98
7. FRACTURES 121
8. MID-WINTER BLUES 138
9. GEA ONE 154
10. PLAYING WITH FIRE 172
11. THE HERON 196
12. REALITY BITES 218
13. DECEPTION 231
14. NO MAN'S LAND 247

To Jack Johnstone

CHAPTER 1

A BOLT FROM THE BLUE

Captain JD Kelly was leaning against a large porthole, on the observation deck. His head rested on the cold, pressurised glass panel, arms crossed in front of him. He was enjoying a moment of peace, a rare occurrence in what was the otherwise busy environment of his spaceship. With the exception of the six years developing his mind-skills in Tijara School, Kelly had grown up on the Zed space station Terra I, before he had been appointed to the ship Ahura Mazda, working his way through the ranks until he became its captain. He was used to airlocks, holodecks, nullifying bins and resequencers and he knew the gentle noise of his ship's engine—the way it purred under his feet while he walked the corridors. His whole life had been spent in space, without even a single day on Earth.

Every so often he would fancifully plan a visit to one of the old continents, telling himself that the next leave would be different and he would actually go. Perhaps he would even take Lieutenant Elian Flywheel with him, if she would consider going anywhere with her superior officer. He didn't believe he was the worst man of the lot, but he feared a beautiful, intelligent woman like Elian would never settle for a rough case like him. They were close in age, but for some reason 38 looked more like 48 on him. Maybe it was the scar that ran from his left jaw up to his cheekbone which made him doubt his chances with her; maybe it was the sheer dread of being refused, but after 12 years he had still not found the guts to ask her out.

The life of a captain sure was tough, and a lonely one at that. There was always something to do, a new location to explore or, as had been the case for the last three months, someone to train. On the first of July 2857, a 2 Mizki Junior from the Tijara School had been sent to his ship, the Ahura Mazda, for his Summer Camp. Kelly had been sceptical at first, since no Mizki had ever been allowed on board his ship for training before, but the request had come from the Grand Master of Tijara himself, Carlos Freja, and no one could refuse Freja, especially not Kelly. Fortunately for him though, the boy in question was more than just your average 14 year old; in fact, Julius McCoy was anything but.

Since joining the Zed Academy two years before, the boy had not only proven himself as a natural White Child—someone with incredibly strong mind-skills—but he had also played a vital part in defeating the Arneshians, sworn enemies of all Earthlings. After foiling their queen's plans twice, Julius McCoy, who dreamt one day of becoming a Starfleet commander, had just spent three intense months on board, learning with the same passion and eagerness that Kelly himself had demonstrated at that age. Kelly was convinced that the boy would go far; the talent was plain to see—it had only to be harnessed. Now, Summer Camp was drawing to a close and tomorrow Julius would return to Tijara to begin his third year at the school, as a 3 Mizki Apprentice, with a whole world of opportunities at his feet.

When he heard the door slide open, Kelly looked up. 'Over here, McCoy.'

Julius bowed his head respectfully and moved over to the porthole. 'Captain,' he said.

'Did you pack your bag?' asked Kelly.

'I'll do it later. I don't have much,' he answered.

Kelly watched as Julius leaned against the glass panel, staring intently at the Moon, with its orbiting docking station and the surrounding protective bubble that was the Zed Lunar Perimeter. He thought that the boy had grown a bit over the summer—a good two inches perhaps. His messy black hair hung down in jagged, loose strands, framing his bright blue eyes. He switched his gaze back to the Moon outside the window. 'They've started,' he said, pointing at Zed.

Julius looked toward the lunar perimeter, where several wide, flat ships were moving into place in a tight formation around the upper portion of the shield. 'What's going on?' he asked.

'Zed is getting a revamp, and about time too.'

'Why?'

'The defence systems needed some updating, as well as some serious repairs, especially after the last attack.'

'That's good, right?'

'Sure, but it should have been done a few years ago.'

'Why wasn't it? What happened?'

'It's more like, what didn't happen,' Kelly answered. 'Queen Salgoria and the Arneshians lulled us into a false sense of security. They'd been quiet for so long that we stupidly believed we were at peace. Until the last couple of years, of course, when they caught us with our trousers down. We've been at red alert ever since.'

Julius nodded his head, knowingly.

'They began relocating Sield School back in June and they're almost done. Tuala is next,' said Kelly.

'Are they moving us?' asked Julius, pressing his hands against the glass.

'Yes, they are. But Tijara won't go till January.'

'Where will they take us?'

'See that round space station in the lunar orbit? That's where. It'll just be for a few weeks though.'

'A bit like a school trip, then.'

'Yeah, something like that,' said Kelly. Then he shook his head. 'Heck kid, you picked the wrong time to join the Academy. I don't like it where we are with the Arneshians, this calm before the storm. I can feel it brewing. Salgoria is planning something big and I don't like it one bit.'

'I'd rather be here than stuck on Earth worrying about them. I don't know how my parents can stand it.'

'Simple. They don't really know.'

'What do you mean, sir?'

'They only get the news that the Curia deems suitable to release. Telling the Earth leader the whole story about kidnappings and genetic experiments isn't really something that ranks as a priority for Colonial Affairs.'

'But folks have the right to know.'

'For what purpose, McCoy? Why worry, when there's nothing you can do about it? If Zed is defeated, Earth would be lost in an instant. We are the defence system. Let us worry for everyone else.'

'It still seems unfair.'

'It's one of those diplomatic decisions. I'm not too good at that stuff. I'm a man of action; I leave politics to the politicians.'

'My friend, Skye Miller, has gone to the Curia, for his Summer Camp.'

'Has he then? I remember him, of course. Miller didn't strike me as the desk type.'

'I guess he was curious. But he probably also did it for his star-rep. He says girls are attracted to power.'

Kelly burst out laughing. 'He's got that right!'

'Not all girls, surely?' said Julius, sounding slightly defensive. 'Morgana isn't like that at all.'

'Who, your friend the pilot?'

Julius nodded.

Kelly thought briefly of Elian, and how easygoing she was with everyone, no matter what rank they held. 'Maybe you're right. But if that's the case, she's a rare one. I would keep her close if I were you, and judging by the way she hugged you last year, after we rescued her from Angra Mainyu, she wants you to keep her close too, if you know what I'm saying!'

'Naaaah! She doesn't ... I don't ... I mean, she's like a sister, or ...'

The captain laughed again and patted Julius on the back, hard enough to make him bump against the glass. 'Blessed youth!' he said. 'All right, all right. So where's the fourth musketeer, anyway? The big-mouthed Irish kid.'

'Faith spent the Summer Camp at Pit-Stop Pete's, as always, assembling engines. He'd stay there the whole year if they let him.'

'A techie, huh?'

'He's great. He says he'll build me the best spaceship ever one day.'

'No one can beat the Ahura Mazda, kid.'

'I'm prepared to bet on it, Captain.'

'You're on. But I'll believe it when I see it, and by then I'll probably be long dead.'

Julius grinned at him and they both looked out at Zed again as the ship drew closer to it. Kelly returned to his thoughts. It had been a good summer. He would be sorry to see McCoy go, although he knew it wouldn't be long before the next time. Just then, the boy activated his Personal Information Planner and looked down at its small holographic screen, which was hovering over the palm of his left hand. He seemed anxious. 'Everything all right?'

'I'm waiting for my folks to call me. Michael—my little brother—is having his Zed admission test today. But there are no messages on my PIP yet.'

'Wait—aren't the tests done in April anymore?'

'They are. It's just that he only turned 12 in July, so he had to wait for the end of August session.'

'I see. He'll be fine, I'm sure. With a brother like you ...'

'I hope so, Captain. I really do.'

Kelly thought he detected just a hint of doubt in Julius' voice, though.

'Why aren't they calling?' growled Julius to himself. He was now feeling utterly frustrated. He had been pacing up and down in his cabin since leaving Captain Kelly on the bridge two hours ago. He had tried the home line several times, but no one had been there to answer. He couldn't understand why his parents hadn't called yet; after all, the test should have finished by now. He sagged heavily onto his bed, where he lay, staring at the ceiling and trying to calm himself down. After a couple of minutes, his PIP screen lit up, signalling an incoming vidcall. In a flash, Julius was on his feet again. 'On screen!'

'Ahoy, there!' said Faith's smiling face.

'Oh, it's only you.'

'Thanks! It's good to see you too, mate,' answered Faith sarcastically. He was busy polishing his conical hover-skirt, which allowed him to stand despite his disability.

'Sorry. I haven't heard anything about Michael yet,' said Julius, anxiously.

'Bummer,' said Faith.

'I don't understand why it's taking so long. It's almost ten at night, and they're still not home.'

'You sure they didn't go out to celebrate, or something?'

'Without telling me? Unlikely. I'm starting to think that-' Just then, a second incoming vidcall made his PIP vibrate. 'It's them, Faith. Gotta go, gotta go!'

'Right you are. Call me later,' said Faith, before disappearing from view.

Julius took a deep breath. 'On screen.' His dad's face came into view, and he felt his stomach sink around his ankles as soon as he saw the downcast expression on his features.

'Hi son,' said Rory McCoy, who was sporting two dark bags beneath his eyes. 'You'd better sit down.'

Julius didn't need to be asked twice. He plucked the holographic image of his dad's head between the fingertips of his right hand, and threw it into the centre of the room, where it expanded to full length, showing Rory in all his tired glory, bumble bee-shaped slippers and all. While Julius sat back on his bed, his father's hologram sank down onto a chair.

'He didn't make it, did he?' asked Julius, quietly.

Rory shook his head. 'No, he didn't. Between getting in for the medical examination and being escorted out of the main premises, it took about ten minutes.'

'Escorted out?' said Julius, visibly alarmed. 'What do you mean? Did he play some silly tricks on the officers?'

'No Julius, he didn't.' Rory passed a hand through his hair. He looked completely worn out. Julius could see thin white strands among the familiar brown ones. 'Your mother and I were waiting with the other parents—like I did when you and Morgana were doing your test—when suddenly an officer came into the waiting room, asking for the McCoys. Everyone was looking at us, wondering what had happened. We thought that Michael had had an accident. He couldn't give us any information, so we followed him to another office, behind the main test centre. When we entered, Michael was waiting there, looking confused and scared. Other than that, he seemed fine, even though he kept saying that he hadn't done anything wrong. Eventually, after waiting for almost half an hour without a clue as to what was happening, one of your Tijaran teachers came in to meet us.'

'Who was it?' asked Julius.

'Master Cress.'

At any other time, Julius wouldn't have seen anything odd in that, given that it had been Master Cress himself who had told Julius about being accepted into Zed, at the end of his own test. But these were not normal circumstances, it seemed. 'Go on,' he prompted his father.

'He introduced himself, apologised for the situation and, on a screen, showed us a series of tests that had been run on Michael during the medical exam. I don't know how to say this Julius ...'

'Say what, Dad?'

'Michael is ...' he paused, and drooped his head.

'Michael is what?' asked Julius, unable to suppress the impatience in his voice.

'He's an Arneshian!' Rory blurted out.

Julius looked at his father, stunned, waiting for him to say that he was only joking, but there was only an uncomfortable silence. His mouth had gone dry. 'An Arneshian! What are you talking about?' sputtered Julius. 'He can't be an Arneshian! He's one of us.'

'Yes ... Of course he is, son. Sorry, I'm not explaining this very well - he's a Nuarn.'

Julius flinched at that word: Nuarn was the term used to describe any Earthling born with the advanced technological Grey Arts skills of an Arneshian after Clodagh Arnesh's banishment.

'How ... how is this possible?'

'They don't know. They even tested your mum and me, to see if we carried some weird gene, but from their first analysis it looks like we're just plain humans.'

'Wait a sec ... what about the socks? He always made the socks fly. Surely that counts as telekinesis, and that's a mind-skill, right?'

'Yes, they did find that odd, but apparently it can happen with Nuarns. The side of his brain that controls logic,' continued Rory, 'computation and all sorts of Grey Arts, is off the charts. His technological skills are very advanced, with very little presence of mind-skill development. You had plenty of both, that's why you made it into Zed.'

'What's going to happen now?' asked Julius, incredulous.

'Nothing is going to happen, Julius. It's not like Nuarns are shipped off to Queen Salgoria. Master Cress said that your brother is not allowed on Zed, except to visit you during the mid-winter break. He'll just live here like any other human. There are many Arneshians on Earth, you know. They just blend in.'

'But he did get tagged.'

'Yes. They gave him the choker,' said Rory, more than a trace of sadness in his voice.

Julius nodded. He knew all about the later generations of Arneshians on Earth, but it wasn't really big news back home. People didn't tend to discuss their presence; in fact, it was safer to say that they were practically ignored—except for the choker, a device which blocked all Grey skills. He had never liked those grey, metallic neck bands, a constant reminder that the person wearing it was someone potentially dangerous, and essentially an outcast. 'Where is Michael? Can I talk to him?'

'Not just now. He was so upset that the doctor gave him a sedative. Your mum is with him. She says she'll speak to you soon.'

'All right. Tell him I'm thinking of him, and when he feels ready, tell him to call me.'

'Of course. Are you all set for tomorrow?' asked Mr McCoy, quickly changing the subject.

'Yes. I'll be back in school by tea time,' replied Julius, absently.

'Good. Take care, son. Your mother and I wish you all the best for the new year ahead. We're very proud of you, son.'

'Thanks Dad,' said Julius, attempting to smile.

'We'll get through this together. Don't worry.'

Julius nodded half-heartedly. 'Good night, Dad.' When his dad's hologram vanished, he rubbed his eyes with the heels of his hands. How could this be happening to his family? There was obviously nothing wrong with his parents, as today's tests had shown. Yet, both of their children had turned out to be at opposite ends of the spectrum of mind-alterations—the long-lasting legacy of the Chemical War of 2550.

The Arneshians represented all that Zed and its officers stood against. For 232 years the Earthlings had fought with this breakaway sect of humanity, who were devoid of mind-skills, but rich in technological know-how, for control of the planet. In the last two years of his life, Julius and his friends had been at the forefront of that battle twice already, sending Queen Salgoria and her holographic army packing.

For months, Julius had formed an image in his mind; one in which he and his brother would be fighting the enemy together, side by side. He had even created a folder on his PIP, containing a personal guide to life on Zed, which he had been planning on giving to Michael upon arrival, as a late birthday present. In between lessons and games, Julius had listed the coolest shops to visit on Satras, tips on how to win in the games at the Hologram Palace and the best ways to earn Fyvers at school.

All of this was worthless now, shattered by a medical exam. Michael would never get to use the information in that folder and he would never be able to receive Zed officer training. Not only that, but he was also tainted in such a way that would forever be greeted with distrust by his fellow humans. Mind-alterations of any kind made a person "abnormal"; the difference was that if someone had mind-skills, they were set for life, with a future career in space guaranteed, but if someone was a Nuarn, then the only place for them was Earth, under constant surveillance.

Julius suddenly felt very tired and confused. He decided not to call Faith back, but to rather leave it until the next day. He knew he'd have to tell his friends sooner or later, but he couldn't bring himself to do it when it all still seemed so impossible to him. He took a quick shower, slipped under the covers of his bed and let himself drift off into an uneasy sleep.

CHAPTER 2

3 MIZKI APPRENTICE

'Computer, terminate session 2MJ McCoy,' said Julius aloud. The holoscreen on the desk in his room flickered for a moment, and then vanished. His last day aboard the Ahura Mazda was at its end. Julius stretched lazily in the chair, and ran his fingers through his hair. The three months of his Summer Camp had flown by and although he would have loved to remain with Captain Kelly and his crew, he was eager to see his friends. Trying to digest the news about Michael was proving very difficult. His sleep had been restless and he had woken up several times with a deep sense of dread in his heart. Dreams of Michael being taken away by Zed officers, and shipped off to the planet Arnesh like a traitor, had filled his night.

At breakfast that morning, Kelly had taken one look at him and immediately realised that something was wrong. Julius hadn't been able to bring himself to lie about the fact that Michael had failed the test, but he certainly hadn't wanted to share the rest of the news with him either. Still, he had had to spend the entire day avoiding Kelly's curious glances.

Julius stood up and moved to the locker where his bag was waiting, already packed, then swung it over his shoulder and headed for the door. Before leaving the room he had a good, last look around, partly to check that he hadn't left anything behind, and partly to say goodbye. He was pretty sure he would be back, but not before next summer.

When he reached the docking bay, Captain Kelly and Lieutenant Flywheel were waiting by the small shuttle pod that would be taking him back to Zed. 'Captain. Lieutenant,' he said, bowing to them.

'I'm sad to see you go, Julius,' said Elian, sincerely. 'It's been great having you here.'

'I really enjoyed the summer. Thanks for all your help. And thanks for having me, Captain Kelly.'

'You did good, kid. You've earned your placement for next year, if you're still interested in stealing my job,' said Kelly.

Julius grinned. 'Sure.'

'Run along now.'

With a last quick bow, Julius boarded the shuttle pod and strapped himself into the free seat next to the pilot. The hatch closed silently, and a few minutes later the engine hummed into life. The bay outside quickly emptied, and the large airlock below the pod yawned open. Julius' stomach turned a little as the shuttle dropped into space; their descent only lasted a few seconds thankfully, before the pilot steered them towards the Moon, setting their course for the Zed docks.

As they entered orbit, Julius threw a quick glance at the platforms stationed above a section of the shield encasing Zed's lunar perimeter. To their left, he could see Pit-Stop Pete, which served as the orbital repair station. It was a flat disc, with a central spherical structure set in its middle. Several ships were docked all around its edge which, to Julius, made it look a bit like a giant daisy. Behind Pete's core floated the repair bays, rectangular metal frames which encased a spacecraft during its maintenance. There was plenty of activity going on, with numerous sky-jets zooming in and out of hatches, carrying people and various bits of equipment. Faith and Morgana had already driven one of those space-scooters during their first Summer Camp at Pete's, the previous year. The students had been asked to help out retrieving all the debris left behind after the battle between Zed's Cougars and the Arneshian fleet. Julius was sure Skye would also have had a shot at it, seeing as he had grown up on a space station, which meant that he was the only one of their group who still had not tried it. Perhaps he could ask Faith to take him with, next time he visited Pete.

Slowly, the shuttle pod began to pass through the shield. Julius had the impression that its membrane was stretching over their windscreen like a thin layer of jelly, which was pliable enough to allow them to push through it but at the same time not allow any room for the air inside to seep out. The Zed shield had many useful functions: as well as protecting them from attacks and the harshness of the space environment outside, it generated the air they breathed, using specially designed filters. It was also equipped with an illumination system that mimicked the sunrise and sunset of Earth, as timed at the Greenwich meridian. Seasonal changes in temperature were the only thing that Zed lacked, but Julius didn't mind the perennial spring too much; besides, if he really wanted to have cold feet and see his breath puff up in little clouds, all he had to do was enter a simulation room.

A few minutes later, the pilot landed smoothly inside Zed's dock, and the hatch swung open. Julius grabbed his bag, thanked the pilot, and disembarked. He headed straight for the Intra-Rail System, hoping not to meet any of his classmates. He had been so sure that he would soon be welcoming Michael to Zed, that he had told everyone in his year group about the test, so he knew there would be questions about what had happened. Julius had already decided that when anyone asked, he would give the same explanation he had given Captain Kelly: his brother just didn't have enough mind-skills. Yet, as soon as this thought formulated in his mind, Julius felt a pang of guilt as he realised the truth was he was ashamed to tell people that Michael was an Arneshian. He really needed to work on it, because spending the rest of his life lying about it was definitely not an option.

As soon as the train arrived, he jumped on board and in the short time it took him to reach Tijara, he used his PIP to send a note to Morgana, Faith and Skye, who were listed under "Skirts" in his contact list, the name their gang had adopted from their gaming sessions. In the message, he asked them to meet him in the school garden, at the foot of their favourite oak tree, in twenty minutes. Given that he had been incommunicado since the night before, he knew they had probably already guessed that something was up. They were his closest friends after all and, with them at least, he was ready to come clean.

'Surely they've made a mistake,' said Skye, staring at Julius and sounding completely bewildered.

'Nope. Michael has been certified and tagged,' answered Julius, grimly.

'What are the odds?' added Faith. 'A White Child and a Nuarn, both from the same parents.'

'I'm so sorry, Julius,' said Morgana, squeezing his arm gently. 'How is Michael?'

'I haven't spoken with him yet. He's still very upset. Mum will let me know when he's ready to talk.'

'Have you ever noticed anything odd about him?' asked Faith.

'Michael has always been odd,' answered Julius. 'But if you mean, Arneshian-odd, then no. Sure, he's very talented when it comes to building things, but other than that ...'

'Man, I would be gutted,' said Skye, shaking his head. 'Do pass our ... our ...'

'See,' said Julius, the frustration he was feeling seeping out into his voice, 'that's the thing—I don't even know how to feel! What should I pass on to him? Our pity? Our best wishes for a swift recovery? He's not dead, he's not ill and he's certainly not going to get better. Yet, he's everything we hate.'

'Come on now,' said Faith. 'That's too harsh. Plenty of Nuarns have lived among us in the past 200 years, and not one of them has ever done anything wrong or shameful.'

'Faith is right,' added Morgana. 'They may be singled out, but they get by just fine.'

'Get by, huh?' said Julius. 'Is this what I have to wish for my little brother's future? That he gets by?'

'What did you have in mind?' asked Skye. 'Did you think he would become the next Grand Master of Tijara, or something?'

'And what if I did?' said Julius, a little louder than he meant to. A couple of Seniors and a group of first years sitting nearby, turned their heads towards him. Julius saw them and, lowering his voice, he turned to Skye once more. 'What are *you* hoping to do with your life? Get by?'

'Hey, I'm just happy to exist, man. Everything on top of that is a bonus for me. We all get by. Some of us better than others, but we all do. And since when did this conversation become about me, anyway?'

Julius leaned back against the oak. 'Sorry. I didn't mean to take it out on you.'

'I know, mate.'

'That's why we're here, Julius,' said Morgana. 'Vent away.'

Julius breathed deeply. 'This one is gonna be hard to digest.'

'Have you told anyone else?' asked Faith.

'Cress and Freja know, of course. As for the others, I'll just say he didn't make it. For now anyway.'

'Of course,' said Morgana, quickly. 'We'll back that up.'

The boys nodded in agreement.

'Look,' said Morgana, pointing at the garden entrance. 'The rest of our year is arriving. Let's go say hi.' She stood up and held her hand out to Julius. 'He'll be ok.'

Julius looked her in the eyes for a few seconds, wanting with all his heart to believe her. Then he grabbed her hand and pulled himself up. 'I hope you're right.'

Seeing his classmates after the long summer gap was always good for Julius; it felt like a reunion party for old friends, with everyone eager to share their stories from the past few months. There were a few recurring after-dinner activities among the students that night. One of these was the moustache check, where all the boys' faces were scanned for the faintest trace of hair, something that they seemed to find hilarious. Of course, Skye being Skye, he quickly grew bored with talk of facial hair and instead took to examining something he found far more interesting: the girls' body development. This was the cue for Julius and Faith to let him talk by himself while trying not to look at whatever he was so blatantly pointing at.

All night, Morgana was surrounded by her closest girlfriends, Isolde Frey and Siena Migliori, and they chatted excitedly right up until bedtime. Julius often wondered what could have possibly happened to them over the summer that justified such an intense conversation, especially since he knew that it would be like this for the entire year. But it quickly occurred to him that he didn't much care to know anyway, given that it was most likely about clothing or hair or whatever else girls discussed. The fact that they may be discussing the boys was something that rarely crossed his mind since, in his opinion, Morgana would always be too young to be interested in relationships.

In a corner of the mess hall, Barth "The Menace" Smit was comparing scars, bumps and scabs with Lopaka Liway. All of Lopaka's were surf-related—something that he was definitely proud of. In Barth's case though, they were all the result of sheer clumsiness and, judging by the grin on his face, it seemed that Barth was beginning to embrace his awkwardness a little too much, in Julius' opinion.

Before the evening was over however, Julius knew that most of the students would be discussing the games in the Hologram Palace. Everyone on Zed knew who the best players were: the Skirts. As a group, they were formidable and had already set unbeaten records among the first and second year students, in both the Flight and Combat simulations. It was only natural that all eyes would be on them this coming year, as they entered the third year competitions. Technically, they were allowed to compete against any age group, but the Skirts had decided they would stick to their level, and no one had been able to make them change their minds, much to the frustration of the older students who were itching to challenge them. As if this wasn't enough, Julius had also set a personal record for Solo, the single player version of the regular games, where players used their actual mind-skills to fight against the computer. As the reigning champion, he was allowed to wear the black metal ring on his finger, which had the word "Solo" engraved on its inner surface.

Strangely enough, no one had asked Julius about Michael yet. Whether they had simply forgotten, or just noticed how he was keeping to himself and so drawn their own conclusions from that, he couldn't tell. Either way, he was grateful for it.

Eventually, it was time to retire for the night. As 3 Mizki Apprentices, their year group would now have their dorms on level -4.

'Another three years, and we'll make it to the surface,' said Faith, waving goodbye for the night and following Barth into their shared room.

'Not quite to the surface,' added Skye. 'I feel like a mole sometimes.'

'You are a mole,' said Julius, pushing him along the corridor. 'And I'll take the bed nearest the door.'

There was a brief struggle, as the two of them tried to squeeze through their bedroom door at the same time, much to the amusement of the rest of the boys in their dorm.

'Come on—I want to see our new uniforms,' said Skye excitedly, even though Julius' hand was parked on his face. 'Look, they're on my bed!'

'It's *my* bed,' said Julius, who had Skye's thumb lodged firmly in his right ear. He managed to pull Skye back by his jumper and rushed to claim the bed he wanted. Julius' new wardrobe was neatly laid out. There were new socks and underwear, two pairs of tracksuits, a pair of combat trousers, short and long-sleeved t-shirts, two round-neck jumpers, a pair of trainers and some new boots. Everything was navy blue: Tijara's official colour. All of the outer garments had labels on them with the words "Julius McCoy—3MA—Tijara", written in silver. The sight of those tags brought home his new reality to him: his two Apprentice years had officially begun.

On the morning of Thursday the 1st of September, Julius woke up feeling rested and decidedly more cheery than he had been the previous two days. He had been thinking about it a lot and had decided that there was no reason why he should feel embarrassed about Michael's situation. He knew that it would take time to fully accept it, but to be sad, or ashamed, was not fair on his brother, who had done nothing to deserve that. He would talk to Michael and let him know there was absolutely nothing to worry about and that he could still realise his dreams, even if it meant doing it through an institute other than Zed.

By the time Julius was showered and dressed, Skye and Faith were patiently waiting outside in the hallway, sporting their new uniforms. Faith's metallic, panelled skirt had even been freshly polished for the occasion.

'You finished putting your makeup on, Julia McCoy?' teased Skye.

'You look ... sparkly,' said Julius, ignoring him and admiring the hovering device wrapped around Faith's waist. 'Very shiny.'

'Fresh start and all that,' said Faith, pirouetting for his friends. 'However, I do seem to have a problem.'

'What's that?' asked Skye.

'Me legs are outgrowing the skirt,' explained Faith, hovering upwards slightly and pointing at his feet.

Julius looked down and, sure enough, he could see feet and ankles dangling from the bottom of the skirt. Then he turned to Skye, and chuckled.

'I look funny, do I?' said Faith, in a deadpan voice. 'I'll show you funny; I'll turn you into the Flying Scotsman, McCoy.' He charged towards Julius, who spun on his heels and made a dash for the stairs. Faith quickly caught up, deftly slipped his arms under Julius' armpits and, gripping him tightly, lifted him off the floor and whisked him up the stairs.

'Let me down, you crazy Irishman!' cried Julius, thrashing about in the air.

Soon enough, the commotion attracted students from all the other dorms. As they zoomed up the stairs, Julius had to face a barrage of flashes as the Mizkis snapped away on their PIP cameras at each floor landing. Skye and some of the 3MAs led a parade behind them, hollering and clapping away. Gustavo Perez, one of their classmates from Terra 2, was walking beside Skye, grunting and crying with laughter.

'That's it,' said Julius, once they reached the level -1 landing. Stretching out his hand, he aimed for the wall directly ahead and gave a strong mind-push. He immediately felt the energy rush out of his body, and although no one could see the actual stream, they all heard the whooshing sound and a thump as it rebounded off the wall. To the general amusement of everyone, Julius and Faith were blasted backwards by the strength of Julius' push and sent tumble-weeding down the stairs.

'I've recorded it, Skye! I've recorded it!' Manuel Valdez, a dark haired Mexican boy who had proved a valuable source of Spanish pick up lines in the past for Skye, was loudly crying out while leaping about excitedly. '*Tus amigos son locos!*'

Julius and Faith couldn't even disentangle themselves from each other, for how hard they were laughing and how sore they were. Eventually, Skye and Lopaka had to pull them apart.

'You girls can carry on messing about if you like but I'm starving,' said Skye. 'We've only got twenty minutes until first class. I could eat a space freighter.' And with that he started up the stairs.

The thought of being left without food until break, combined with the sudden urge to discover what subjects they would be studying that year, spurred Julius and Faith into action and they hurried after him. As they approached the mess hall entrance, the smell of bacon and pastries grew maddeningly strong and inviting.

Julius noticed that no timetables had been left for them by the door, as had happened the previous year, but instead there was only a single message on the monitor beside the doorway, instructing all 3MAs to assemble in the garden at 09:00 hours.

Faith and Skye shrugged their shoulders and motioned for Julius to hurry up.

The canteen was packed with all the returning students and a fresh batch of 1 Mizki Juniors, who were all intently studying their new timetables. Julius grabbed a large latte, plus a carrot-and-hazelnut muffin, and headed for a table which was occupied by Morgana and Siena, followed by Skye and Faith.

'Hi guys!' said Morgana, cheerily.

'Ladies,' said Julius, sitting down next to her.

'Hi Siena,' said Faith. 'Good to see you again. How was your summer?'

Suddenly, Julius noticed a little wisp of bright pink shooting out of Siena's head, like a tiny firework. He flinched, caught off guard by it. The wisps and threads that came out of people's heads were something that apparently only Julius could see, as far as he knew anyway. It didn't always happen, but when it did, Julius was able to tell what a person was feeling at that moment.

'What's the matter?' asked Skye, noticing his friend's discomfort.

'Oh, nothing,' answered Julius quickly. 'Just banged my knee against the table.' He really didn't want to share what he had seen; besides, if he had read that wisp correctly, then Siena had a crush on Faith and Julius certainly didn't want to get involved in that. He had never been the best when it came to girls and their strange ways.

As the start of period one approached, all the Mizkis began to slowly file away and head to their respective classes. Julius looked around and realised that only his year group had remained behind.

'Let's go, guys,' said Morgana to her table and stood up.

They quickly returned their empty trays to the counter and headed outside. Julius stretched happily in the morning sunshine. He knew that the heat he was feeling wasn't really from the sun, but the illusion of it was good enough to make it seem real. As he walked into the clearing at the centre of the garden, he spotted a man there, sitting cross-legged and beckoning to them with his right hand.

'Over here, Mizkis,' called the man, pleasantly.

They walked towards him and were invited to take a seat on the grass. Faith's skirt, interacting with the sensors implanted in his legs, was able to make him kneel quite easily and he gently lowered himself to the ground. Julius sat next to him, and turned his attention to the stranger. He wondered who this man was and where was he from. His skin was slightly darker than Julius', and his hair was jet black.

Once all eyes were fixed on him, the man bowed to them, and they bowed in return, as was customary on Zed. 'Good morning Mizkis, and welcome to the first of your Apprentice years. My name is Hamza Patel, and I will be your guidance teacher for the next two years.'

'Sir,' Dhara Sundaram, a petite girl with long straight hair, said shyly. 'Are you Indian, sir?'

'Indeed, Miss Sundaram,' answered Mr Patel, amiably. 'From a village not too far from yours, actually.'

Dhara looked pleased, and nodded her head.

'Mrs Cruci has passed all of your files on to me, and with them your ideas for possible careers,' said Mr Patel, his eyes examining them. 'As you know, from this year you will be able to select two of your subjects, according to your own wishes, while the rest of the timetable will be the same for all of you. As always, you are required to keep a record of all of your classes in your student log, as it allows you to analyse the choices you make, as well as the weaknesses and strengths you may have in any given area.'

'Sir,' said Morgana, eagerly. 'When can we choose our new classes?'

'That is what you'll be doing today and tomorrow, Miss Ruthier,' answered Patel. 'We have prepared a special career fair in the assembly hall, where the relevant teachers will be answering all of your questions. We have also invited representatives from different professions, so you can pick their brains about the ins and outs of each job. How does that sound?'

An excited whisper ran through the group.

'What a nice way to start the year,' said Faith, merrily. 'Two extra days off!'

'Double agreement,' added Julius.

'Now,' continued Patel, visibly satisfied by their reaction, 'as you enter into the hall, scan your PIP chip on the sensor by the entrance, and a map of the fair will be downloaded into its memory. It's a bio-interactive app, which responds differently to every individual. Your own special set of mind-skills will make certain career paths flash brightly if they are suited to you.'

'What if you like a subject that doesn't suit you, sir?' asked Barth, sounding very worried.

Patel smiled affably. 'Then choose it. In October, and again at the end of the year, we will have our usual reviews and if you've changed your mind, so be it.'

Barth looked relieved at that, as did a few of the other students.

'Visit every station. By 16:00 you must make an initial selection, which you will submit to me, via your PIP. Tomorrow morning I will send it back to you, confirming the subjects that you are allowed to take, and if there are any that you need to change. It is very rare that you aren't allowed to do a certain subject, but it can happen. The final decision rests with Grand Master Freja.' Patel stood up, nimbly. 'Let's go Mizkis. I'll be at the fair with you if you need to ask me anything.'

Julius waited for Faith, Skye and Morgana to join him, and together they headed indoors. A small queue formed as they approached the black doors of the main hall. Julius watched eagerly as the Mizkis ahead slowed down by the entrance, before disappearing inside. When it was his turn, Julius scanned his PIP chip on the sensor and felt a little shiver run up his arm. He moved inside and stood off to the side, waiting for the others.

The rows of chairs that normally occupied the hall had been replaced with a multitude of colourful stands, peppered across the floor. Each station was shared by the particular subject teacher and the representatives for each job. The lighting inside the hall had been turned to its full brightness, in contrast to the usual softer ambience.

'I say we divide and conquer,' said Skye, examining his new map, which was hovering above the palm of his hand.

'Good idea,' added Morgana. 'Later,' she said, walking away towards the centre of the room.

'All right then,' said Julius, activating his own map. As it flashed into life, he was surprised to see that every single stand was glowing brightly. 'Great,' he said, disheartened. Being a White Child sure had its downsides: according to the screen, no matter what he chose, he would do well, so there was no guidance for him there. He decided to approach the floor the old fashioned way, stand by stand, left to right. The first one in his path, he was pleased to see, was occupied by none other than Captain Kelly himself.

'McCoy, are you following me?' said Kelly, pretending to be serious. 'I've told you a thousand times, I will never let you anywhere near a spaceship.'

'Good morning, Captain,' answered Julius, grinning. 'I didn't expect to see you here.'

'The Grand Master asked me to,' he answered, dropping the joke. 'It's hard to say no to him.'

'I bet,' said Julius, under his breath.

'Anyway, McCoy. What are you doing here? You know you'll pick this subject, so go visit the other stands. You're not having second thoughts, are you?'

'Oh no, Captain,' answered Julius quickly. 'I'm just exploring, that's all.'

'Good. Why don't you go and meet your new teacher, then?' said Kelly, pointing at the next section.

'I wouldn't want to presume that I get to do this subject, Captain.'

'Presume away, and get lost,' said Kelly, half seriously. 'I have other candidates to meet.'

Julius bowed and moved to the right. There was a woman in the next section, under a sign that read "Starship Management." Julius approached her hesitantly. 'Good morning,' he said, politely. The woman turned towards him, and bowed. She was tall, with auburn hair gathered in a tight bun behind her head; her nose was thin, its tip pointed slightly downward, and her eyes were wide and black. Julius knew he had seen her before, coming and going in Tijara, but he had never properly met her.

'Good morning,' she replied cordially. 'I'm Professor Farshid, Starship Management.'

'Julius McCoy.'

'Pleased to meet you. Are you interested in becoming a captain?'

'Yes, very much,' answered Julius.

'This is the course for you then. It's very comprehensive and will teach you all the different aspects you need in order to successfully command a ship and its crew. From leadership skills, diplomacy, intergalactic protocols—in case we should ever encounter another race—to the everyday run of the mill stuff: what you need, who you need, basic maintenance and, of course, piloting. You will have a helmsman for that, but it is important you are an excellent pilot yourself. You will also have all sorts of technicians and civilian personnel to direct.'

'It sounds pretty full on,' said Julius.

'It is, but in my opinion, it's *the* job to have. Nothing beats it!' said Farshid, brimming with infectious confidence. 'Here,' she said, holding a hand-held device out for Julius. 'Bring your PIP-chip closer. I'm transferring the prospectus to you. It contains everything you need to know about this course and the career options at the end of it. Read it before you sign on.'

Once the transfer was done, he withdrew his hand. 'Thanks, Professor.'

'You're very welcome.'

Julius bowed, touched by her comment, and moved along to his right. The next three stations were marked as Starship Engineering for Pilots, Technicians and Architects respectively. Sure enough, Julius spotted Morgana anxiously jumping up and down in the queue for the first of them and Faith desperately trying to keep his place in both the second and third queues, by zooming between them. 'Mental, those two,' he chuckled to himself. He decided to skip those stations for the time being, given how busy they were, and headed for the far side of the hall, opposite the entrance. There were two stations there: Pilot, and Catalyst Training. Julius did like flying and was very good at it too, but given a choice between the two courses, he knew his strengths leaned more towards the use of catalysts and therefore, combat. He still stopped by the first one though, where Professor Clavel, who also taught Pilot Training as a core subject, was handing out his own prospectus. 'Can I have one, Professor?' called Julius, over the heads of the classmates gathered there in front of him.

'Here you are, McCoy,' said Clavel, holding out his device over Yuri Slovich's head.

Julius stretched his hand towards it to receive the file. He was pleasantly surprised to see that one of the real life pilots at this stand was none other than Lieutenant Elian Flywheel but, seeing as she was completely surrounded by students, Julius didn't stop to say hi, and moved on to the next stand. The Catalyst station was shared by four men that Julius had never seen before. The first one on the left was holding the same kind of device that Clavel and Farshid had, so Julius assumed that he must be the teacher. He was a man of broad build, with dirty-blonde hair and small chestnut eyes. Julius walked up to him and bowed. 'Julius McCoy, sir,' he said. 'Could I have one of those, please?'

The man looked at Julius with curiosity. 'I am Professor Gould. Your PIP, please.' As Julius did so, Gould added, 'I was wondering when you'd turn up.'

'Were you?' asked Julius.

'When a Mizki Junior is allowed to spend his first Summer Camp in the Fornax constellation doing an intensive Catalyst Training course, believe me, I am the first to know about it.'

'That was a brilliant summer, sir,' said Julius excitedly.

'If you pick this course you'll get more of the same.'

Julius nodded. 'Oh, I will, sir.'

'I would still like you to read the prospectus though.'

'Of course. Thank you,' said Julius. He quickly bowed and left.

There was no real need for him to stop by the catalyst operators, since he had already met a fair few of them during that first summer. Along the right side of the assembly hall, there were just two large stations: Colonial Affairs, and History and Politics. Julius saw Skye talking with one of the female Curia workers, at the Colonial Affairs desk, and couldn't suppress a chuckle. He was leaning over the counter, his head resting on the heel of his hand, looking dreamily at the young woman. In the three years Julius had known Skye he had come to accept the fact that his friend was a magnet for girls and, most importantly, that he knew exactly what to say to attract them. No matter who they were—students, Zed officers or teachers—if he liked them, he would work his way into their consciousness somehow. At the tender age of fourteen, Skye "Black Hole" Miller—as he had been affectionately dubbed, due to the amazing amount of food he could consume—was the guy you talked to, if you needed advice on relationships. Julius grinned and moved along. Working at the Curia wasn't really that appealing to him since, in his opinion, there was nothing exciting about being stuck behind a desk. However, perhaps History and Politics would be a nice change, he thought, since he liked history anyway, so he stopped to pick up a prospectus, just in case.

The last station sat in the middle of the assembly hall and seemed rather empty in comparison to the others. It was Spaceology and, at the sight of Professor Lucy Brown, Julius let out a groan. He had fallen asleep more times than he could remember during her core classes, so there was no way he was going to choose it as one of his extra subjects. He stopped at the stand though, more out of diligence than any other reason.

As he finished and headed out of the hall entrance, Mr Patel took him aside. 'McCoy, I was asked to tell you that you'll be busy in the infirmary every Thursday at 11:00.'

'What for, sir?' asked Julius, shocked.

'The Grand Master has his reasons, of course, but Dr Walliser will be able to explain them to you at your first session.'

'When will that be?'

'Probably not until October, but they'll notify you.'

Julius nodded, feeling quite annoyed that Freja had made plans without discussing them with him first. Unfortunately, he knew complaining about it wouldn't make any difference, so he pushed the news to the back of his mind and began to count the prospectuses he had collected. He was required to gather some more before he could leave the room, so he began his sweep from the left again and stopped at the stations he hadn't visited during his first round. By the time he finished up and reached the mess hall, it was eleven o'clock. He grabbed some fresh orange juice and headed for the garden, where he lay under the oak tree, with his PIP switched on. Morgana and Faith joined him an hour later, eventually followed by Skye. The four of them sat there for the rest of the afternoon, comparing ideas and advising each other on what they thought were the best courses. Lunch came and went, and by four o'clock they had still not made a choice.

'There's too much to take in,' said Morgana, sounding thoroughly frustrated.

'Everything seems interesting,' said Skye, flipping from prospectus to prospectus on his holoscreen. 'I really don't know what to pick.'

'I like a couple of courses,' said Faith, looking dejected, 'but they clash on the timetable, so I have to settle for one, which is easier said than done.'

Julius opened his blank timetable and noticed that some of the spaces were greyed out. 'Those must be our core lessons then,' he said.

Faith leaned in to look at it. 'The personal choices are every Tuesday and Wednesday morning.'

Julius looked at his options and, although he really wanted to share as many classes as possible with the others, he knew he had to decide what was best for him.

'Come on, let's do this!' said Morgana practically. 'Tuesday mornings—I'll go for Starship Engineering for Pilots.'

'SS Management for me,' added Julius.

'Technician's path, here,' said Faith.

'Colonial Affairs,' finished Skye.

'Next, Wednesday Mornings,' called Morgana again. 'Pilot Training all the way, boys.'

'I thought so,' said Julius. 'Catalyst Training for me.'

'SS Architecture, if you had any doubts,' said Faith.

'I must do History and Politics. No choice there,' said Skye.

'Shame we can't be together,' said Morgana. She pressed a few buttons and sent her programme off to Mr Patel.

'I know, but can you imagine me sitting in Colonial Affairs?' said Faith, mimicking slipping a rope around his neck and giving it a tug upwards.

Julius laughed, and sent his schedule off. 'Well, that's that then,' he thought to himself.

That evening, the 3MAs were abuzz with discussions about their timetables, trying to find out who chose what, and why. The excitement was such that, on the Friday morning they just couldn't wait until nine, and pleaded with Mr Patel to start earlier. Fortunately, the guidance teacher had no problem with that, since all he had to do was send them their approved schedules back.

When Julius opened his, he was delighted to see that his subjects had been confirmed.

With the course choices out of the way, Mr Patel, to the great surprise of the Mizkis, left them free to do as they pleased. As Apprentices, they weren't allowed on Satras until the second weekend of October however, so they had to find other things to do, to pass the time.

Morgana went off to meet up with her girlfriends, so they could resume their seemingly endless, cosy conversations. Julius, Faith and Skye, together with seven other classmates, started a match of five-a-side mind-ball in the garden, the Zed version of football, whereby instead of using their feet, the players would pass the ball overhead using only their Telekinetic abilities. Needless to say, Barth managed to run straight into a tree, giving himself a bloody nose and a severe headache as reward for his clumsiness. Every time ten points were scored, some of the other Mizkis would substitute in, to give everyone a chance to play, and the ones who had been playing a welcome breather. After lunch, even Morgana decided to join in, challenging the class to a boys-against-girls competition. The game got so intense that, when the Friday lessons ended, most of the Tijaran students ended up gathered around to watch and cheer. Eventually, tea time came, and they decided to call it a night, with the boys' team leading, 568 to 540.

Julius and Faith were dripping with sweat, so they headed back to their rooms for a quick shower, and then headed back up towards the mess hall for dinner. As they were walking, they passed a group of 5MS girls, and caught a snippet of their conversation.

'Yeah,' said a red haired girl, 'and she told me that Skye Miller saved them all single-handedly from the evil Arneshians.'

'It would be so exciting to have someone like him come to your rescue!' giggled a brunette.

'She told me that after Skye rescued her, he took her out on a date! And then they ...' whispered a third one, her voice tapering off as the two boys moved away.

Faith and Julius stared at each other, stupefied. Apart from the fact that no one was supposed to know the details of their mission, to believe that Skye had rescued the girls all on his own was quite preposterous. There were tears in their eyes, and they were making particularly odd noises as they tried hard to suppress their amusement. Once they were sure they were out of earshot of the girls, they fell against each other and howled with laughter. It was too funny not to share, so when they got inside and spotted Skye, Morgana and Siena, they quickly sat down at their table and shared the tale.

While Skye and Morgana were suitably amused, Julius thought that Siena didn't really look like she was enjoying the joke, but maybe she just hadn't found it that funny. After all, she had been one of the kidnapped girls, along with Morgana, and she knew all too well the real scale of the rescue mission, which had required the intervention of a whole team of officers, as well as the three boy members of the Skirts.

'And you know what's even funnier, Miller?' said Faith, waving a fork in the air. 'It's the fact that you sit here, stinking to high heaven after twelve hours of physical exercise, and not one of these girls here has said anything. Me Irish sense of comprehension is officially baffled.'

'It's nothing to do with "Stinky" here,' answered Morgana, promptly. 'It's more to do with the fact that we haven't washed either.'

'Fanks Mofgana,' said Skye, chewing noisily.

'No, seriously, look at him,' she said, her voice caught halfway between mirth and mock disgust.

'Yeah, yeah,' said Faith, still looking unconvinced.

The morning after brought more mind-ball in the garden; this time the other year groups joined in too, creating an improvised mini tournament that ran throughout the entire weekend. By the time that Sunday night arrived, there were plenty of sore necks among the students, as running around with their heads tilted back, fixed on the hovering ball, was seriously hard work.

One curious episode that left the Skirts puzzled, was that by bed time the story of Skye Miller rescuing the hostages had somehow changed. According to the female consensus, the unsung hero of that day was now none other than Faith “The Skirt” Shanigan.

‘What can I say,’ said Faith, still chuckling about it. ‘It’s me Irish charm.’

Given the sudden satisfied grin on Siena’s face, Julius wasn’t too sure that his charm had had anything to do with this strange turn of events.

CHAPTER 3

THE AMBASSADOR

On Monday the 5th of September, the 3MAs gathered in the mess hall for breakfast. There was an air of anticipation among the Apprentice and Senior Mizkis, as they awaited their new timetables.

Julius had just started his honey and cinnamon porridge, when his PIP vibrated, announcing an incoming message. Judging by the sudden drop in noise in the room, it was clear that the rest of the students had also received one. There was a rush to activate their devices, followed by a general chorus of comments that ranged from enthusiastic to horror-stricken. Julius avidly scanned his new schedule.

'We're starting Pyrokinesis!' cried Skye excitedly.

'Finally!' added Faith, exchanging a high five with Julius. 'Bring on the heat!'

'Ahem,' coughed Morgana. 'I don't mean to be a spoil-sport, but it says here that we don't start Pyrokinesis until January.'

'What?' said Julius, double-checking his planner. 'Why?'

'It doesn't say,' answered Morgana.

'On a Friday morning there's a class of Biomathematics, run by Cress,' said Skye.

'It says here that it's an opt-in subject,' said Julius.

'That's right,' added Morgana. 'Kaori told me that MAs can study towards a medical career if they want to.'

'Hmm,' said Julius, not convinced. 'It doesn't sound like much fun to me.'

'Probably because it isn't,' replied Skye.

Julius nodded. 'So, what exactly do we study in this Bio-thingy anyway?'

'It's math applied to biology,' explained Faith, simply. 'They use it for genetic research and computer simulations ... among other things, but that's as much as I know.'

'Wow,' said Julius. 'That's a lot more than I care to know.' Then he remembered his conversation with Patel the previous day. 'Speaking of doctors, apparently Freja wants me to see Walliser every Thursday morning.'

'Really?' asked Morgana. 'When did he tell you that?'

'Yesterday.'

'I get it,' said Faith, patting him hard on the shoulder. 'It's the W.C. business again!'

'Don't call me W.C.,' said Julius, flicking a lump of porridge at his friend with the tip of his spoon.

Just then, the loudspeaker bellowed, 'Attention Mizkis—all 3MAs must report to the infirmary at 09:00.'

Julius looked around the room, feeling quite puzzled. A table of senior students were chuckling away disconcertingly, and pointing at them.

'Infirmary?' gulped Faith. 'Why the infirmary?'

Skye shook his head. 'No idea, mate.'

'Please don't tell me they're going to add a few more gadgets to me body,' continued Faith, the distress obvious in his voice.

Body augmentations were a necessary part of their Zed training, and they were always done to enhance the students' abilities. In his second year Julius was implanted with the Personal Information Planner chip into his left hand and two shield chips—one in each of his forearms. He could understand Faith's anxiety, though. Because of his disability, the school had already given him his famous Skirt, which responded to the many sensors embedded all along his legs. Julius had joked with him before about how he was slowly being turned into a cyborg.

They tried to guess, and even resorted to begging some of the Seniors to tell them what was happening, but no one was able to extract even a hint from them, so the 3MAs made their way to the infirmary feeling a mixture of curiosity, and suspicion.

Dr Walliser, the Tijaran physician, was waiting for the students. Resident nurses Ms Federica Primula and Mr Dorian Finch were by his side, together with ten other members of staff. The students were invited to take a seat on the many sofas occupying the waiting area. When they had all done so, Dr Walliser bowed to them. 'Good morning,' he said, 'and welcome to your Apprentice years.'

The students bowed back to him, still looking quite anxious.

'As you can see from your timetables, the first two hours of lessons on Mondays are for Pyrokinesis, but you will not be able to do this training until January.'

A few murmurs of complaint ran through the room.

'I know it seems unfair but, trust me, you must be physically prepared for the intense pressure you will be putting your body through once you start.' Dr Walliser began to stroll in front of them, hands nestled in his lab coat pockets. 'I'm sure all of you have experimented with your Pyrokinetic skills at one point or another but, of course, always during simulated game play. You will be trained to a completely different level, pushing boundaries you didn't even know you had. To do this, you must prepare, and that is why every Monday morning you shall come to the infirmary for your Pre-Pyro dose.'

More whispers spread around the room.

'I don't want anyone to worry unnecessarily though,' the doctor continued. 'All you will be required to do is to lie on a bed while we administer the treatment. There is a very important reason why all students undergo this procedure. Using Pyrokinetic abilities on a regular basis exerts sustained and irrevocable harm on all internal body organs, and to the circulatory system, due to the heat that is generated by your mind-skills. In the past, Mizkis were not able to fully develop this White Art, as they could end up severely damaged by it. Today's technology however, has allowed us to bypass these problems, and that is why we must properly prepare your bodies.'

'It doesn't sound too bad,' ventured Julius unconvincingly.

'I know what you're really thinking about, McCoy,' said Faith. 'An extra chance to sleep.'

Julius grinned and winked at him.

'The treatment lasts approximately 90 minutes, so we are going to start right away. Wait here until your name is called. Zolin Acalan, come with me.'

Zolin, a short boy with brown hair, stood up quickly and moved over in front of the doctor. Julius watched as he was led off into one of the rooms. As soon as he had gone, the nurses started to call names alphabetically, and the next twelve students were summoned. Julius was among them, and followed his designated nurse to a nearby room.

The doctor hadn't lied—all Julius was asked to do was lie on a bed and relax. He watched intently as Ms Primula inserted a needle into his left arm, flinching just a little when it went in. The little tube was attached to a machine, which Julius assumed was the Pre-Pyro dispenser.

The nurse pressed a few buttons on the machine, until a long steady beep was heard. 'There, you're all set. If you want to watch something, the screen in front of you is voice-activated. Just say the channel and it'll select it for you. Any problems, here's the call button, by the bedside. I'll be back in a little while.'

Julius nodded. Once the nurse had closed the door, he decided a little nap was just the thing for him, so he closed his eyes and dozed off.

'Wake up, McCoy.'

The voice brought Julius back to full consciousness. He looked at his arm and saw that the needle was gone.

'There's some juice in the waiting room,' said Ms Primula. 'Have a drink; it'll make you feel better.'

Julius stretched slowly, before jumping off the bed. He stood still for a few seconds, to see if he could feel anything weird about his body. Everything seemed fine however, so he left the room. A few of the other students were already in the waiting area. Julius grabbed a glass, filled it with juice from a jug and sat down on one of the sofas. It was true: the tangy liquid gave him a nice kick, which awoke all his senses. It wasn't long before all the 3MAs were out of their rooms, sipping some juice and comparing first impressions of the Pre-Pyro treatment. All in all, it hadn't been a bad experience; strange perhaps, but perfectly acceptable.

When Dr Walliser released them at 11:00 hours, the Mizkis headed straight to the Grey Arts sector for their Draw lesson. Professor Cathy Turner was waiting by her door, spectacles precariously propped on her long, bony nose.

'Welcome back, Mizkis,' she said, twitching in her usual manner. 'Let me show you to your new classroom.'

Julius followed her eagerly, wondering what new plant she would let them use to practice their draws. So far they had worked on cacti and more delicate pot plants, trying to control the amount of energy drawn each time.

'I hope we get to practice on a big ol' tree,' said Julius, rubbing his hands together.

'I agree,' said Faith. 'I'm tired of stinky, puny sticks. I want me hands on a right trunk.'

There was a snort, followed by a chortle from behind. Skye and Manuel Valdez were turning redder by the second.

'What?' asked Faith, puzzled, 'What did I say?'

Morgana, shaking her head, leaned closer to Faith and whispered something in his ear which made him turn crimson.

'You guys are bad!' said Faith pointing at them both but, by then even Julius and Morgana had joined in. Faith shrugged, and began to chuckle himself.

Amidst the laughter, Julius noticed that they had descended a couple of floors, and that Professor Turner was now standing in front of a new entrance, ushering the Mizkis inside. When Julius stepped through the double door, the sight before him took his breath away.

'Is this a zoo?' asked Morgana, clearly impressed.

'As close as we can get to one on the Moon, Miss Ruthier,' replied Professor Turner. 'Come, let's go and sit at those picnic tables for a moment.'

The students followed her and took a seat, exploring the environment around them with their eyes.

Even after two years on Zed, the holographic facilities of the Lunar Perimeter never failed to astonish Julius. The virtual zoo was set inside a vast park, with green hills rolling off in the distance under a blue sky. Rows of trees stretched off in every direction, and a cacophony of mixed animal voices echoed through the air.

'This simulation room is specifically calibrated to perform draws on animals,' explained Turner. 'As Apprentices, you must now learn to take advantage of different types of life forms, in a responsible manner. As I explained to you in your first year, the smallest amount of energy can save your life in combat.' She then turned to her right and whistled sharply. From a nearby path, something scampered her way.

Julius glanced in that direction and found himself staring at a bouncing Border collie.

A chorus of 'Awww!' came from the girls, but to their disappointment, the dog didn't even notice them, and instead sat obediently at Professor Turner's feet.

Julius knew very well what was coming, since he had also performed a draw on a sim-wolf during his first Solo game, some two years ago. He watched as Professor Turner placed her hands on either side of the dog's head, her face fixed in concentration, looking the animal directly in its eyes. She then took a long, deep breath and held it. Julius saw several yellowish threads of energy passing from the animal's fur to Turner's fingertips, which then spread over her hands until they were completely absorbed into her skin. The collie yelped weakly and swayed to the left, before hunching down in exhaustion.

'Just enough for a pick-me-up,' said Turner, satisfied.

And indeed, she did look perkier than before, in direct contrast with the dog, who was now practically asleep.

'So, for this year's training, you will be free to choose an animal for your weekly practice. Start small, and work your way up. And to stress the importance of responsible drawing, every time you harm a sim-animal by drawing too much, Fyvers will be docked off your account, so be careful, or you'll be left with nothing but a string of detentions.'

Lopaka Liway raised his hand.

'Yes?'

'Professor, I don't mean to be cheeky, but ... what are the odds of finding an elephant on a spacecraft?'

'Fair question,' answered Turner. 'However, you seem to forget the importance of the exploration and repopulation programmes that Zed has been conducting throughout the galaxy. There are many habitable planets out there, and although no one has seen an elephant on a space station, more than three million animals live on Kapaldi 22. So, you see, Mr Liway, it is better to be prepared than sorry. And now Mizkis, go explore the zoo and find your first animal. And don't forget to update your logs as you go along. Off you go.'

Julius exchanged a glance with the rest of the gang. 'Not too bad for a Monday morning.'

'Agreed,' said Skye, 'but let's try not to kill anything, or we can say goodbye to the game season this year.'

Julius nodded eagerly. In fact, he was so worried about the idea of having Fyvers removed from his weekly wage that he decided to try his draw only on the sturdiest of any small animals he could find. So it was that he ended up spending the rest of the morning staring intently at a particularly uncooperative tapir.

Professor Turner had given each of them an energy receiver, so that by the end of the lesson they had a precise log of the type of animals used and the amount of energy drawn each time. At lunchtime, as the students returned their receivers to the teacher, they saw Barth walking up the path, soaked from head to toe.

'What happened to you?' asked Faith.

'That nasty platypus just wouldn't stand still,' he said, trailing water all over the place. All the Mizkis collapsed into fits of laughter so contagious that even Professor Turner found it hard to stifle a giggle.

After their meal, Julius and his classmates made their way to Professor Clavel's classroom in eager anticipation of their Pilot Training lesson.

'I wonder what we'll be doing this year,' said Morgana to no one in particular, as she was bouncing along the promenade.

'Look at her,' said Skye, nodding in her direction. 'We aren't even in class, and she's already hyper.'

'Wait until she starts her chosen subjects,' said Julius. 'Then you'll see her really take off. Her head will be so high up in the clouds she won't even notice us lot.'

'Huh?' asked Morgana, suddenly turning around. 'Did someone say something?'

They looked at her in amusement.

'See? What did I tell you?' said Julius to the boys; then to Morgana, 'Nothing dear, just talking about the weather.'

When they arrived at their classroom, Clavel was already inside.

'Welcome back Mizkis,' he said. 'I'm glad to see that even after two years you're still punctual.'

Julius looked around at the enthusiastic faces of his classmates. There was no doubt that Clavel was one of the most liked teachers in Tijara, so their constant punctuality didn't surprise him at all.

'We have a very special destination set for you this year, and this is what you'll need to pilot in order to get there,' he said, touching a section of his desk. Immediately, a holographic image appeared in the space behind him.

Julius looked up and saw a shuttle pod revolving slowly on its own axis. He had been in one of them before: a four-seater used to carry people to and from spaceships.

'I wondered when we would get to piloting them,' said Faith, sounding quite pleased at the prospect.

'What's the destination we're going to, Professor?' asked Morgana, who looked about ready to leap up and down in her seat with excitement.

'Your destination,' continued Clavel, 'is Gea One—our very own space station.' A new holographic image appeared above his head, leaving the students in stunned silence. The Gea was a metal sphere, surrounded by two rings crossing over each other in a perpetual motion. 'The Gea can hold 300 people, and for three months it will be Tijara's new school.'

'Holy Fagioli!' cried Faith, shaking Julius by the shoulders. He looked at Clavel. 'Professor, please, no more! Me heart can't take it!'

'Too bad, Mr Shanigan,' said Clavel, 'since I was about to show you the last surprise. But if you don't want to ...'

'No, no! Don't listen to him,' cut in Morgana, flushed cheeks and all. 'Tell us, Professor!'

'Here it is, then,' he said, smiling and pointing upwards. 'The Heron.' The two holograms suddenly shrunk and moved to the side, leaving centre stage to a starship.

Julius had seen this model before, and he was aware of it being a larger version of the Cougars. The Heron was a water drop-shaped, flat ship with two fins sticking out from the middle of its upper and lower sides, capable of carrying 100 passengers.

'Awesome,' whispered Barth, full of wonder.

Although Julius had already been given the heads up by Captain Kelly about their impending stay in orbit, his concerns about Michael had driven it clear out of his mind, which was why he had not mentioned it to the others. Remembering his chat with Kelly however, made him think of his brother again, and the sadness that fell over him dampened his excitement about Gea One. In the confusion around him though, no one had noticed his sudden change of mood, so Julius had a chance to breathe deeply, compose himself and force a smile onto his face.

For the rest of the lesson, the Mizkis explored the contents of their class programmes in some depth, so that they had a schedule of what lay ahead in the coming weeks. Learning to pilot and maintain the shuttle pod was going to be their focus until the mid-winter break.

On Tuesday morning Julius woke up well before his eight o'clock alarm. After a quick shower, he headed for the mess-hall, and bumped into Faith in the food queue.

'Really looking forward to me new classes, mate,' said Faith, filling his plate with scrambled eggs and smoked salmon.

'Same here,' said Julius. 'Starship Management: I wonder who else has chosen it.'

'I know that Lopaka's in me class. I didn't think he'd like engineering. Apparently it's a family thing. Go figure.'

'Shame we have to split, though.'

'It sucks, actually. At least it's only for a couple of mornings.'

Julius nodded. He didn't like the idea, but there was nothing to be done about it. He would never have chosen engineering just to be with Faith for a few hours on a Tuesday morning; he would have hated it and probably failed the course. Besides, they would have plenty of time to catch up afterwards.

At 08:50, Julius went to the holographic sector, on level -6, and waited for Professor Farshid to arrive. A few minutes later, three of his classmates—Zolin Acalan, Kaleb Kashny and Yuri Slovich—came around the corner, and greeted him cheerfully. Julius waved back.

'Great!' said Yuri. 'I knew you'd be here, McCoy.'

'Julius,' said Kaleb, 'it looks like it's us two against these spacemen. All-boys teams.'

Julius smiled at the joke: he and Kaleb both came from Earth, while Zolin was from Colonial 1 and Yuri, like Skye, was from Terra 3.

'Ahem.' The group turned to look in the direction of the sound. 'Did you really think there would be no ladies present?' said Leanne Nord, walking towards them in her usual confident stride.

'You know, Leanne,' said Jiao Yu, who was walking next to her, 'I think they did.'

'Tut, tut,' added Astra Evangelou, who was a few steps behind the other two girls. 'I bet we can teach you a thing or two.'

'I bet you could,' answered Zolin, grinning cheekily. 'Right, guys?'

'You're so immature,' said Leanne, shaking her head, and pretending to be offended.

The banter continued like that for the next few minutes, with more goodhearted retaliation from the boys, matched equally by the girls. Julius, who still wasn't much good at chatting with girls, found himself suddenly wishing for Morgana's reassuring presence. Seeing as that wasn't possible right then, he quietly stepped back, happy to watch them from the sidelines.

It wasn't long before Professor Farshid arrived and opened up the classroom. Inside, it had already been set up with eight single desks, forming a circle. Julius sat between Yuri and Astra, facing Kaleb.

'My, my—seven students,' said Farshid, raising an eyebrow. 'More than I was expecting.'

Julius tried to read her, but couldn't quite get any sense of whether she was genuinely pleased by the turnout, or not. She seemed quite different from his other teachers, that was certain. She didn't have the warmth of Morales, or the natural ease of King and Clavel; at the same time she wasn't as stern as Chan or Beloi either. Truth to be told, the only person Julius could compare her to was none other than Grand Master Freja: someone who inspired authority, but still managed to be quite accessible at the same time. You wouldn't want to joke around with Freja, but you could be sure he would help you when the chips were down. Were those the qualities of a good captain? Julius wasn't entirely sure, but he knew that was what he was here to find out.

'This tends to be a small class,' explained Farshid. 'Five is the average number of students who generally sign up.

Being a captain is a dream for many, but a reality for few.' She let her words hang in the air for a moment, to let them sink in. 'It's not my intention to scare you, Mizkis, but you need to know that if your ship is under attack, its shields are down and the engines offline, every single crew member will be looking at you, demanding a solution. And you must give it to them. In the face of death, you must be larger than life. It is unthinkable for a captain to be anything less than that.'

Julius felt a shiver run down his spine—her words had definitely hit home for him.

Professor Farshid looked down and touched a point on her desk. Suddenly, the room disappeared, and was instantly replaced with what looked like the engine room of a large spaceship. There was a collective gasp from the students at the sudden change, since they were now sitting in the middle of a bustling environment, with holographic crew members hurrying to and fro, and a massive plasma core engine to one side.

Julius shifted in his chair, looking wide-eyed at the scene unfolding all around him. His classmates were equally captivated by their surroundings, their heads turning left and right, trying to take everything in.

'A captain has many responsibilities,' she continued. 'Although you will not be expected to actually fix an engine, attend to a sick crew member, cook a meal or even pilot your ship, you must know everything that goes on onboard.' As she spoke, she continued pressing different points on her desktop, and every time she did, the scene around them altered.

From the engine room they found themselves in the sick bay, followed by the canteen, and the bridge. In each of these areas, there were always dozens of the holo crew walking around them, and even sometimes through them, attending to their duties.

'During the course of this year,' said Farshid, 'you will familiarise yourself with all the areas that make up a spaceship, from the living quarters to the bridge; the amount of staff required to man these areas and the tasks of each individual under your command, whether they be your tactical officers, your science officers, or your chefs.'

Julius continued looking around avidly, even though he had already been on spaceships before, and had a pretty good idea of what was expected from a captain, thanks to Kelly's help.

'Check your PIP before coming to class,' continued Farshid. 'Some days we will work in here, others in the Grey Arts sector. So Mizkis, still think you have what it takes?'

'Yes, Ma'am,' they replied as one.

'So let it be,' nodded the teacher, satisfied.

Certainly, Julius knew in his heart that this was his calling; it would be hard, but he was up for it. The simulation faded slowly away, and on each desk appeared a blueprint for the Heron.

'Professor Clavel has already told you that you'll soon be manning this ship,' said Farshid. 'I want you to go over every nook and cranny of it, taking extensive notes of the different sectors. In two weeks time I want you each to hand in a detailed report on the essential areas required to create a fully functional ship, and the minimum number of crew members needed to man them.'

The students liked the idea of this so much that, when Julius asked if they could start straight away, they all eagerly backed him up.

Farshid had no problem with that, and spent the next three hours answering their questions and raising any issues with their planning. 'I know it spoils your design, Mr Kashny,' she said tapping on Kaleb's sketch, 'but a toilet is a necessary part of a spaceship, and the bridge is not the right place for it.'

Julius was pleased to see how easily this new subgroup was forming a bond right from the start, though he suspected that at some point there would come a time for competitiveness. But ultimately, each of them wanted to be Zed captains, and so were all on the same side.

That afternoon, at lunch, The Skirts met up as usual, and had to force themselves to take it in turns telling each other about their morning, since they were trying to all talk at the same time. The excitement was so great that, when Morales took them to the infirmary for their annual shield-chip update, Faith didn't complain, and instead volunteered to go first. His good mood wasn't even dampened when Dr Walliser asked him to remain behind to fit his skirt with an extra panel at the bottom (to make up for his growing height), along with the corresponding sensors inside his legs. To Julius' amazement, he was still chatting away about engineering when he joined them later for tea, seemingly oblivious of the fact that he had just spent the afternoon being poked and cut in various parts of his body.

Wednesday morning saw the 3MAs maintaining the same level of excitement as the previous day, as they went along to the first sessions of their second chosen subjects.

Julius headed for the holographic sector, to meet Professor Jeremy Gould, who was head of Catalyst Training in Tijara. As he stepped into the room, he was surprised to see Isolde Frey there. He had never thought of her as a fighter.

'Hi Julius,' she said, her long, dark braid swaying behind her shoulders as she turned. 'Guess who the only two Mizkis attending this class are?'

'Hi,' he replied. 'Just us two, huh?'

'Yes. And you look surprised to see me, I'd say. Or maybe you're just disappointed.'

'Uh, no ... well, ok, yes. A little,' he answered, awkwardly. Then, realising his blunder, he hurried forward, waving his hands in the air. 'I didn't mean that! I'm not disappointed, honest. I meant what you said first, surpr-'

'Whatever,' Isolde interrupted, turning away from him, the cheeriness gone from her voice.

Julius rolled his eyes, mouthing the word "idiot" to himself, then sat at the desk to her right. This was just perfect, he thought. By the look of things, Tuesday mornings would see him stuck in the middle a bunch of hormonal classmates, happily engaged in romantic bantering, while Wednesdays would see him one-to-one with a touchy girl. All in all, two of Julius' worst nightmares. On the bright side, he knew Isolde a little better than the girls in his other class, on account of her being such close friends with Morgana.

Professor Gould arrived at 09:00, on the dot, and nodded curtly to his students before activating his terminal. Julius had discovered that Gould was from Terra 1, same as Grand Master Freja; the only two Tijaran teachers from outer space. There was a long-held rumour about him, supported by many of the Senior Mizkis, that he slept with his Gauntlet under his pillow, just in case. Julius thought that, if it was true, he must either be one hardcore fighter, or a complete pillock.

'Miss Frey,' said Gould, examining a file on his desk, 'Professor Clavel believes you capable of becoming a catalyst specialist.'

'Yes, sir,' she replied.

'And what practical experience have you had so far?'

Julius looked at Isolde, also quite curious to find out.

'As well as maintaining excellent grades in class, sir,' said Isolde, a hint of nerves in her voice, 'I have used the Hologram Palace regularly, each week, for the past two years. I rank third overall in the female Fight chart for the whole of Zed.'

Julius was definitely impressed by that. He regularly checked the Solo scores and the progress of the Skirts against similar teams, but he had never thought to check any of the other types of charts, which was why Isolde's record caught him completely by surprise.

Professor Gould nodded. 'It's a good start.' Then he turned to Julius. 'Mr McCoy, you come highly recommended for this course. Between your Solo record, the Skirts' endeavours, and your past two Summer Camp experiences, I am sure you can easily prove your worth to me. Remember though, arriving at the top isn't difficult; remaining there is. Don't become complacent in your success, or you may lose your status before you even realise it.'

'Yes, sir,' answered Julius, glad that Gould, while acknowledging his past achievements, hadn't made too much of a big deal about it.

Professor Gould picked up two virtual files from his desktop, pinching each one between thumb and forefinger. 'Open your PIPs, please.'

Julius activated his, and watched as Gould flicked the file in his left hand toward him. To the eye, these data files always appeared like luminous, tiny specs of gold, as they travelled between two points. Julius knew though, that they contained a massive storage of information. The file floated briskly towards his activated PIP, accelerating as it got closer, and was rapidly sucked into the holographic screen on his palm.

'This is your 3MA programme,' said Gould. 'I want you to read it before next Wednesday. As well as a breakdown of topics, it has the dates of a series of checkpoints scattered throughout the year. We don't have exams on Zed, as you know, but by each checkpoint you must have mastered the topics up to that date, or you will not be able to progress. If, by the end of the year, you have not cleared all of them, you will not be allowed to continue on this course as a 4MA. Is this clear?'

'Yes, sir,' they quickly answered.

'Good. Let's start from scratch.' A screen flickered to life behind his head, displaying an image of a Zed officer manning a spaceship catalyst. His hands were clenched tight around the lever, seemingly releasing a vast amount of energy. 'As you know, a catalyst channels your energies and shoots them out in the form of a yellow laser beam. Meditation is what gives you focus and precision for shooting; this White Art is especially useful when you are piloting a Cougar. Why is that, Miss Frey?'

'Because, on a one-man vessel, such as a Cougar, you fly it using only your mind-skills, since your hands are busy operating the catalyst,' she answered promptly. 'Therefore Meditation is vital, as it helps you concentrate on doing the right things at the right time.'

'Correct, Miss Frey. A fleet is only as strong as the fighters in it; if you're having a bad day, or you're distracted for whatever reason, and without a way of replenishing your energies, you will not be able to attack an enemy, or defend your ship.' The image behind Gould slowly changed to one of a fighter looking increasingly tired, while the beam from his catalyst was growing weaker. 'You must know how to manage your powers, and how to reload quickly.' Again, the image changed. This time the fighter was firing short bursts of energy, rather than one continuous stream, and intermittently drinking some kind of liquid from a long tube connected to the wall right behind the catalyst. He appeared to be very lively now. Professor Gould dismissed the screen with a wave of his hand, and looked at the two Mizkis. 'A catalyst is just a piece of metal—you are the real weapon.'

Even if he hadn't been able to see the orange wisps in Gould's aura, it was clear enough to Julius that the professor was passionate about his work. As the teacher talked, it wasn't just words that Julius heard; behind every gesture and facial expression, there was a story to tell. To Julius, being described as a weapon was particularly strange, especially now, in a society where conventional weapons no longer existed.

Before the Chemical War of 2550, someone like Julius or Isolde would have been seen as a threat to humanity, or as someone to be used in the then common wars between nations. The death of some twelve billion people in that war had changed all that though, leaving the remaining three billion-odd to face up to their own mortality. After a global promise of never again, weapons had been completely banned and the planet became the D.R.E., the Democratic Republic of Earth, under the guidance of the Earth Leader and the five Voices of the Earth, representing each of the five agreed continents. It was only because of the Arneshians that words like "weapons", and "military" had been reintroduced into everyday vocabulary, although Julius was glad they were now more commonly used in reference to defence, rather than offence.

'We shall start this course by examining a catalyst up close and personal,' said Professor Gould. 'Behind you, there are three basic types of catalyst, one set for each of you. You've seen them before, during Pilot Training. Today, instead of using them, I want you to take them apart.' He walked towards the back of the room, motioning for them to follow.

Julius let Isolde choose first, and then moved to the remaining empty table with the catalysts propped on it. There were all manner of screwdrivers, pliers and tools of different shapes and sizes that Julius had never seen before, all neatly arranged on a large tray to the side of them. Julius looked at them with apprehension. 'Faith would be able to do this in a jiff,' he whispered to Isolde.

'Yeah, and we need to learn how to do it just as well as he would,' she replied.

He was pleased to notice that some of the coldness had left her voice.

'I want you to make a note of the name and function of each individual piece,' said Gould. 'By the end of October you must be able to assemble each one of them in less than a minute; this will be your first checkpoint. And now, to work!'

'To work then,' repeated Julius softly, looking at his catalysts, not sure where to begin.

By one o'clock neither he, nor Isolde, had managed to finish the task. Professor Gould however, wasn't especially displeased and pointed out that to fully catalogue each piece and understand its function for the first time certainly wasn't a job for one lesson. Those words reassured Julius greatly and, judging by the greenish wisps visible in Isolde's aura, they had had the same effect on her.

Later that day, Julius bumped into the rest of the Skirts in the promenade, and they headed for lunch together, once again eagerly sharing every detail of their new subjects with the others.

'Wow,' said Skye, swallowing his last French fry whole. 'Isolde's a fighter. Who would have thought?'

'You should have paid more attention to the girls' charts,' said Morgana.

'No, please,' cut in Julius. 'He already pays enough attention to girls as it is.'

'I'm honing my diplomatic skills,' answered Skye, defensively. 'In my position it's very handy to be as close as possible to as many people as possible, I'll have you know.'

'I'm not even gonna ask what position that is,' muttered Julius.

'Your *position*?' said Faith. 'Have you already replaced the Curio Maximus, then?'

'Not yet,' said Skye, with a cheeky grin, 'but I'm working on it. I found out that his daughter works at Colonial Affairs too.'

'You're unbelievable,' said Morgana, rolling her eyes.

'Moving on,' said Julius, punching Skye on the shoulder, 'how was Starship Architecture, Faith?'

'Really grand,' he answered. 'It's going to be the best course yet for me, and there's this competition as well, you know.'

'What competition?' asked Morgana.

'Apparently every few years Pit-Stop Pete runs it and you have to design a spaceship from scratch. It's open to all Mizki Apprentices and Seniors and, if you win, they actually build it as a one-off.'

'That's just, Faith,' enthused Julius.

'You should definitely go for it, mate,' added Skye. 'Who better than you?'

'I'm not too sure,' said Faith, sounding a bit worried. 'It's packed with older Mizkis and I really don't want to shame meself by making something horrible. I mean, I just started the course, I couldn't possibly-'

'Faith,' interrupted Morgana, 'when was the last competition held?'

'Nine years ago.'

'So this could be your only chance to realise the biggest dream you've ever had, and you're still debating about entering?'

'Well ...'

'That's it,' she said, standing up abruptly. 'You've lost your marbles. Come with me, now!'

'What ... hey!' uttered Faith, as Morgana grabbed him by the waist of his skirt and dragged him out of the mess hall, fork still in hand, past the staring eyes of a group of 1MJs.

'That girl's a handful,' said Lopaka Liway, stopping next to their table, holding an empty tray. He was looking at Morgana with a longing expression on his face.

'Too big of a handful for you, my friend,' said Skye, standing up and patting him on the shoulder.

'I'll show you both a handful, if you don't drop that kind of talk right now!' said Julius, brushing past them and returning his tray to the counter.

'What's with him?' asked Lopaka. 'I can never talk about girls with him.'

'Late puberty,' said Skye.

'I heard that,' Julius called from behind them.

'Oops. Better go,' he whispered to Lopaka. Then to Julius, 'Coming dear!'

When Morgana and Faith joined the others in Professor Beloi's Telepathy class, Faith was positively beaming. 'Professor de Boer said that Pete was counting on me signing up,' he told them, clearly chuffed by that.

Morgana just sat there, a little satisfied smile on her face.

'*Well done, you,*' Julius told her with his mind.

'*Someone had to,*' she replied.

Professor Beloi announced himself to the students in his customary way, with a sudden mind-message, taking them all by surprise. They should have known better by now really, especially since their Russian teacher had not uttered a single word in forty-one years, which was probably the reason why he was the best telepathist the world had ever known. '*Good afternoon, Mizkis,*' he said, entering the classroom. '*Take a seat.*'

The students quickly complied.

'*In light of our recent encounters with the Arneshians, we are going to step up the pace this year. I have already sent my programme to each of you, and I expect all of you to-* '

'All personnel and Mizkis, please activate Space Channel one immediately!' a voice boomed over the loudspeaker.

The students looked at Beloi, who appeared to be as surprised as they were. '*Very well,*' he said, and activated a large screen on the front wall, so the entire class could see it.

Julius exchanged a worried look with the others. Interrupting lessons so the whole school could watch the Space Channel wasn't exactly an omen of good news, and judging by the grey wisps above Beloi's head, that was exactly what he was thinking too. There was complete silence as the words "Breaking News" rolled across the screen.

'Good afternoon Zed,' said the anchorwoman, Iryana Mielowa.

Julius recognised her immediately, with her dark wavy hair and bright red lipstick—she was probably the most familiar face on the Lunar Perimeter. She was sometimes also half-jokingly referred to as "the harbinger of moon."

'We are interrupting our regular broadcast to report an unprecedented event: less than thirty minutes ago Earth Channel News received a recorded vidcall from Manuel T'Rogon, the High Ambassador of the Arneshians.'

'The what of who?' said Faith, incredulous.

'The video has already spread like wildfire throughout Earth and the regular colonies,' continued Ms Mielowa, 'creating considerable unrest. Here, now, we will be showing it on the Space Channel in its entirety.'

Julius shifted uncomfortably in his seat with a growing sense of unease. What could the Arneshian ambassador possibly have to say to Earth? He could feel the tension in the air, as no one uttered a sound.

Professor Beloi had also taken a seat next to Barth, and was staring at the screen like the rest of them.

The image switched from Ms Mielowa to that of a hefty man, seated behind a dark, mahogany desk. When Julius saw him, he unconsciously leaned forward, so as to observe him better; after all, this was the first time he was seeing an *actual* Arneshian, as opposed to one of their holographic servants. To his surprise however, Manuel T'Rogon looked just like any other human, and nothing in his features suggested otherwise: he had pale blue eyes and a thin, pointy nose; his short, pearl-white hair shimmered as the light caught it. He was wearing a metal circlet around his head, while his body was garbed in what appeared to be a long silver tunic, with gold details embroidered on the front. Still, there was something odd about him, but Julius couldn't quite pinpoint what. All in all though, T'Rogon was a bit disappointing, perhaps because a tiny part of Julius' brain had half-expected to see tentacles sprouting out of his head or, at the very least, an extra set of ears.

'Earthlings, on behalf of Queen Salgoria of Arnesh, I bring tidings of peace and goodwill,' said the ambassador.

His voice was calm and welcoming and Julius immediately noticed a distinct absence of any accent. T'Rogon was using the common speech in its purest form, untouched by the regional variations that he was used to hearing on Zed.

'For the past 200 years our people have been at war. No more, we say. Let us bury the hatchet of hatred and division, in favour of a new era of prosperity and peace. Let us build bridges, not walls. Let us bring to life the dream once shared by Clodagh Arnesh and Marcus Tijara. Words cannot fully express the sentiment of regret that we Arneshians feel for what we have done against Earth, our mother world. Nonetheless, I am here to formally lay at your door the most heartfelt apologies from my queen and my people, with the hope that you will allow us to demonstrate our sincerity. Thank you,' he concluded, bowing his head.

The image faded to black, then switched back to Mielowa. 'Ambassador T'Rogon and his entourage will enter the lunar orbit within the next two weeks. More news in tonight's edition. Iryana Mielowa, reporting live from the Space Channel.'

'Is this a joke?' said Skye, breaking the astonished silence.

'*I'm afraid not, Mr Miller,*' answered Beloi, returning to his desk.

'He's not seriously expecting us to let him waltz in and park his ship in our backyard, is he?'

'*But that's exactly what he'll do,*' answered Beloi. '*He has diplomatic immunity, and he is going to use it.*'

'I don't believe this!' cried Skye, jumping up, his cheeks flushed.

Morgana delicately placed a hand on his forearm, to calm him. It had the desired effect, because he took a deep breath and slowly sat back down.

Julius knew how sensitive Skye was when it came to the Arneshians—his opinion was very much black-and-white when it came to taking sides in that regard. As was the case with anyone who had grown up on a Zed space station, he had been raised with the fear that attack could befall them at any minute; he had never forgiven the Arneshians for letting him, his family and friends grow up in such way. 'Professor,' said Julius, 'isn't there a danger that they may try to attack us while in our orbit?'

'Yes!' added Barth, looking agitated. 'What if they detonate their ship near Pit-Stop Pete?'

'Oh no, they won't!' answered Faith quickly, fist in the air. He was very protective when it came to Pete Kingston.

'*Mizkis,*' said Beloi, '*do not fret. There will be no explosion, at Pete's or anywhere else. Every visiting ship that comes within our orbit is always completely encased within a magnetic field, for everyone's peace of mind. And if they do "detonate", Mr Smit, they would be blown to smithereens within their own containment field. Now please, excuse me for a few minutes.*' Excited whispering broke out among the students, while Beloi moved towards the back of the room and activated his PIP.

The Mizkis gathered up into small groups, to discuss the situation and try to figure out what T'Rogon's real intentions were. Skye continued to vent his frustration with those students who, like him, had grown up in outer space, feeling that only they could truly understand what it meant to feel the enemy's breath on the back of their necks. Faith and the other engineers, who were apparently not convinced by Beloi's reassurances, were discussing the defence system of Pete's docking station and just how big an explosion it could sustain, while Morgana was simply listening to his words and at the same time keeping a worried eye on Julius, who had fallen completely silent.

Julius' mind had left his classmates' concerns far behind and had drifted off in a different direction: he was focused only on Michael. Had his brother already seen this video? How would he react to it, now that he knew he was one of them too? Would he even understand properly what any of this meant? Julius had no answers to those questions, but deep down he had a feeling this abrupt change of heart from the Arneshians was not going to play out easily at all.

CHAPTER 4

LONG LOST FRIENDS

In the weeks that followed T'Rogon's video appearance, all conversation boiled down to just one topic: the armistice with the Arneshians. Every inhabitant on the Lunar Perimeter was very sceptical about the idea of any possible truce. There was no great love of the need for any military action, but their distrust of Salgoria's people had grown deep over the last two centuries.

Many of Julius' classmates were quite prepared to voice their views on the Space Channel, should they be asked, but all the students had been instructed to refrain from doing anything of the sort until the official position of the Curia was known. Still, that didn't prevent the Mizkis spending most of their waking hours discussing the Arneshians' real intentions, much to the annoyance of their teachers, who found it difficult to get them to focus on even their most basic exercises.

On Monday the 26th of September, Julius and Faith were in the Apprentices' lounge, tackling their homework. Even though they were enrolled in different subjects, studying together still made things easier. Faith was lying on one of the sofas with an e-book about plasma cores propped on his belly, and his metallic skirt flattened around his legs; Julius had taken over the large rug in the middle of the room, with the various bits and pieces required for assembling a catalyst spread out in front of him. Professor Gould had set the first of their checkpoints for the end of October and occasionally, Faith would offer Julius advice on quicker ways of doing things, which was gratefully received.

Later that evening, Skye and Morgana entered the lounge in a hurry, followed by Barth and Siena.

'They're here,' said Skye, heading straight for the large TV screen on the back wall, and switching it on.

Julius instantly knew who he was referring to, and a little shiver ran down his back. They had been waiting the whole day for this: the Arneshian delegation was about to enter lunar orbit. Faith sat up, making space for Morgana and Siena next to him. Skye and Barth sat down on the floor beside Julius. No one spoke as Iryana Mielowa appeared on the screen.

'I'm standing inside the Zed docks, surrounded by the lunar leaders, awaiting the most anticipated event in modern human history: the visit of the Arneshian delegation. The tension here is tangible, and the last of the preparations have now been completed. The Curio Maximus, Aldobrando Roversi, has just arrived, accompanied by some of the Curiates. Behind me, you can see them talking to the Grand Masters and the Masters of the three schools.'

'Wait a minute,' said Morgana. 'What are the Cur ... the uh, Curi ... the whatchamacallems doing there?'

'The Curiates,' volunteered Skye. 'They help Roversi make important decisions. They're like his council, that's why they're here. I've just studied that actually, but don't ask me their names.'

Morgana nodded, clearly impressed.

Julius scanned the people in the background and easily spotted the faces which were familiar to him: apart from Freja and Cress, he recognised Roversi and the other Grand Masters, Kloister and Milson, having met them a few months earlier, during their rescue mission aboard Angra

Mainyu. That left seven people he had never seen before, and he guessed that five were the Curiates, and two would have to be the Masters of Tuala and Sield.

A minute later, the image switched to a view looking out into space, with Pit-Stop Pete's docking station in the left of the screen. Mielowa continued her commentary of events but, for the moment at least, nothing was happening.

'Where are they?' asked Morgana impatiently.

Suddenly, as if in answer, a large, dark blob blinked into view, filling the screen. Mielowa's tiny yelp of surprise was most likely echoed by numerous others watching the coverage. Slowly, the formless mass began to stretch out in all directions, and gradually took on a spherical shape, until it was a hulking, solid, steel structure, which looked big enough to fit the entire lunar perimeter inside it.

'Oh my,' gasped Siena.

'Will you look at that,' said Faith, his jaw dropping open in sheer admiration.

'It's just a ship,' added Skye, pretending not to care.

'Miller, that is *not* just a ship,' Faith retorted. 'I would guess that Zed has never seen the likes of her. I get how you feel about those fools, but when it comes to starships, man, they seem to know what they're doing.'

Skye shook his head and didn't reply.

Julius was with Faith on this one. He didn't even know that starships could morph like that, never mind that it seemed it had made the journey to Zed in a shapeless state. 'How's that even possible?' he said, pointing at it.

'I'm dying to find out,' replied Faith, leaning forward towards the screen. 'And I bet Pete is pretty keen too.'

'Taurus One,' said Morgana. 'Look, the name is written under that hatch there.'

'Maybe it's because they come from the Taurus constellation,' offered Barth.

'I would so love to pilot one of those,' continued Morgana. 'Mind you, I can't even tell where the front of this thing is.'

'You know,' said Siena, sounding puzzled, 'for a diplomatic mission, they sure brought a large ship with them.'

Skye snorted in reply and crossed his arms, a disapproving expression etched all over his face. 'Diplomatic mission my a-'

'Look,' cut in Julius. 'There's a port opening up.'

They all watched as a cavity appeared, creating a dark patch in the steel body. A small shuttle pod emerged from it, making a direct course for the Zed docks. The camera followed the vessel until it crossed the Zed shield, then switched to Iryana Mielowa, back on the platform. She had moved closer to the landing area where, being the only TV station allowed access, there was no need for the cameramen to fight for a good spot.

'Look at Freja's face,' said Barth. 'He doesn't seem very happy about this.'

'Who would be?' snorted Skye. 'He's probably wondering where the trap is.'

Julius had no way of knowing what his Grand Master was thinking about, but he could see plenty of dull, grey wisps radiating from him, and the others around him, causing a kind of ghostly puddle on the concrete floor beneath them. They were definitely worried about something and, on that score, Skye was correct—who wouldn't be?

Silently, the shuttle pod landed and everyone held their breath. The hatch slid open noiselessly, and a moccasin-clad foot appeared. The Arneshian ambassador stepped out, the thin metal circlet on his head glistening in the light. Manuel T'Rogon had arrived.

Julius stared, transfixed, at the screen. The ambassador was wearing the same gold-detailed tunic that he had on the day of the first broadcast; he could see now that it reached almost to his feet. He was taller than Julius had previously thought, and broadly built. His head was held up with pride, his stern features softened a little by just a hint of an enigmatic smile. Roversi, Freja and the other Zed leaders bowed their heads in the customary lunar fashion. T'Rogon responded in kind.

'Is it just me, or is his skin slightly ... greyish?' asked Morgana.

'That's it!' said Julius, slapping his thigh. 'I knew there was something odd about him during that broadcast, but I couldn't tell what.'

'Apparently it's to do with the atmosphere on Arnesh,' explained Barth, timidly.

'Well well, look who's been doing his homework,' said Faith. 'I'm impressed.'

Barth blushed vividly, smiled, and resumed his viewing in silence.

Once all the protocols for receiving guests had been followed, four more Arneshian delegates stepped out from the shuttle pod. They were clothed in similar robes, and each had matching circlets around their heads. After they had all been greeted, Roversi and T'Rogon led the way, followed by the Grand Masters, while the Masters and Curiates escorted the remaining Arneshian delegates. As they disappeared off the screen, the cameraman zoomed in on Ms Mielowa. She was positively beaming, no doubt fully aware what a honour it was to be giving witness to such an event. 'You saw it here first, ladies and gentlemen. Iryana Mielowa, for the Space Channel.'

'Don't you think it's odd,' said Morgana, a week later over breakfast, 'that people back on Earth seem to be a wee bit too positive about this whole ceasefire thing?'

'To be sure,' agreed Faith. 'You would have thought they'd be more concerned about their real intentions. I mean, everyone knows how dirty they've played recently.'

'Actually they don't really,' said Julius, looking up from his food and meeting their surprised gazes. 'I was talking to Captain Kelly about it, and he told me that the Curia doesn't pass all information on to Earth. They only communicate with the students' parents, as you know.'

'But, that's not right,' said Morgana.

'That's exactly what I told Kelly,' answered Julius

'What do you mean?' asked Skye. 'Why?'

'Well, he says it's because there's no point scaring folks with stories of kidnappings and the like when they can't do anything about it.'

'Good grief,' said Faith. 'Can you imagine if they did ever find out about the kidnappings? Not to mention the truth about old Bastiaan Grant's death all those years ago. They would have kittens!'

'It certainly wouldn't look too good for Colonial Affairs,' said Julius.

'Or Zed,' added Faith. 'Let's hope they never find out.'

'I think it may be too late for that,' said Skye, pointing at one of the mess hall screens. 'Look.'

Julius, Faith and Morgana turned quickly in that direction, while from a nearby table, Leanne Nord shouted, 'Everybody! Quiet.'

Iryana Mielowa was speaking above a "Breaking News" sign, with "T'Rogon reveals Grant's fate at last" written underneath that. As someone turned up the volume on the TV, the seriousness of this latest report immediately became apparent. 'As a token of goodwill, Ambassador T'Rogon has delivered several top secret files to Earth Leader, Paulo

Trent. These files include the shocking truth behind the death of Bastiaan Grant, the Tuala Master who disappeared six years ago, and the recent series of abductions from Zed, all at the hands of the Arneshians. In a statement, T'Rogon said, "We wish to come clean about all of this." As the contents of these top secret files leak their way around the global media, we are hearing more and more reports of people in favour of peace negotiations with the Arneshians, while the Curia's reputation seems to be at a major low for the first time in the history of Zed.'

'I can't believe he gave those files to Trent,' said Morgana, sounding completely stunned.

'Oh, he has his reasons, I'm sure,' said Skye bitterly. 'No doubt he wants to discredit us in the eyes of our own people.'

'He's very clever,' agreed Julius. 'By apologising for what they've done wrong, they're showing their good side, while we look like the ones scheming to keep secrets from Earth.'

'If you think about it,' said Faith, 'not even me relatives back home—apart from Mum and Dad—knew what happened to those girls last year. Did you tell your aunt or uncle, Julius?'

'No, I didn't. Academy honour code, rule five: a student may only report to their immediate family, and they must not disclose anything therein to anyone else.'

'Exactly. And now that code has landed us in deep trouble. I bet you anything, every Zed student will be getting a call from home asking if it's true,' continued Faith.

'Yes, and straight after their kids, they'll be calling the schools, demanding an explanation,' concluded Julius.

'If you ask me,' said Morgana, 'the Curia brought this on itself. They're supposed to be the bridge between Earth and Space, not the gate.

'I wonder what's going to happen now,' said Skye.

'Whatever it is, it won't be good,' answered Julius with a sigh.

Julius realised just how accurate his prediction had been only a few days later. On Wednesday the 5th of October, it was Faith's fifteenth birthday, and thoughts of the recent events were put on hold for a little while. Skye, who had puppy-eyed his way into the heart of Felice Buongustaio, Zed's head chef, over the course of the previous two years, had now convinced him to create his deliciously deadly Supernova, a cake so called because of the untold amount of calories it contained. It was crammed with so much chocolate, nuts and fudge, that it could stall a nuclear reactor. It was, in fact, the only cake that carried warnings about its possible side effects, which included violent cramps, rashes on the scalp, and gout. Felice had made this cake only twice before and, after each occasion, he had promised Dr Walliser he wouldn't do it again. However, when it came to Skye, the chef had no will of his own.

Although Faith's party was being organised by his classmates, there were also other Mizkis in the garden, all of whom had heard of the Supernova at one point or another, but never actually seen one. When the 3MAs caught sight of the brown monster being carried into the garden, their cries of "Happy Birthday" abruptly died in their throats, giving way to a deferential silence.

'It does exist,' whispered Yuri Slovich and Ferenc Orban in chorus.

'Am I supposed to say thanks for that?' asked Faith, breaking out in a cold sweat.

Carefully, Felice placed the cake on a table, while the Mizkis gathered around. He looked at Faith and opened his hands. 'I could-a say Happy Birth-a-day, but-a maybe good luck it's-a better,' he said.

Faith looked at the 15 fat candles sticking out of the glossy, chocolate coated top, which looked more like lit sticks of dynamite, and gulped.

'Make a wish-a!' said Felice.

'I wish to still be alive tomorrow,' said Faith, looking at the cake with dread.

'Too bad-a,' said Felice. 'You told us the wish-a. Now it don't work no more.'

'What?!' gasped Faith.

By then Felice had already turned around and was heading back towards the kitchen, while the others laughed nervously.

'Miller!' cried Faith. 'This is all your fault. You go first.'

'No way. It's your party, dude.'

'Go on Faith,' said Julius. 'We'll all have a bite. Right guys?'

'Yeah, go on!' said Morgana.

'I've alerted Nurse Primula,' added Julius. 'She's on standby for the night.'

'Great,' said Faith, half-heartedly. He took a deep breath and blew out the candles while his friends cheered. Morgana and Siena removed them, being careful not to pour the hot wax over the surface of the cake. When they had removed the last one, Faith picked up the knife and placed it over the centre of the cake, looking very nervous.

'It won't explode, you know,' said Lopaka.

'Are you sure about that?'

Just then, a boy cried out from one corner of the garden, making Faith freeze. 'This can't be true!'

There was enough panic in his voice to instantly claim the attention of all present.

Julius looked to his left and saw a 4MA Mizki standing there, staring wide-eyed at his PIP screen, which was hovering above the boy's left hand.

'What's happened?' asked Morgana.

'They've stopped recruitment,' the boy said, his eyes not leaving the screen.

'What recruitment?' said Julius.

'The Zed Test Centres on Earth have all been shut down.'

Julius activated his PIP immediately, quickly followed by most of his classmates. Faith leaned in to look at Julius' screen. Sure enough, as soon as Julius clicked onto the News page there it was: the familiar "Breaking News" banner emblazoned beneath a picture of a test centre. Julius pushed the play button and watched as the video showed security personnel closing and locking the gates of the building.

'In an unprecedented move,' said Iryana Mielowa, 'Earth Leader Paulo Trent has declared that all Zed recruitment should be suspended until further notice. A full enquiry is to be launched into the various revelations contained in the files from Ambassador T'Rogon, to judge Zed's actions in all these matters.' The images continued to show the closure of various test centres around the world. Julius recognised the British one as it flashed up briefly. 'After the shocking discoveries of the past few days, more and more people are warming to the idea of negotiation with the Arneshians, with many growing extremely uneasy about the level of secrecy which has developed in the Lunar Perimeter. The decision to suspend recruitment was issued this afternoon and, although the consensus is still mixed, there seems to be many who would support a total closure of Zed.'

Julius closed his PIP. 'I can't believe this.' As he glanced around, most of the 3MAs had also finished watching the report, and were looking quite bewildered.

'Can they actually do that?' asked Morgana. 'I mean, Zed isn't controlled by the Earth Leader.'

'Aye, but we come from Earth,' said Julius. 'Obviously they must have some sort of power.'

'What if they keep them closed forever?' asked Barth.

'Unlikely,' replied Skye. 'They can't just abandon the space program. They'll need the technology, and it's all here.'

'What if they get the gear from the Arneshians?' asked Siena. 'We all know they're a lot more advanced than us.'

'And what?' said Faith quickly. 'Bypass us completely, like we don't exist?'

'They couldn't shut down Zed,' said Julius. 'Freja wouldn't let them, and neither would I.'

Faith sighed. 'Happy birthday to me. I think I'm ready for the Supernova now.'

'I think I may need a slice too,' said Skye. 'This news sucks, big time.'

'Well,' said Julius patting Faith on the shoulder, 'normally it's my birthday being spoiled by some Arneshian trick but this year the honour's all yours.'

'There's still time, McCoy,' he said glumly, raising an eyebrow. 'Mark my words.'

After Julius had finished a slice of the cake, which was indeed delicious, but which had also given him quite the sugar rush, he realised there was no way he would be able to eat any dinner. So he decided to instead call home and see how the latest news had been affecting his family. He was also hoping he would finally be able to talk to Michael, and see firsthand how he was coping with his new reality. To his surprise Skye, who was looking oddly indisposed, headed back to the room with him.

'You ok?' Julius asked.

'Not sure, actually. I don't think I should've had those slices.'

'Slices? How many did you have?'

'Four ... or five?'

'You know,' said Julius, opening the door to their room and allowing his friend to enter first, 'if you're sick tonight, you deserve it.'

Skye walked straight into the toilet and closed the door behind him.

'Shout if you need me to fetch the doctor,' called Julius, taking a seat at his desk. 'Computer, call home,' he said.

After a few seconds, Jenny McCoy's face appeared in the panel. 'Darling,' she said, a smile lighting up her features. 'I'm so glad you've called. We were just thinking about you!' She turned her back to Julius momentarily. 'Rory! Come here, quick. It's our boy!'

'Did you hear the news?' asked Julius, scanning the living room behind his mother, hoping that he would see Michael there somewhere.

'All of the news,' she replied. 'But I still can't believe Trent would want to stop recruiting like this.'

'Hiya son,' said Rory, taking a seat next to his wife.

'Hi Dad. How are things?'

'I guess we're all a wee bit shaken up. That T'Rogon though, I don't like the looks of him. It's fishy what he did with those secret files. Makes Zed look bad.'

'That's what we think he's trying to do,' agreed Julius.

'Is it true about Bastiaan Grant?' asked Jenny, sounding a little alarmed.

Julius nodded. 'Everything they've said is true. Hey, so where's Michael? Why hasn't he called me yet?'

'Your brother has been so gloomy since the test,' said Jenny. 'He really wants to talk to you, but I think he feels ashamed, because he failed.'

'But it's me. I don't care what they say he is.'

'That's the problem, Julius. It's because it is you and not some other random person,' said Jenny.

'I don't understand.'

'I thought you would have by now. Michael idolises you. He's always wanted to be like you. So to then fail that test, for him, it's like letting you down.'

'But I'm not perfect. I make mistakes: big ones too!'

'Julius darling, you'll always be his hero, no matter what you do.'

Julius wasn't sure what to answer. He felt genuinely touched but, at the same time, undeserving of such admiration. 'So, he won't talk to me?'

'Just give him a little more time. We'll tell him you called, and that you love him very much.'

Julius nodded sadly. 'Have you told anyone else about him being an Arneshian?'

'Some,' answered Rory, 'but no one really needs to be told, thanks to the choker he has to wear.'

'Has he had any problems because of it?'

'Not at all. Of course, people are surprised when they find out, but he's not the first, nor will he be the last. To a certain extent, it's only Michael who has to find a way to get over it. Everyone else isn't really that bothered.'

Julius, however, wasn't entirely convinced.

'Believe me son, here on Earth folks have a very different opinion of the Arneshians.'

'What's that? You don't approve of them, do you?' said Julius, sounding a bit more defensive than he meant to.

'It's not what you think darling,' said Jenny. 'We don't get to see the enemies of Zed, like you all do out there. We only know the Nuarns who live with us; the ones who work alongside us and contribute to our society. That's why people have a different perception here; it's a matter of habit.'

'Sure,' said Julius curtly. 'That's why they put collars around their necks, to remind them who's boss, right?'

'That's not the reason and you know it,' said Rory, calmly. 'The only reason Zed wants them to wear the chokers is because it blocks their Grey Arts. It prevents them from developing too fast, and ensures they don't-'

'Don't what, Dad?' blurted out Julius, realising that the conversation was taking a wrong turn, but unable to stop himself.

'That they don't become a threat,' finished Rory simply.

'A threat,' repeated Julius. 'That's what Michael is: a potential threat. You can embellish the story as much as you like, but no one treats them the same. Not even you, and he's your own son.'

Jenny's eyes began to fill with tears. She quickly stood up and disappeared from view.

'Mum!' Julius called. He leaned back against his chair, shaking his head. 'I ... I didn't mean it's her fault.'

'She knows that,' said Rory. He sounded exhausted. 'Look, we've been through some pretty big changes in the last month, all of us. Everyone's on edge. You have your own worries up there without having to deal with all this. Michael will come around, you'll see. As far as T'Rogon is concerned, he's done as much damage as he can. We'll recover and move on. Zed is still part of Earth and it won't be dismissed lightly. You, on the other hand, I know that you can't always tell us what happens in Tijara, but your mum and I would really appreciate some more news from you. I think any parent deserves that.'

'Sure,' he said. 'Listen, I need to go now, Dad. Say hi to Michael for me.'

'I ... yes, of course son. You take care now.'

Julius waved and closed the link. With the unhealthy sounds that Skye was producing next door, and the cake still rocking his stomach, he realised that maybe calling home just then hadn't been such a great idea. He had upset his mum for no good reason and he now felt quite miserable himself. Perhaps it was true: the people back home didn't think of the Arneshians as a constant threat, but as the guy or the girl next door. So when T'Rogon had come waltzing in, asking to make peace, no wonder they didn't really think there was anything odd about it. And on top of that, Zed was being made to look like it had something to hide, with no accountability to Earth or its citizens. Morgana was right: the Curia had brought this on itself.

Before retiring for the evening, Julius switched on his PIP, opened a new message addressed to his mum, and sent it. In it, he wrote just four words: *Sorry. I love you.*

CHAPTER 5

THE CHALLENGE

The morning after Faith's birthday, Professor Lao-Tzu had to cancel his Meditation lesson on account of more than two-thirds of his students being under the care of Dr Walliser. News soon spread around Tijara that the after-effects of the Supernova were taking their toll, which only added to the legendary status of Felice's cake. Julius wasn't feeling great but, since he had only eaten one small slice, he succeeded in removing the nasty aftertaste with a long lie-in and a glass of fresh mint water. With three hours of Martial Arts in the afternoon, he decided that he really should eat a little because, cake or no cake, Professor Chan would no doubt relentlessly put him through his paces. That said, given the amount of calories unleashed by the single slice Julius had eaten, he knew he could do with some serious exercise to help work it off.

When he got to class, Morgana was also there, along with Siena—the three of them bringing the class number up to five. The professor had activated the scenery panels in the walls, floor and ceiling so that they were now displaying a park, the leaves on the trees tinged with yellow-brown hues of Autumn. Clumps of the fallen virtual leaves swirled around their ankles as they jogged along the path for their warm up.

'So glad I only had a little taste of that dratted cake,' said Morgana, who was running with Julius on her right and Siena to her left.

'I thought more girls would have done the same thing,' said Julius.

'Why's that?' asked Morgana.

'You know ... waistline and all that. Skye says you girls are always talking about fitness and ... stuff.'

'Does he now?' replied Siena stiffly. 'That's not all we talk about, I'll have you know.'

Julius began to regret even mentioning anything about it. Was he supposed to ask about their other interests at this point, he wondered. He looked at Morgana, but her gaze stayed fixed ahead of her, a little smile curling one corner of her mouth.

'Hmm, what else do you talk about then?' he asked.

'Loads of stuff,' answered Siena. 'Life, school, love.'

Morgana giggled and Julius could feel his cheeks flushing. Why had he let himself get dragged into this?

'Come on, Julius,' said Siena. 'Don't you guys talk about girls too?'

'Not really. I mean, Skye does, and others, but we ... I don't ... Girls like Skye, and ... um .... no one's quite like him,' he finished awkwardly.

They laughed at his answer, in a friendly manner, and Julius knew there was nothing mocking about it. Still, he felt so embarrassed that he would have given anything for a change of topic just then, or even an Arneshian attack.

'McCoy,' said Siena, 'do you mean to tell me that you're completely unaware of the way some of the girls look at you? Because if that's the case, let's just drop this chat right now and re-open it when you wise up a little.'

He felt so stupid. Of course he did, he wasn't that blind. But right now he just wanted this conversation over, so he played dumb and shook his head. Thankfully, that was enough for Siena and she didn't push the subject any further. For the rest of the lesson, as they went through various training drills, the two girls chatted away about future shopping trips to Satras and various party ideas, while Julius tried his best to blend in with the walls, especially when they started discussing bra sizes.

As dinner time drew near that evening, the rest of the students were dismissed from their respective classes and Julius was gratefully reunited with Faith and Skye. He had never been so happy to chat with them about engines and plasma cores.

As the first week of October came and went, Julius felt the familiar anticipation for the gaming season ahead growing in his mind. He had been working extra hard in class to earn as many Fyvers as he could. Plus, he and the rest of the Skirts had managed to avoid killing any sim-animals during their Draw sessions, so none of them had lost anything either. On Monday the 10th, as they made their way to the infirmary for their Pre-Pyro therapy, they eagerly discussed what games they would be playing that Saturday.

'Ok so, first year we did Flight,' said Julius, as they waited in the lounge for the nurses to arrive. 'Last year it was Combat. Maybe we could go back to Flight again.'

'I don't know,' said Skye. 'I did enjoy the Combat scene more, to be honest.'

'I'd always choose Flight over Combat,' said Morgana, 'but I guess you know that, right?'

'And there's another issue to consider too,' added Faith. 'Are we sticking to the usual plan of competing only against students from our year?'

'Aye,' said Morgana.

'Definitely,' agreed Skye. 'Besides, it's a great way for us to hold on to top spot.'

'I bet the Seniors are gonna say we're too scared to play against them,' said Faith.

'Let them,' answered Morgana. 'They said the same thing last year. Who cares?'

'They're just jealous because we're top of the chart overall, and they can't get there,' continued Skye. 'If they're as good as they think they are, their names would be up there, instead of ours.'

'Right then, let's think about an action plan, and at lunch we can decide,' concluded Julius.

The others agreed and moved off to their respective areas for their treatments.

Ms Primula was waiting for Julius as he entered the room that had been assigned to him. 'Good morning Julius, how are you today?'

'All good, thanks. And you?'

'Still recovering from Wednesday's night shift, actually.'

'Supernova night?' asked Julius, and he couldn't help but laugh. 'That bad, huh?'

'Felice should know better,' she replied, her hand inserting the needle with practiced experience as Julius lay back on the bed. 'Dr Walliser went mental when he saw the first patient. He knew it immediately, even before that poor Irish boy could open his mouth. I think it was his birthday, actually.'

'It was. My roommate Skye wasn't feeling too good either.'

'I remember him. He came in around five in the morning, and he had to be put on a drip.'

'Yeah. I did hear him ... uh, losing loads of fluids that night. But that's his prize for eating five slices!'

'Did you say five?' asked the nurse, sounding understandably startled. 'I don't think we've ever met anyone who ate more than two and wasn't sick for a week.'

'Well, we don't call him The Black Hole for nothing.'

'I need to tell the doctor right away. We may need to study him more closely. Call if you need anything,' she said, leaving the room in a fluster.

Julius grinned and closed his eyes. Hearing about all the post-Supernova ailments made him even more grateful that he had only just had a taste of it. 'Faith will remember this birthday for a while,' he thought. Maybe they should buy him something in Satras, just to cheer him up a bit. After all, it couldn't have been great spending his birthday suffering from severe cramps, in a semi-conscious state. Julius opened his left hand and activated his PIP. The screen sprang to life, hovering over his palm. He selected the Hologram Palace page from his bookmarks and started browsing the charts, to remind himself of where everyone had been sitting in the rankings before the summer break. He was halfway through the Mizki Juniors when his PIP vibrated, signalling an incoming vidcall.

'On screen,' he said. Morgana came into view. 'Hey, what's up?'

'Go to the Space Channel, now,' she said, hurriedly.

'O ... Ok,' he said. Then, to the empty room, 'Computer, Space Channel News.'

T'Rogon's toothy smile instantly appeared on the room screen. Julius pushed a button on the side table, and the top half of the bed rose up, allowing him to sit properly. 'Now what?' he said. It was too early for this kind of surprise. Julius quickly saw that T'Rogon was being interviewed by Iryana Mielowa, who today was wearing the reddest shade of lipstick he had ever seen. Her dark hair had been gathered upwards, and she was batting her eyelashes much too seductively for his liking. 'Is she flirting with him?'

'My thoughts, precisely,' said Morgana disapprovingly from his PIP. 'Apparently the programme started forty minutes ago and is also being broadcast on Earth.'

The camera panned to the left of Mielowa and focused on Paulo Trent, or at least his holographic image. Julius had seen him on TV many times before—he had grizzled hair and dark eyes. Trent had been elected to lead the Democratic Republic of Earth when Julius was just eight but, despite his young age, he still remembered watching coverage of the exciting party that had been thrown for him in his homeland, Brazil—having the Earth Leader come from your country was a huge honour. Sitting next to Trent were Grand Masters Freja, Kloister and Milson, each wearing their particular school's uniform.

'Moving on from the issue of the Zed Test Centres,' said Mielowa, 'we now come to the last item on today's agenda. Mr T'Rogon, tell us about the children you brought with you from Arnesh.'

'What children?' cried Julius and Morgana in unison.

'But of course,' answered T'Rogon, flashing a bright smile at her. 'It was the wish of my Queen that you should meet our offspring. After all, we are proud parents too. They represent the best in us, and are the most advanced of our civilisation.'

Julius watched Freja intently: as the ambassador spoke those words, the Grand Master had not moved a muscle; his face was a blank mask, in stark contrast to Trent's cheeriness.

'If we are to begin dialogue,' continued T'Rogon, 'then the new generations should be involved. They had no part in all that went on before; their hands are clean.'

Ms Mielowa was nodding her head vigorously in agreement, reminding Julius of one of those toys with the springs in their necks, which people sometimes placed in the rear windows of their fly-cars.

'Ambassador,' Mielowa asked, 'what are your children like?'

'Just the same as yours, Iryana—may I call you Iryana?' he replied, making her blush furiously.

'Oh, p-lease!' groaned Morgana, rolling her eyes.

'Children are children,' continued T'Rogon. 'They like to learn, build, expand their minds and most of all, they like to play. As a matter of fact, just last night, they were expressing their interest in your magnificent Hologram Palace. After all, it was their ancestor, Clodagh Arnesh, who built it.'

'Well Ambassador,' said Trent, 'in that case I think that a visit is in order!' He turned to the Grand Masters. 'Don't you think so?'

Edwina Milson forced out a smile that could have grated steel, and nodded. Kloister looked at Freja, then back at Trent.

Eventually, it was Freja that spoke. 'Mr Trent is right,' he said, calmly. 'What do you have in mind, Ambassador?'

'A challenge, perhaps?' replied T'Rogon. 'Wouldn't it be great if our peace negotiations were to start with a friendly game between our children?'

'I think it's a marvellous idea, Ambassador!' said Trent, looking pleased. 'And I am sure that our facilities will be perfectly able to accommodate such an event.'

'What type of challenge would that be, Ambassador?' asked Mielowa. 'One on one, perhaps?'

'I was more inclined toward a team effort, actually,' answered T'Rogon. 'We have ten of our best youths onboard the Taurus One and they would all love to compete.'

'Then it's settled,' said Trent. 'Freja, why don't you choose ten of our best players and- '

'Oh no,' cut in T'Rogon. 'Not Freja. We want this challenge to be as fair as possible now, don't we?'

'I can't believe he said that!' cried Morgana.

'What does he even mean?' said Julius, feeling completely outraged. 'Is he expecting Freja to select ten crappy students?'

'Let your best player select the team,' he continued. 'And from what I've heard, you do have a Solo champion at your school.'

Julius' mouth fell open involuntarily. 'Wha ...' was all he could manage to say.

'Who is he, Freja?' asked Trent, seeming more and more like a kid in a candy store with each passing minute.

Freja seemed unwilling to answer at first, but eventually he did. 'Julius McCoy, one of our third year students.'

'Yes—McCoy,' said T'Rogon. 'He's quite the celebrity on Arnesh.'

'Is he now, Ambassador?' asked Trent, sounding quite chuffed.

'Oh yes, didn't Freja tell you? He's very much responsible for disrupting our plans over the last two years ... of which we are very glad, I might add. He's what you call a ...'

'No!' cried Julius at the screen, realising with horror what the ambassador was about to reveal.

'... White Child,' finished T'Rogon.

Julius slumped back, feeling as if someone had punched the air out of him. Everyone who was watching this interview would know now: his parents, Michael, all his classmates; even old Mrs Mayflower. Freja, Kloister and Milson, however, hadn't so much as flinched, and Julius wondered how hard they must be trying to not betray any emotion.

'Is this true, Carlos?' asked Trent.

Freja simply nodded.

'We are very grateful for him, you know,' said the ambassador. 'It was, in fact, McCoy's efforts which made Queen

Salgoria rethink her actions. How could she allow the destruction of such talent; such skills? Do you want to know what she said to me?' T'Rogon leaned towards Mielowa, who was hanging on his every word by that point. She nodded, captivated, so he continued. 'She said to me, "T'Rogon, my friend, go to Earth and make peace! I have realised the beauty of the human race once more and I want the dream of Clodagh and Marcus to finally come true. T'Rogon, I don't have much longer left to live—make this my lasting legacy."'

'Salgoria's dying?' sputtered Trent.

Even the Grand Masters flinched at that.

'Not quite,' explained T'Rogon quickly. 'But she's getting on in years; we all are.'

'Well folks,' said Mielowa, wrapping up the interview with a triumphant smile. 'You heard it here first. This is Iryana Mielowa, from the Space Channel.'

Julius shut his PIP off abruptly, forgetting that Morgana was still online, and ordered the room monitor to switch off. He lay back and stared up at the ceiling, too astonished to do anything else. Thankfully, the Pre-Pyro session wouldn't be over for another hour, so he had some time to try regain his composure. He felt torn in two: on one hand T'Rogon had just revealed his secret to the entire world, which would no doubt expose him to the unwanted attention of people who didn't even know him, and for that he hated the ambassador's guts; on the other hand though, the ambassador had selected him, over everyone else, to lead a team in the most important challenge Zed had ever faced. As he brooded over the events, his PIP vibrated, signalling an incoming message. Julius opened it and saw that it was from his dad.

"Is it true?" is all it read.

"Aye. Sorry I was asked not to tell," he typed back.

"I knew it! Be more careful than ever, J."

"Will do."

"Very proud."

He closed the screen once more. 'That was quick,' he said to himself. His parents had always known that his mind-skills were strong, ever since his first visit to the family Mind Doctor and he felt very grateful to his dad for dealing with the news so quickly and simply. He wondered what Michael would make of it; he was afraid that it could make him feel even worse. But there was no helping it now. T'Rogon had seen to that.

At 10:30, Nurse Primula came into the room and removed the needle from Julius' arm. He was expecting some sort of remark, but she didn't say anything, so he went back to the infirmary waiting room for the usual orange juice and biscuits. The rest of his classmates were just finishing up, and Julius grew conscious of the darting glances directed at him and the quiet whispering. He saw numerous wisps of mixed reds and greys floating throughout their auras, as if their excitement at the news was tainted by a sense of apprehension. When Faith, Skye and Morgana emerged from their rooms, they immediately joined him on the sofa.

'That was so OTT,' said Morgana. 'He practically insulted Freja and led Trent and Mielowa about by their noses.'

'I thought those two were the worst,' said Faith. 'At least the GMs were cool as cucumbers, rather than jumping through the hoops T'Rogon was holding out for them.'

'He really knows how to take centre stage,' said Skye. 'I hate to admit it, but he's good at his job.'

'What job?' asked Faith, sarcastically.

'Undermining Zed's credibility,' answered Julius, dryly. 'And steering opinion in favour of this armistice. But I don't buy it.'

'I think you've got more pressing matters than that now, Julius,' said Morgana.

'The challenge,' he said. 'I know.'

'At least that shouldn't be a problem,' said Skye. 'I mean, we are pretty good ... aren't we?'

'For starters, I've never been responsible for more than three people in a team—none of us has; second, we don't know zilch about these Arneshians or their abilities; and third, who says I'm gonna pick you?'

Skye was momentarily lost for words, but then he saw Julius, Faith and Morgana chuckling, and he punched Julius on the arm.

'Seriously though,' said Julius, 'this is one big responsibility I could do without. I mean, Earth against Arnesh!'

'McCoy,' said Faith, 'do you want to be a captain or not? If I'm going to entrust one of me babies into your care, I want to make sure you don't chicken out at the first problem.'

Morgana laughed. 'He's right, you know? Show us your stuff!'

Julius sighed and was about to reply, when he saw Dr Walliser approaching them.

'Master Cress would like to see you in his office at 11:00 hours,' the doctor said. 'All four of you.'

'Thanks Dr Walliser,' said Morgana, as he left them.

'I guess we'll be missing Draw then,' said Faith. 'Shame, I was looking forward to seeing me monkey.'

'Come on, let's go,' said Julius standing up. He was all too aware of numerous eyes following them out of the infirmary.

Julius knocked on Cress' door, which immediately slid open. He entered, followed directly by the others, and found the Master waiting behind his desk. They bowed to him and four chairs materialised in the centre of the room, courtesy of the inbuilt replicator.

'I take it you watched the interview,' said Cress.

'Yes sir,' answered Morgana.

'I won't deny that he has put us in quite a spot with this challenge. I take it you will be picking all of the Skirts, yes McCoy?'

'Yes sir,' answered Julius.

Cress nodded. 'Given the Arneshians' lack of mind-skills, it has been agreed that you will face each other with Sim-Gauntlets in a mixed flight/fight simulation, to the last man, or woman, standing. McCoy, you are the leader of a toon of ten players, chosen from across each of the three schools and all year groups.'

'Sorry, a what, sir?' asked Julius.

'A toon,' repeated Cress. 'As in a platoon.'

'Of course,' said Julius. 'How will I select the players, sir?'

'Gabriel List and the technical department have arranged a video conference for tonight at 20:00 hours.'

'A conference?' said Julius, suddenly worried.

'Yes McCoy, a conference. Speaking to people and all that?' said Cress, sounding amused. 'You better overcome that particular fear soon. Mr Miller can teach you how, I am sure.'

'Yes, sir,' answered Julius, ignoring the stifled giggles to his left.

Then Morgana's voice popped into his head: '*Told ya!*'

'Talk about how you will be selecting the players, and what roles you will be looking for. The Tijaran students will be physically present; the students from Tuala and Sield will see you as a hologram in their respective Assembly Halls. Should you choose someone from the Sield School, they will be housed in Tijara until the day of the challenge since, as you know, they are currently in a space station orbiting us. Once the Zed toon is created, the Grand Masters will need to approve it.'

'Zed Toon ...' said Faith. 'I like the name. Can we use it?'

'Go right ahead.'

'When is this event taking place, sir?' asked Skye.

'On Saturday the 5th of November; you have twenty-five days to prepare. I've booked a room exclusively for your practices in the Palace. Mrs Mayflower will give you the details. You are not allowed to skip lessons, but your team can stay behind to practice beyond curfew if needed; once you're allowed to game again of course.'

'Thank you, sir,' said Julius.

Cress stood up, walked around his desk, and stopped in front of them. 'Everyone would just love to see you win this challenge, Mizkis, but there's more than the Skirts' reputation at stake this time. The Arneshians are looking for ways of discrediting us in the eyes of Earth and we cannot afford that. Play fair and be careful. Dismissed.'

'The hall is absolutely heaving!' said Morgana.

'Don't need to know,' said Julius, dusting off his clothes and flattening his hair. He couldn't remember ever being so nervous. They had jotted down a few selection rules during lunchtime, and then Morgana had spent the last two hours helping Julius to calm down with some meditation. It was only after Faith had accused him of being worse than a pregnant woman an hour before delivery, that he had forced himself to regain some composure.

At 19:55 Gabriel List fetched him and led him to a spot near the stage. 'The link is ready. Just take a deep breath and remember there are worse things in life than this.'

'Like what?'

'I could be testing the mic by telling everyone that our very own White Child had to take remedial Meditation lessons, in first year,' said List with a grin.

'Thanks Gabriel, and I thought you were my friend,' he answered back.

'So did I! Jokes aside, how did the Mizkis take it?'

'Funnily enough, no one has said anything to me about this White Child business. I see them looking at me, but they don't come forward. I think they're scared.'

'Of you? Nah. Go on now—it's time.' List gently pushed him forward. 'Good luck!'

As Julius stepped onto the platform, the voices hushed down, until there was complete silence. Julius moved over to the centre of the stage and stopped before the podium that had been placed there. He pressed a button set into its top ledge and activated a screen which displayed the notes he had written up that day. Having so many Mizkis staring at him was rather intimidating; however, he knew that right then they were looking at the leader of a unique squad, a leader chosen because of his particular abilities, so he couldn't afford to show any weakness or doubt.

'Good evening Mizkis,' he started. His voice cracked a little, but he cleared it with a small cough. 'As of tonight, we will start the selection for the Zed Toon. Anyone who is interested can send their names and game stats to me. I am looking for the best nine players on Zed, to compete in a flight/fight simulation. Therefore, the squad will need to be balanced. You all saw the interview today, so you know what is at stake. If you are chosen, you will represent Zed and Earth in a unique competition. Do not enter lightly!' That was it. He had said all he needed and, knowing that, allowed himself to relax a little. 'Are there any questions?'

A few hands shot up. Julius pointed to a blonde boy in the third row, who he thought he recognised as a 4MA student.

'Are the Skirts taking part?' he asked.

'Their names have been entered.'

'So you're not really looking for nine players, then. Figures,' said the boy wryly. There were a few chuckles at that.

Julius raised an eyebrow: who did this guy think he was? Suddenly he didn't feel so shy that he couldn't answer back. 'I'm sorry, I didn't catch your name. Is it because you're not in the gaming charts, unlike The Skirts?' A much larger burst of laughter greeted Julius' reply, which encouraged him immensely. 'Miller, Ruthier and Shanigan are at the top of the overall and individual charts, and they have been there for the last two years straight. No one can contest that. Next!'

There was a smattering of applause which quickly faded away, but it gave him a few seconds to calm himself again. The mixture of adrenaline and nerves had made him grip the podium tightly, and he could see his knuckles turning white. Once again, he took a deep breath and continued answering questions. Fortunately, no one made any more silly remarks, and the conference ended just before 21:00 hours, which left Julius and the Skirts free to grab a bite to eat.

'That went well,' said Faith, once they were seated with their food.

'Thanks for sticking up for us, Julius,' said Morgana.

'No problem. Who was that guy anyway?'

'Forget about it,' said Skye, 'and rather check the mail. I want to see if anyone has applied yet.'

Julius activated his PIP, and as soon as he did, his inbox filled up with 123 messages. 'This is going to be harder than we thought. Look how many already, and they keep arriving.'

'I don't think picking people will be a problem,' said Morgana, waving her chopstick in the air. 'I'd be more concerned with those you don't pick.'

As she said that, Julius looked around the mess hall. Suddenly, he was very aware of tiny little smiles and looks of approval being thrown at him, which were soon followed by numerous friendly shoulder pats and thumbs up as people passed by his table.

'You have a whole bunch of new friends now, McCoy,' said Skye.

Julius knew then just how right Morgana was. This was not going to be an easy job.

With less than a month to go, and no access to Satras for another week, the Skirts decided to spend the next few days selecting the players. Faith was in charge of filtering the entries, according to their individual placing in the charts. Anyone below tenth rank was automatically excluded. Julius and Skye had decided to focus on the fighters, and Morgana and Faith on the pilots.

As well as poring over player files, one Wednesday evening Julius received a call to see Dr Walliser the following morning. With everything that was happening on Zed, he really could have done without this extra treatment, or whatever it was that Freja wanted him to do. At the end of their Meditation class he quickly mentioned where he was going to his friends, promising that he would tell them all as soon as he got back.

Dr Walliser was waiting for him in the foyer. 'Mr McCoy, follow me.'

Julius was taken into one of the familiar rooms, where he sat on the bed.

'You must be sick and tired of this place,' said the doctor. 'Second time this week?'

'Third,' specified Julius.

Walliser nodded. 'Grand Master Freja has decided to use one of our gene therapy enhancement procedures on you.'

'A what procedure, sir?' asked Julius.

'The simplest way to explain it, is that we want to improve your DNA, McCoy.'

'I don't understand,' said Julius, trying to hide the concern in his voice. 'Why me?'

'As a White Child, you will receive certain special treatments during your development on Zed,' answered Walliser, preparing a tray with various instruments. 'Not that we've had that many like you, though. You are special, as far as Zed officers go, and a most precious asset for our defences. Salgoria has already moved twice to get you and, even though she has failed, we need you strong and in peak condition. I have to admit, I've never met a White Child in my career, so I'm really looking forward to our weekly meetings. So McCoy, what do you say?'

'Do I have choice?'

'Do you want out?'

'No, sir,' answered Julius.

'Then you don't,' said the doctor, not unkindly. 'Shoes and socks off, please.'

Julius removed his boots and lay down on the bed. Walliser got to work, nimbly attaching sensors around Julius' head and neck, and on the backs of his feet and hands.

'Thanks to the advances in Biomathematics,' explained the doctor, 'all you need now is a quick injection in the neck, and a small pill.'

Julius looked suspiciously at the red pill that Walliser was handing to him on a dish. He put it in his mouth and swallowed. 'Ugh,' he said, disgusted. 'It tastes horrible.'

'Here, have some juice,' said Walliser.

Julius drank gratefully, trying to remove all trace of the acrid taste.

'You'll need to stay in here for half an hour, McCoy. That's all that's required from you for this treatment. Ms Primula will let you know when the time is up.'

'Thanks doctor,' said Julius, lying back down. With time to kill, he decided to carry on his player search so, once he was alone in the room, he activated his PIP and skimmed through the files. The thirty minutes flew by and soon the nurse came to let him know he could leave. In fact, it took him more time to explain what had happened to him to the Skirts, than to actually do the treatment. Faith had far too many questions about it that Julius couldn't answer and, in the end, he told him he should ask Cress during their next Biomaths lesson since, no doubt, the Tijaran Master would know a lot more than Julius ever could about it. Skye found the whole thing quite cool, while Morgana seemed a little anxious about it, but didn't say anything.

On Friday the 14th, Julius and Morgana were sitting under the oak tree in the garden, looking over pilot choices. Skye had to finish an assignment for the following Monday, while Faith was developing his project for Pete's competition.

'I'm not sure who to go for,' said Julius, switching between three files. 'Who would you choose?'

'Charlie Dolan, 5MS Tuala. He's the best of the three,' answered Morgana quickly. 'But if you're looking for a pilot-slash-fighter, then it's between our Isolde, or Celia, from 6MS Sield.'

Julius closed Charlie's file and read over the stats for Isolde and Celia.

'You know Julius, I think we should go for Isolde. She does have a good reputation and, besides that, she'd love to fight by your side.'

'How so?'

'I think she fancies you, which wouldn't surprise me in the least. I mean, most of the girls in our year think you're cute,' she said, matter-of-factly.

'I wish you hadn't told me that,' he said, shaking his head. 'How am I going to look at her in class now? It's just the two of us!'

'You're far too shy for your own good, you know? When it comes to ladies, I mean.'

'It's just a distraction, and I don't need that.'

'Don't forget what they say—behind every great man, there's a great woman!' she said, teasing him. Before he could think of a reply, she promptly stood up and left him there under the tree.

Julius looked at Celia's file again, and then at Isolde's. If he picked her, there would be nothing strange about it; after all, she was good and had high stats. And she *was* pretty, he had to admit. 'See—just a distraction,' he said to the empty garden, then stood up and headed inside for dinner.

It was during dessert that the final list was decided. Julius sent it to Freja, and they waited patiently for a reply. At 21:00 hours, the list was returned to him with a seal of approval from the three Grand Masters, and a personal note from Edwina Milson, the only GM who still played in the Hologram Palace. '"Excellent choice, McCoy. Good luck.",' said Julius, reading out the message. 'That was nice of her.'

'And here's the message for the lucky winners,' said Faith, clearing his throat. 'Congratulations, such-and-such. You have been selected to represent your planet in the most exciting challenge ever! The Zed Toon depends on you. No pressure. Meet tomorrow morning at 09:00 hours by Mrs Mayflower's kiosk. Signed, JMWC.'

'What's that last bit?' asked Julius, suspiciously.

'JM, that's you; WC, for White Child,' answered Faith, with a grin.

'Oh no you don't! No one is going to call me WC. Off my case, Irish,' growled Julius.

'You're no fun,' said Faith, typing on his PIP. 'There, just JM. Better?'

'Much better. Right—let's send them.'

As soon as Faith had pressed the send button, Julius felt as if a weight had lifted from his chest. Tomorrow morning they would start training and he really hoped that the new toon would blend well.

The next morning, Isolde joined the Skirts on the Intra-Rail platform, looking suitably excited. Morgana was very happy to have her there, since she was one of her two best friends. When the train arrived, Julius looked around the carriage hoping to see the other players and, sure enough, huddled in a group at the back were five faces that he recognised immediately, having poured over their files for an entire week.

'Hey there,' he called.

The five Mizkis waved back and moved over to the front to join them. Wearing the dark red Tuala uniform were Maks Suraev, a blue eyed 5MS from Russia, who was renowned for his piloting skills, and Nalani Liway, Lopaka's big sister. She had been chosen by Faith once he had found out that, like her brother, Nalani had a real passion for technology, not to mention her seriously deep dark eyes, which grabbed Faith's attention a little too often. The three fighters who had been chosen were all from Sield. They were, a lively American girl called Ellie Gibson from fifth year, plus two

6MS: the tanned Inigo Vega from Spain, and the red haired Maya Berg from Norway.

'I hope you guys don't have any problems with me being in charge,' said Julius, after they had all shaken hands. 'I mean, I'm only a 3MA after all.'

'You're kidding, right?' said Maks. 'You're a Solo champion *and* a White Child. I'm more than happy to leave you in charge.'

The others readily agreed, making Julius feel more at ease. 'I'll do my best, I can promise you that, but it won't be easy. There will be plenty of eyes on us for this game, so let's make sure we give it our all.' As he looked at the newly assembled Zed Toon, he started to get a good feeling about them. The new guys seemed friendly enough and, if they were as good as their stats suggested, then his job wouldn't be too hard. Of course, he also had the Skirts there to help him out.

As the days passed, and the 5th of November drew closer, things started to get pretty hectic. Faith was dividing what little free time he had between extra practices and his competition, often not going to sleep until the small hours of the morning, while Julius worked on assembling and disassembling catalysts with Isolde. With them working together both in school and in gaming, Isolde soon forgot about Julius' earlier blunder in class and became much more relaxed around him. However, after the conversation he had had with Morgana about Isolde's apparent feelings for him, Julius started to feel a bit more awkward around her.

Morgana and Skye were also dealing with their fair share of homework and practice. And, not being totally blind,

Julius had also begun to notice Skye's extra-curricular activities with Maya Berg which, as Faith had put it, had been only a matter of time really. To everyone's delight though, their practice sessions were going well, and they all seemed to be working with, and around, each other in a pleasingly fluid way.

When the time came, Julius and Isolde sat, and passed, their checkpoint exam with Professor Gould, managing to assemble three different types of catalyst within a minute. Julius felt so good about it that he didn't even flinch when Isolde gave him a congratulatory hug, on their way out of class.

The night before the big game, Julius called home and was delighted to be greeted by the sight of Michael's face appearing on screen first. Although they didn't exchange too many words, just the fact that his brother was sitting there, between his parents, was the best possible way to end his day. They told Julius that they would be watching the game with Morgana's family, over at their place. As he signed off that night, and got ready for bed, Julius felt on such a high that he was ready to take on the entire world.

CHAPTER 6

ZED TOON

On the morning of the challenge, Julius met his team by old Mrs Mayflower's kiosk in the Hologram Palace. The game would not start until midday, but they had been asked to arrive three hours early to avoid the crowd and leave time for last minute preparations.

'Eeeeh! Look who's here,' said Mrs Mayflower, flashing her usual cheeky, although less toothed, smile at them.

'Good morning!' said Morgana. 'Will you cheer for us, Mrs Mayflower?'

'I will be doing more than that, dear!' Saying this, she turned around, disappeared beneath her counter and re-emerged holding a silver-grey t-shirt, with ZED TOON emblazoned on it. 'Ta-daa! What do you think?'

'Brilliant!' said Ellie and Nalani together.

'Really shiny,' added Skye.

'They will be on sale in every shop in Satras, and not just for today. They'll become serious memorabilia.'

'Make sure you keep some for us,' said Faith. 'I'm sure me mum would love one.'

'Have the Arneshians arrived yet?' asked Julius.

'Yes. They got here an hour ago and went straight to their dressing room.'

'What do they look like?' asked Maks.

'Kids,' she said, simply. 'A bit greyish perhaps, but just like you.'

Julius nodded. 'So, what's the deal today?'

'The cameras will go live when the game begins. There will be a small ceremony at the start, where you will meet your opponents for the first time. It'll be a fast paced game, but you can do it. However, first things first, there's breakfast waiting for you downstairs, courtesy of Global Brioche.'

'All right!' said Skye, clearly pleased with that last bit of information.

'Thanks Mrs Mayflower,' said Morgana. 'Where do we go?'

'Follow the corridor to Combat,' she said, pointing at the stairs that led down towards the simulation levels. 'They're waiting for you.'

Julius led the way, and when they reached the split in the corridor they took a left. Once at their destination they were met by Miss Logan, the blonde technician in charge of that sector, and Mr Smith, who took care of Flight simulation.

'This way please,' said Miss Logan. 'Have your breakfast in here, before you get changed.'

Julius was surprised by all the trouble they seemed to have gone to for them. The normally bare reception room had been fitted with three small tables and ten chairs; each table was laden with juice, coffee, milk and at least eight different types of pastries. Julius loved Global Brioche, purely because of their ability to cater for whatever type of sweet you craved, from Turkish Baklava, to Hungarian Dobosh, and even Polynesian Malasadas, which Julius liked very much. He looked at the spread eagerly, but he knew that he must not overindulge, no matter how tempting it was. 'Miller, don't-' he started.

'I know,' Skye cut in quickly. 'I promise I'll leave space for dessert.'

For the next two hours, they went over the possible scenarios they may encounter, hoping that the computer hadn't inserted too many surprises for the occasion. At 11:00, Julius couldn't wait any longer and walked over to the desk. Mr Smith gave him a holosuit and he went to get changed.

The monitors in the dressing room were switched on, but instead of broadcasting the games, as they would normally do, they showed Satras and the Hologram Palace arena, packed with students and Zed officers glued to whatever screen they could find. Julius saw his classmates in a corner of the main courtyard. They were all wearing the silver grey t-shirts over their uniforms; he was overwhelmed by the sight, and it was then that he truly realised what this game actually meant for the Lunar Perimeter.

Slowly, the rest of the boys joined him and with ten minutes to go, the familiar green light appeared on the side door. As they entered onto the game-floor, an eerie silence met them. On a Saturday morning the whole place would have been teeming with Mizkis, but not today; it had all been shut down because of this game.

'This way,' said Mr Smith, leading them towards the closest row of machines.

Julius stopped by the first one and waited as each member of his team passed by, giving them high fives as they did. Morgana was the last, and she winked at him on her way to her sphere. He grinned back before quickly climbing into his own frame, as he had done countless times before. He then placed his feet on the two small platforms and grabbed the handles. When the holosphere was activated, all sound disappeared; the headrest slipped behind his head, while invisible straps secured his hands, ankles and waist. The sphere's membrane became visible and slowly began to vibrate. Julius shifted in his restraints and closed his eyes, feeling weightlessness entering his body. It was time.

He came to in a town square, surrounded by the quaint façades of small, brick houses. He looked around and saw that his team was all there. In-game, they were now clothed in silver, fitted jumpsuits, with their surnames printed in shimmering white on the front and back, which Julius guessed must be for the benefit of the spectators. Faith had regained the use of his legs, exactly as had happened during last year's games, which made him mighty pleased. They all had triangular devices pinned on their chests, above their hearts: Julius knew these were their com-links, which were small communication devices.

'That colour really suits you,' said Skye, winking at Maya. 'It goes nicely with your eyes.'

Faith pretended to puke behind his back, making everyone snigger.

'I would refrain from doing that in front of the cameras, Mr Shanigan,' said a voice suddenly. 'The audience will not be able to hear you, but they will see you quite clearly.'

They all turned and saw Professor Chan atop a small podium. He was wearing his usual loose, black tunic, and standing there with his hands behind his back.

'Professor,' said Julius, surprised. 'What are you doing here?'

'I will be the master of ceremonies for this game. The Arneshians are about to arrive and, as soon as they do, the game will go live. Create a row in front of me now; gaze forward. McCoy, you first.'

Julius stood before Chan, and the other players positioned themselves in a line behind him. Chan examined them thoroughly, and looked pleased. 'Remember who you represent today.'

'Yes sir,' they answered as one.

Suddenly, there was a flash of light and ten figures appeared in the square. As tempted as he was to stare and examine them, Julius continued looking ahead, hoping to look professional. After all, from that moment, the world's eyes would be fixed on them.

'Arnesh Glory, welcome,' said Chan. 'Please stand next to a member of the Zed Toon, your leader at the front.'

Julius was aware of feet approaching and, out of the corner of his eye, saw that someone had stopped just to his left.

'Face each other and bow,' ordered Chan.

Julius turned left and found himself staring at a boy taller than he was. He was wearing a black jumpsuit, with the com-link device pinned to his chest; his eyes were blue and his hair pure white—it shimmered in the same way as T'Rogon's. To top it off, a thin circlet crowned his head. In the sunlight his skin looked slightly dull and greyish. The name printed on his suit identified him as K'Ssander. The boy kept his face straight, betraying no emotion. Julius wondered just how old he was because, quite frankly, he didn't look much like a "youth", as T'Rogon had said; not quite an adult, but certainly not as young as the Zed students. He quickly threw a glance at the other Arneshians, and was taken aback when he saw that, as well as having the same hair colour as their leader, they were all as tall and looked just as old too. The surprise must have been visible on his face, because suddenly he heard Chan's voice in his mind, '*Don't show any weakness, McCoy.*' He immediately relaxed his face and stared back at the other captain.

'Players, I want a fair game from you. You all have Sim-Gauntlets and, as per usual, all mind-skills have been blocked, so you are now equal. The com-link on your chest will allow you to communicate with your own team. Every time you hit a player, their health bar will decrease, until it's depleted and the person will then disappear from the game. The last player standing will represent the winning team. Are you ready?'

'Yes, sir!' they all cried.

'Let the game commence.'

As Chan pronounced those words, a white light engulfed the square once more and, as Julius opened his eyes for the second time, he found himself sitting on a tree branch with Faith, in the middle of an empty field. 'What the ...' he started.

'Where's everyone?' asked Faith, sounding worried.

Julius touched his com-link. 'Zed Toon, state your position,' he said, scouting his surroundings and looking down carefully.

'Skye and Inigo, standing in a pond,' replied Skye.

'Morgana and Maks, chicken house,' said Morgana.

'I'm with Maya in a tunnel,' added Isolde.

'Nalani and I are in a stinky bakery,' said Ellie.

Julius looked at Faith, feeling totally at loss.

'So much for teamwork,' said Faith.

'Look for a big landmark, anywhere around you,' said Julius. He began to scout the horizon as well, until his eyes rested on a tall building in the distance. 'Toon, can you see the building with the neon sign at its top?'

'The one that says, "Fly me"?' asked Skye.

'That's the one,' answered Julius.

The others confirmed that they could see it too.

'Right. Let's meet there and shoot anything that moves along the way. Good luck.' He turned to Faith. 'We have to jump. Are you ready?'

Faith nodded and slid off the branch until he was dangling by his hands. After a brief hesitation, he let go. Julius followed suit.

'Now what?' asked Faith.

'Now we run!' said Julius, suddenly grabbing him by the arm.

'Wait, what-' Faith turned his head and saw an armour plated stegosaur pelting towards them, making the ground shake. 'Why is it looking at us like that? Doesn't it eat grass?'

'I refuse to stand here and discuss dietary habits with it!' shouted Julius. 'Run!' Julius leapt forward in the direction of the landmark ahead, keeping an eye out for any possible Arneshian attacks. The two boys had been sprinting for almost a minute, the dinosaur's footsteps booming behind them, when finally Julius spotted a large clump of trees to his left. 'Over there. We'll hide and ambush it!' They instantly steered in that direction and, as Julius made a sharp bend behind one of the thick tree trunks, he saw a jet-bike parked in its shadow.

'Move over,' said Faith, jumping on the vehicle and pressing the start button. It roared to life and slowly rose from the floor. 'Hop on!'

Julius swung his right leg over, hooked his left arm around Faith's waist and turned to look back, Gauntlet at the ready. Faith accelerated and the jet-bike zoomed forward. A few seconds later, the stegosaur broke through the tree line.

'Shoot it!' cried Faith, while he sped in the direction of a nearby rocky terrain, hoping to discourage the animal from following any further.

Julius tried to steady his right arm but, with all the tight turns that Faith was having to make, that was easier said than done. He aimed as best as he could and, when he thought the beast was more or less centred, he fired. The first energy ray whisked past it, well above its head; Julius continued shooting at it, and slowly lowered his arm until he hit the stegosaur's forehead. The animal stumbled, let out a primeval roar, and crashed to earth in a cloud of dust. Seeing that it wasn't about to get up again, Julius turned forward and patted Faith on the shoulder. 'Good driving, speedy. Now, take us to that building.'

As the landmark loomed closer, Julius saw that it was set in the middle of a ruined city. As they arrived at the edge of it, Faith stopped the bike. The place was eerily quiet, except for the occasional chattering of the birds that had made a home in the long abandoned structures. Where the road began, cracked asphalt replaced dying blades of grass. 'Zed Toon,' said Julius over his com-link, 'we've just reached a ghost town. I'd say it's about 3000 feet to the meeting point.'

'How did you get there so quickly?' asked Inigo. 'We just made it out of the pond!'

'About that,' interrupted Skye, 'we would have been a lot quicker if it wasn't for the giant octopus that tried to drown us.'

'Giant octopus?' said Morgana. 'For real?'

'We believe you, Skye,' said Faith. 'Julius just downed a dinosaur.'

'These games get weirder by the day,' commented Nalani. 'Anyway, we're out of the bakery and right under the building. If you-' Nalani's voice cut out abruptly and was replaced by the sound of screams and running footsteps.

'What's happening?' shouted Julius. 'Nalani? Ellie?'

Faith revved the engine. 'Hold on!' He lurched forward, aiming for the building.

'Ellie?' Julius kept calling her name over the com-link. 'Nalani, come in!' No one answered his call, but he could hear hurried steps and voices he didn't recognise.

'Can you see them, Julius?' asked Morgana, breathing heavily—it sounded like she was running.

'Not yet, but we are getting closer,' he replied.

Faith had the jet-bike at full speed, and Julius had to hold on to him with both arms to avoid being blown backward by the wind. They were forced to zip in between the fly-car carcasses and sometimes just above them; for some reason their ride wouldn't take them higher than ten feet above the ground.

'Ellie!' screamed Nalani. 'Stop, no!' Then silence.

Faith spotted the bakery and skidded to a halt outside it.

'Zed Toon: Gibson, Liway, eliminated,' the monotone voice of the computer announced over the com-link. 'Arnesh Glory: F'Saner, eliminated.'

'Shoot!' cried Julius, running a hand through his hair.

'At least they took one of theirs with them,' said Faith. 'Let's get inside our meeting point. We're too exposed out here.'

'Toon,' Julius said, 'we are going in. Meet us there.'

Cautiously, keeping their Sim-Gauntlets at the ready, they backed into the building. Faith checked that the foyer was clear before letting Julius in. Once inside, they secured the ground floor, checking behind any closed doors and corners.

'I'll go check upstairs,' said Faith, heading toward the stairwell.

Julius crouched by the main glass door, sheltered by the branches of a pot plant. Losing two players so early wasn't good, but there was nothing to be done about it now; they would just have to be extra careful from here on.

'Julius,' whispered Isolde, over the com-link. 'Can you hear me?'

'Yes, where are you?'

'Across the road from you. See the wrecked Bumble-Bee? We're right behind it.'

Julius identified the fly-car immediately, as it was the same model as his dad's, and saw two pairs of feet shuffling beneath it. 'I see you. Want me to cover you?'

'That would be just swell,' she replied.

Julius shifted over to the door, opened it slightly and had a quick glance around. He couldn't see any movement. 'Ready ... Go!'

Isolde and Maya jumped up and slid over the roof of the car, and ran as fast as they could towards Julius, who was waiting, ready to open the door wide for them. That was when the shooting began.

'Run!' he shouted at the girls. Isolde ducked down and Maya shielded her head with her arms. Julius spotted K'Ssander leaning out of a window on the first floor of the building opposite them. He lifted his Gauntlet and returned fire. A further series of energy bursts streamed at the girls from his left, this time from inside a burnt-out fly-car. He began to panic as he realised he wouldn't be able to hold off both attackers. To make things worse, the girls had stopped running and were now caught smack bang in the middle of the crossfire.

'Faith!' Julius shouted over his shoulder. 'Could do with some help here!'

A few seconds later, Faith had joined him and started firing at the opponent to their left.

'They won't be able to resist much longer,' said Julius.

'Hey!' cried Morgana suddenly. 'Over here, you big bullies!'

Julius looked right, and saw her standing over a capsized nullifying bin, her Sim-Gauntlet aimed at the Arneshian leader, a look of stern defiance on her face. The energy beams shifted towards her, but Morgana was quicker. She back-flipped and landed effortlessly a few feet back, then sprinted towards the side of the building with the neon sign.

'That's what I call a crowd pleaser,' whooped Faith enthusiastically.

'Where did she learn that?' said Julius, wide-eyed.

At the same time that Morgana was attracting the shooters' attention, Skye, Maks and Inigo had entered the fray; shielding their sides with scrap pieces of metal, they ran towards the girls, grabbed them by their arms and dragged them inside the building, where Julius was waiting, and slammed the door shut behind them.

'That was close,' panted Maks, slumping down, exhausted.

'We must have lost a lot of life back there,' said Isolde, who was also breathing heavily.

'At least we're still here,' said Maya. She walked up to Skye and thanked him with a big kiss on his cheek for saving her.

Inigo and Maks grinned and winked at Julius and Faith.

'It's the Miller charm,' whispered Faith. 'You get used to it.'

Suddenly, there was a loud thumping noise, which made them all jump. They whirled to the source of the sound and saw Morgana standing on the other side of a full-length window, hiding in the shadows.

Julius touched his com-link. 'Are you ok?'

'Yes. I think I lost them for now, but you need to let me in.'

'Stay back,' he replied. He aimed his Gauntlet at the bottom of the glass panel and fired a single blast at it; the window shattered and came crashing down. Morgana hurried inside and re-joined the group. They stood for a bit, not saying much and all was quiet. The respite didn't last long however as, a few minutes later, the ominous sound of a low rumble, growing slowly louder, was heard from outside.

'What is that?' asked Inigo, walking over to the main door.

Julius and the others moved cautiously forward and peered into the distance. A billowing cloud of dust hung above the road, rolling slowly in their direction. As it drew closer, the various small pieces of junk sprawled on the floor around them began to vibrate and rattle.

'Look at the fly-cars!' gasped Inigo, pointing.

Julius involuntarily took a step back as he watched one of the vehicles tilt precariously forward, then backwards, then forward again, as if it was perched on the edge of a precipice. It teetered like that for a few seconds, then nose dived and disappeared from view. 'The road is collapsing!' he said.

'It's happening all around us!' cried Inigo.

'Upstairs, quick!' shouted Julius, ushering them up the stairwell.

'Won't we be trapped?' said Maya, holding on to Skye's hand.

'The sign on the roof,' replied Julius. 'It says, "Fly me." I bet there's a way out up there.'

'It's fly-time!' cheered Morgana. 'Let's go, let's go!'

Faith turned to Inigo and Maks, pointed at Morgana and said with a smile, 'That, is also something you get used to.'

'My kind of girl,' said Maks.

Julius tried to ignore the comment, and the fact that there were little red wisps shooting out of Maks' head as he looked admiringly at Morgana. A couple of minutes later, they had reached the roof.

Julius was relieved to see that there were indeed four aircraft parked there, similar in design to the Sim-Cougars, but slightly longer, so as to accommodate two people in each. 'Morgana, Maks, Isolde and Faith,' called Julius. 'You're piloting—take us out of here.'

'Aye, aye Captain,' answered Morgana enthusiastically, rushing towards the first plane with Skye in tow.

Julius followed Faith towards the second one; Inigo went with Isolde and Maya with Maks. The engines fired up simultaneously and the four Cougars lifted upwards.

Julius grabbed the catalyst and began to scout the sky. His seat was raised slightly, allowing him to see over the pilot's head; as in the real Cougars, the top cover was transparent, so that there were no blind spots. 'Morgana,' called Julius. 'Follow us west. Isolde and Maks, head east. Let's find them.'

'Roger,' answered the pilots.

Isolde and Maks performed a perfect 180 degree reverse rotation—just as they had been taught in first year—and headed eastward, still in the upside down position, twisting themselves to face the right way up as they flew. From up above, Julius now had the chance to see the abandoned city in its entirety, or at least what was left of it. The cloud of dust had almost completely settled and he was able to make out the long, black strips of nothing that had replaced the roads. Not a car was in sight, only the buildings, jutting out of the concrete like rotten teeth.

'Where are they?' said Faith, frustrated.

'I bet they're hiding,' answered Julius. 'Keep circling the city, Faith.'

'Guys,' said Maks over the com-link, 'I see movement ahead.'

'There are people on one of the rooftops,' said Maya. 'It's them! I recognise their shimmery hair.'

'Send us the coordinates, Maks,' said Julius. 'Let's go say hi.'

Faith veered right and zoomed forward, lowering his altitude until he was level with the rooftops.

Julius looked into the distance and spotted five small aircrafts, taking off from one of the tallest buildings. 'Faith,' he said quietly, 'take us to ground level. I want to hit them from below.'

'Sneaky! I like it,' grinned Faith, before diving between two houses.

Julius readjusted his grip on the catalyst and kept his eyes on the sky above, while the Cougar moved silently closer to their targets. 'I see them,' he said, a few seconds later. 'Aim for the rearguard one.'

'Roger,' answered Faith. He steered upwards and, as stealthily as he could, positioned himself right below the last Arneshian aircraft, nose pointing at its core.

'Go!' cried Julius.

Faith accelerated instantly, flattening both of them against their seats. Julius took aim and opened fire. Caught by surprise, the Arneshian craft swayed desperately and set off at pace, leaving its group behind. 'Stay with him, Faith!' shouted Julius, still shooting.

'Come to daddy, you shell-head,' said Faith, sticking hot on its tail.

The Arneshian craft twisted and swerved, in and out of empty buildings, in an effort to lose them in the ruins, but Faith was relentless in his chase. As they emerged from one of the buildings, an energy burst rocked their plane.

'We have company,' said Faith. 'Two nasties right behind us.'

'Don't lose him, Faith,' said Julius. Then to the com-link, 'Guys, we need some help here.'

'I'm on it,' said Morgana.

'We'll take care of them,' said Isolde.

'They're all yours, ladies,' answered Faith. 'I've got me hands full with this one.'

Julius continued shooting, and thanks to Faith's flying, he managed to keep a constant stream aimed at the enemy craft. He wasn't quite sure how that would affect the pilots inside it but, since no target had appeared above the plane, as it would have in a regular flying game, he believed that the craft must also have a separate energy bar. 'Come on,' he said through gritted teeth. 'Will you just die already?' As if in answer to his plea, the Arneshian plane suddenly exploded, the force of it enough to knock them slightly off course.

'Arnesh Glory: C'Tardid, T'Namen, eliminated,' announced the computer.

'Yes!' cheered Julius. 'Well done mate,' he said, patting Faith's shoulder.

'Likewise,' said Faith, grinning.

'Congrats,' said Maks over the com-link, 'but leave the champagne on ice for now. I've got two aggros right behind me.'

'On our way,' answered Faith, speeding up. 'Send co-ordinates.'

'Incoming,' replied Maya.

Faith veered upward and headed back toward the city.

'Hmm ...' said Julius after awhile. 'They should be here, but I can't see them.'

'We're here!' cried Maya. 'Look up!'

'Where?' asked Faith.

Julius craned his neck around until he caught sight of a fast-moving shadow in the lining of a cloud. 'There!' he said, pointing.

Suddenly, Maks' Cougar burst out of the cloud, followed by two enemy craft. He was twisting and spinning skilfully to avoid being hit. Faith accelerated and positioned his craft behind the Arneshians.

As he did so, Julius began to shoot. 'Stay still, damn you,' he said through gritted teeth. To his frustration, the two planes in front of him were zipping nimbly around each other, making them incredibly difficult to hit.

A minute later, the computer came back online—'Zed Toon: Frey, Montoya, eliminated.'

'Shoot!' cried Julius. 'Morgana, what's happening?'

'Just ... a ... sec ... almost ... there!' she answered.

'Arnesh Glory: A'Trid, P'Lankot, eliminated.'

'All right!' said Skye. 'Bring 'em on!'

'Well done, guys,' said Julius. 'Come join us.'

'On our way,' answered Morgana.

Julius was still firing determinedly at the planes in front of him, and wondering how low their energy bars were now; unfortunately there was no way to tell, and they seemed to be going just as strong as when the chase had started. He had five players left while K'Ssander had four, and that was a good start, but he knew they really couldn't afford to lose any more.

Without warning, the Cougar banked left sharply. 'Faith, where are you going? I'm in the middle of shooting that guy!'

'It isn't me,' answered Faith. 'I can't control it.'

'What's happening?' said Morgana.

Julius looked around and saw that all the planes, including those of the Arneshians, were now flying in an orderly manner in the same direction, creating a V-formation. He let go of the catalyst and wiped the palms of his hands against his suit. He wouldn't admit it out loud, but this unplanned rest was more than welcome: aiming and shooting was hard enough work, even without the constant spinning and twisting of the last few minutes.

'What's that, right ahead?' asked Maks. 'Can you make it out?'

Julius peered into the distance and saw six tall dark shapes, split into two groups of three. With the sun in his eyes, it was difficult to tell exactly what they were, but soon the shapes began to take on an unmistakable humanoid outline. His mouth fell open, while his brain tried to process what he was actually seeing. 'That can't be.'

'Well, wax me back and call me a surfboard,' said Faith, hypnotised by the view.

As they drew closer, each shape became perfectly clear and visible; standing at roughly 150 feet above the ground were six giant robots, in full armour plating. The three on the right bore the Zed oval emblem on their chests—Julius instantly recognised the full moon in a starry dark sky—while the remaining ones had a symbol that Julius had never seen before: a triangle with a straight line balanced at its peak, contained within a circle. Although he could guess that it must be the Arneshian symbol, he had no idea as to its meaning, and no time to figure it out either, so he pushed it out of his mind for the time being. He focused his attention on the nearest of the Zed robots. The paint on the metal created the illusion that the machine was wearing clothes. Its torso, pelvis, forearms and the sections from the knees down were coated in blue, while the rest of the area was metallic grey; red and gold designs were embossed throughout giving it a vibrant look. Its head was crowned with a spiked, gold circlet. Julius was blown away by the look of it, and judging by the total silence on the com-link, the rest of the toon were just as stunned as he was.

The plane bearing him and Faith steered itself away from the formation and headed for the robot to their far right. They levelled up to it at waist height and slowly ascended toward the head. As they did so, Julius observed the perfect details of its armour. The sun reflected off its surface, creating a kaleidoscope of colours inside their Cougar. When they reached its face, Julius found himself staring at two large black eyes, which had a menacing look about them courtesy of the arched metal eyebrows above them. The nose was straight and almost triangular; the mouth thin, but perfectly shaped. They hovered there for a few seconds, and then the craft began to slide sideways, moving in an orbit around the head, until it was facing the back of it. They rose a couple of feet, paused in front of a large opening, and slowly moved forward, slotting comfortably into the hole, where it locked into place.

'I always knew I was the brains of the operation,' said Faith.

Julius chuckled nervously; they were now literally sitting inside the skull of the robot. There was a gentle humming noise and a new type of control panel materialised over the Cougar's own, and solidified.

'Am I supposed to drive this thing?' asked Faith, looking back over his shoulder.

'I guess,' answered Julius, shrugging his shoulders. He picked up two controllers from his own panel and, as he began to rotate them, the arms of the robot did exactly the same. 'Whoa! It looks like I can control his arms.'

'That means that I've got the legs. I think I need to put me feet in these stirrups here,' said Faith. He added, as an afterthought, 'Good job I've got me legs on today.'

Julius watched as Faith stepped cautiously forward into the empty space below his seat; as he did this, it was mimicked perfectly by the robot. Guided by Julius, the robot lifted both arms and, when he squeezed the catalysts, two violent bursts of energy pelted out of the hands, crashing into a tree in front of them, blowing it to smithereens. 'This is just!'

'There's a funny button here,' said Faith. 'It says UP. I might just press it, you know?'

'Sure, go a-' began Julius, but the words caught in his throat as the robot zoomed upwards into the sky. 'OK, now we're flying again.'

'Incoming!' said Morgana cheerfully, as her robot came to a halt in midair before theirs. 'Come on up, Maks!'

The third Zed robot quickly joined them and, as they regrouped, the Arneshians did the same.

'Let's get 'em!' cried Morgana, leading the attack.

Faith guided the robot after her; Skye and Maya quickly followed suit, and they all released a volley of energy bursts at their targets. The Arneshians weren't about to stand still though, and launched towards them, lasers blazing away in response.

'Guys, I can sense a head-on collision coming our way,' said Faith. 'Shouldn't we move, maybe?'

'Hold your course!' ordered Julius. 'They will move.'

'If you're sure,' replied Faith, sounding unconvinced.

'I'll take the one in the middle,' said Morgana. 'You're so mine.'

'She's a little intimidating sometimes,' whispered Maya, over the com-link.

'Girl, you ain't seen nothing yet,' said Morgana. '*Banzai!*' Her robot hurtled on and collided with the furthest forward of the Arneshians. The sound of clashing metal echoed through the air.

'I'm gonna close me eyes now,' said Faith. 'Here we go!'

Julius felt a rush of adrenaline surge through him, but kept his hand steady as he continued shooting from his catalyst. He braced himself for the impact and, as the Arneshian robot loomed large in front of theirs, he also shut his eyes. As they crashed against each other, Julius was grateful that his shoulder straps kept him safely cushioned in his seat, even though the jolt made the entire robot shake. He opened his eyes and realised that he had grabbed the Arneshian vehicle by its arms, and now had it in a lock.

'Hold on to him. I want to slam-dunk him to the ground,' called Faith excitedly.

Julius kept his hands steady, while Faith manoeuvred into place. Several seconds later, they were in free fall, the ground speeding up to meet them. This time, the landing impact was considerably more brutal, and the two robots were bounced clear of each other.

'I feel like I'm in me mum's washing machine,' whined Faith, rubbing his neck.

From the ground where they were lying, Julius began to shoot again—a steady, powerful stream of energy directed at his opponent's head. Faith wrestled with the controls and managed to get the robot upright again. The Arneshian machine was trying hard to stand up, but was struggling futilely.

'We haven't killed them for real, have we?' asked Faith, walking slowly towards it.

They were within a few feet of it when it flashed brightly and then disappeared, catching them by surprise.

'Arneshian Glory,' announced the computer. 'B'Nold, M'Tard, eliminated.'

'What's with these people and the missing vowels in their names?' said Faith.

'Vowels are so last year, F'Th,' said Julius, grinning.

'Oi, comedians,' cried Skye, 'why don't you come up and play with the big boys?'

'On our way,' replied Faith, taking off.

'Guys,' said Maks, 'we need some serious help here.'

Julius looked around and saw one of the Arneshian robots hovering high in the air, and swinging Maks' robot around by the legs.

'I'm gonna be sick soon,' groaned Maya. 'I'm not kidding!'

Faith lowered his altitude and zoomed up toward the feet of the Arneshian.

'Hold on tight, guys,' shouted Julius. He lifted the arms and fired, blasting the enemy robot up and backwards. Its grip didn't falter though and, as it fell, it took Maks down with it.

'It's gonna land on top of them,' cried Faith, diving down in pursuit.

As they sped closer, Julius grabbed at the Arneshian with the robot's arms, but it was too late; when Maks' robot crashed to the ground, its attacker crunched down on top of it. Faith managed to pull out of their nosedive just in time, narrowly avoiding joining the pile-up.

Julius craned his neck and looked down. The Arneshian robot was slowly getting back to its feet. 'Maks, Maya,' he called. 'Are you OK?'

'Sort of,' answered Maks, 'but this machine has gone dead. It won't move.'

'What about the Sim-Cougar?'

'Gone too.'

'Then get out of there! We're coming down to shield you.'

'Julius,' said Faith, sounding oddly calm, 'I don't want to sound repetitive but, once again, I am not in control of the steering.'

'What do you mean?' asked Julius anxiously.

'We're free falling, and there's nothing I can do about it.'

Julius looked down and saw that indeed, they were plummeting to earth, in the direction of their teammates. 'Guys, get out of there. Now!'

'Julius!' cried Morgana. 'We can't control this thing!'

'Brace yourself and join the club,' replied Julius. 'Looks like we're all going down.'

Maks and Maya scampered out of the back of their robot's head. Thankfully, Maks grabbed hold of Maya's hand just in time to pull her clear of the landing area.

Julius gripped his shoulder straps, bracing himself as they crashed into the ground. As the dust settled, he groaned and opened his eyes slowly. 'Are you all right?'

'I'm fine,' answered Faith, yanking himself free of his seat. 'This is the harshest game, by far.'

'Morgana, Skye, can you hear me?'

'Yes,' answered Skye. 'We're getting out now.'

Julius nodded, relieved that they were all at least still in the game. Hurriedly, he unlocked his seatbelt and opened the hatch in the ceiling. He let Faith go first, then crawled out quickly. When he stood up and looked around, he immediately realised that something was wrong. 'Wait a minute—how come the Arneshian robots are still flying?'

'Hey,' cried Maya indignantly. 'That's not fair!'

The others looked up and, sure enough, the two robots were circling the sky above their heads.

'I don't understand,' said Morgana, shielding her eyes from the sun.

'Well, we can't ask questions now,' said Julius, rallying them. 'We need to go. Head towards that forest. Come on!'

They followed as he ran towards the trees; there weren't really many alternatives. Unexpectedly, a burst of energy struck the ground a few feet in front of them, sending debris flying in all directions and opening up a large hole.

'They're shooting at us,' cried Maya.

No sooner had the words left her mouth when a second shot hit just to their right, creating a huge cloud of dust. Julius skidded to a halt, unable to make out what was around him anymore. Then he heard the computer's voice. 'Zed Toon: Shanigan, Suraev, eliminated.'

'We can't stay together!' he cried. 'Skye, Maya, head east. We'll meet inside the forest.'

Skye grabbed Maya's hand and sped off to the left; Morgana and Julius headed right. Above them, the Arneshians split up and followed, firing relentlessly as they went.

Morgana was to Julius' left, keeping pace as they ran. Out of the corner of his eye he saw a dark shape descending towards her. He threw a glance over his shoulder and saw a large metal hand coming to scoop her up. Desperately, he veered in her direction, leapt forward, caught her in his arms and dragged her to the floor, just as the hand swooped over their heads. They rolled a few feet, then quickly sprang up again and ran.

'I don't think I can go on much longer!' cried Morgana.

'We're almost there. Come on!'

A new explosion opened the ground before them, sending them both tumbling into the newly formed crater. When the second blast hit, Julius was lifted off the ground and sent crashing against the edge of the hole. He kept his eyes shut as he flew through the air, waiting for the inevitable thud as he landed. He knew that, unless the in-game safety protocol failed, he couldn't really get hurt; still, as he landed on his chest, the air was pushed out of his lungs.

'Zed Toon: Ruthier, eliminated.'

'Damn it!' cried Julius.

'Julius, where are you?' said Skye. 'We made it through the forest, but that thing is still above us.'

Julius blinked and searched around him. Spotting a hole in the side of the crater, he quickly scampered inside it. The cloud of dust had not settled yet, giving him a few brief moments of shelter. 'It's not good guys,' he replied. 'Their advantage is far too great. We can't outrun them, so stay put as much as you can, Skye. After a while the computer is bound to give us another way out. It always does.'

'All right, we'll find a hideout, somewhere in-'

An explosion rocked the ground, and Julius felt bits of earth falling on top of his head and shoulders.

'Zed Toon: Miller, Berg, eliminated.'

'Skye, answer me!' called Julius. But he knew that it was too late. He was on his own and couldn't afford to stay where he was, waiting to be picked off. He wiped the dust from his face and caught sight of the forest. Half of it was ablaze. Deciding to try take advantage of the low visibility, he climbed out and made a run for it. As the first line of trees drew closer, he became aware of a shadow descending on him. He only had a brief chance to look up before a large net fell over him. He stumbled to the ground and flailed around inside the meshing. A giant hand came down, plucked him from the floor and lifted him in the air. Julius held on to the net and watched as the ground sank fast below him. When he looked up again, he was staring at the giant eyes of a robot and, above its brow, at the smirking face of the Arneshian leader, K'Ssander. 'What are you waiting for?' shouted Julius. 'End this now!'

The robot stretched out its left arm, dangling Julius in front of it. Its right arm then lifted, laser at the ready, and aimed at the net. Julius took a deep breath and stared back at K'Ssander, waiting for the blast.

CHAPTER 7

FRACTURES

Julius' eyes flew open, as if he had just woken sharply from a bad dream. He moved about as much as he could in his restraints, to get the blood pumping and the feeling back in his limbs. Looking around, he noticed the empty holo-spheres around him and wondered if they had forgotten about him. Just as he was considering calling out to try get someone's attention, Mr Smith came to let him out.

'That was a heck of a ride, McCoy,' he said, deactivating the magnetic field. 'You gave it your best shot, so be proud of it.'

Julius nodded. 'It would be better if we'd won, though.'

'Next time,' he said, patting Julius' shoulder.

Julius clambered clear of the sphere. He was just on his way to the exit when he heard a commotion erupt up ahead of him. He moved forward quickly to find out what all the noise was about and, as the door came into full view, stopped dead in his tracks, stunned. It was like a freeze-frame from a movie, but all the more surreal because of where he was and who was involved in it: K'Ssander was gripping Morgana by her forearm, holding her behind him, while his free arm was stretched forward, index finger shoved against Skye's chest. Skye had his arms down by his side, fists clenched, leaning forward towards K'Ssander.

Four of the Arneshian players were standing around them, watching, and looking very smug.

'Let me go!' cried Morgana.

'You heard the lady, grey skin,' said Skye through gritted teeth.

'Make me,' replied K'Ssander calmly.

The Arneshian leader's answer was enough to jolt Julius out of his momentary trance and he stomped towards them. However, as he started to move, Maks came striding out of nowhere and landed a right hook on K'Ssander's face. There was a sharp thwacking sound as Maks' knuckles connected, and a tiny groan escaped from K'Ssander's lips. Morgana, who was straining to get free, fell to the floor as he let go of her arm. In a flash, the watching Arneshians launched themselves at Maks, sending him sprawling to the floor, and they all collapsed in a heap.

As if moved by the same hand, Julius and Skye threw themselves into the fray, trying to pull the attackers off. Julius locked his arms around the neck of one of the Arneshians, narrowly ducking his head out of the way of a stray punch from the left and a loose kick aimed at him to his right. However, as he did that, his chin collided with someone's heel, making him see stars.

Just then, he heard Professor Chan's voice loud and clear in his mind: *'Get Miller out of there. Now!'* The commanding tone in the professor's voice snapped Julius to attention. He immediately let go of the Arneshian, jumped up, and looked for Skye. Spotting his friend, he grabbed him by the shoulders and pulled him clear, fists still flailing.

Maks, meanwhile, had regained his feet, and was promptly floored again as K'Ssander, who had quickly come back to his senses, launched himself at the Mizki Senior. The two of them were wrestling furiously when Chan and Mr Smith reached them.

'We don't treat ladies like that on this planet,' cried Maks, rolling onto K'Ssander. 'I'll teach you some respect.'

'No you won't!' said Chan imperiously, scooping Maks up by the collar of his shirt. 'Stop! Arneshian Glory, go back to your dressing room. That's an order!' He extended his left hand to Morgana, who was still sitting on the floor, and helped her to her feet. 'You too, Miss Ruthier.'

The Arneshians grabbed hold of their captain and trundled sulkily away.

When they had completely disappeared from view, Chan released Maks. 'What were you thinking?' said Chan angrily, turning to face him. 'Have you any idea of the consequences of your actions, Mr Suraev?'

'He was just protecting Morgana, sir,' argued Skye.

'Be quiet, Mr Miller,' said Chan. 'I did not give you permission to speak.'

'But, sir-' continued Skye.

'Quiet!' ordered Chan. The professor returned his attention to Maks. 'I know very well what that boy was doing, but that does not excuse your childish behaviour. You are a Zed student Mr Suraev, and we don't train you to engage in street brawls! K'Ssander wouldn't have harmed Miss Ruthier—he was just trying to goad you into doing something silly, and he succeeded perfectly.'

Maks shifted uncomfortably on his feet, but not once did he take his eyes away from Chan. Watching him, Julius had to agree that Maks had been reckless, but he had guts too, that much was sure.

'A common brawl!' said Chan, raising his hands in frustration at the ceiling. 'You could have at least used your blinking Mindkatas! Get changed, all of you. And rest assured, this doesn't end here. They will never allow that.'

As Chan stormed out of the room, Julius and Skye turned to Maks and patted him on the back.

'Great job, mate,' said Skye.

'That K'Ssander, man,' said Maks, rubbing his left shoulder and grimacing. 'It was like wrestling with a big rock. I'll get some grief for it, but Morgana's worth it. Sorry Julius, I hope I didn't screw things up too much.'

Julius shook his head, purposely ignoring the remark about Morgana. 'Don't worry about it, Maks. He was well out of order. To tell the truth, I'm more concerned with that game. Something fishy went on in there.'

'Yeah, those bloody robots,' said Skye, rubbing his left cheekbone, which was already starting to swell. 'Why were ours the only ones that stopped working? Do you think they pulled some dirty Arneshian trick on us?'

'I *know* they did,' answered Julius. 'But we need to prove it before we go making any accusations.'

Maks and Skye nodded. That was surely something that could not be resolved with a brawl.

'Take it easy next time, you hear me?' said Ms Primula, disinfecting a cut on Julius' chin. She picked up a handheld device and placed it an inch over the wounded area. 'Don't worry—it's just a Derma-Fix tool. It'll make you heal faster, but the scar will remain for a while. Hold still.'

Julius felt a tickling sensation spreading over his chin, accompanied by a buzzing noise. He guessed that the light, or whatever was in the light, was repairing his damaged skin cells and that, in a few minutes, the cut would be completely gone; the throbbing however, would stay with him for a few more hours. Right now though, Julius wasn't thinking about his chin, but rather about the reception they had received, as he and the rest of the Zed Toon had emerged from the Hologram Palace. Although he had been dreading that moment, it had not been too bad. A few of the watching crowd had shaken their heads miserably; others had actually applauded, and some had even stepped forward to shake their hands. Sure enough, the bloody cuts on their faces had raised a few eyebrows but, no questions were asked. Just before they had joined the crowd, Julius had taken the rest of his toon aside and told them what had happened at the end of the game.

'That pig!' Maya had said, indignantly.

'When this story comes out,' Julius had replied, 'and folks start to bad-mouth us about being sore losers or something, I want you to tell the students in your schools what really happened. Tell your family, your friends, and everyone you know. I'll take my punishment a lot better knowing that at least our people know the truth. Agreed?'

They had nodded, without hesitation. It was only when he had seen Chan talking to Freja and the other Grand Masters that his heart had started to race. What would the head of Tijara make of his leadership skills? Fortunately, they hadn't been pulled up there, in front of the crowd. Freja had simply glared at them, clearly not very pleased about it all, and had allowed them to return to their respective schools. Now, lying on the infirmary bed, Julius realised that this brief rest would soon be over, as he had just received a message, summoning him to Freja's office, along with Skye and Morgana.

'Miss Ruthier,' said Freja, from behind his large, glass desk, 'would you care to explain how this incident played out?'

Julius saw Morgana shifting in her chair. Reddish wisps were filling her aura, a sign that she was quite embarrassed.

'I was walking towards the changing room, behind Skye, when K'Ssander grabbed my arm. I asked him to let go, but he wouldn't. Skye turned around and told him to stop, while the other Arneshians just stood there, watching. Skye confronted him, but didn't engage him physically, at least not until Maks appeared out of nowhere and ... punched him. It forced K'Ssander to let go of my arm and I lost my balance. That's when Skye and Julius intervened and, uh, tried to stop the fight.'

Cress, who was standing to the right of the Grand Master, raised an eyebrow and said, 'Stop it? Join it, more likely.'

'That's not what we were trying to do, sir,' said Julius, quickly. 'I swear!'

'Be that as it may,' said Freja, shaking his head, 'it is not how it will be presented to the world.' He stood up and paced the floor. 'In case it's not clear enough, McCoy, this is what will most likely happen as a result of your actions: Mr Suraev will be used as a scapegoat, because he started the fight, regardless of how admirable his intentions were; you two will receive a serious case of bad press, and by default, so too will Tijara and Zed; worst of all, our already precarious reputation will take another blow, giving more support to the decision of the Earth Leader to close Zed recruitment. Is this clear enough for you?'

Julius looked back at him, trying to stay calm. He knew Freja was right, but the unfairness of it all, coupled with the fact that he had just lost the most important game of his life, was starting to take its toll. 'And the fact that they cheated to win makes no never mind to anyone, I suppose?'

Freja exchanged a quick look with Cress. 'Where's the proof of this, McCoy?' he asked.

'Everyone saw the robots—our robots—stop working in the middle of the game. Surely that should count for something.'

'Such an accusation, just after losing a challenge,' said Freja, 'can only worsen our position, especially when we have no evidence to back it up. Half the world probably think it was bad decision-making on your team's part.'

'You know that's not true,' said Morgana. 'Please Grand Master, have Mr List analyse the footage, or the game records. We can't let them get away with this.'

'We'll look into it, Miss Ruthier, but be prepared, because the worst is yet to come. Dismissed.'

With November truly underway, Julius arrived at the conclusion that Freja's prediction about their immediate future had been right: things were going from bad to outright horrid. Although the Space Channel had tried to remain neutral while describing the events following the game, the terrestrial ones had not been so soft. Blame was placed at Julius' feet for failing to properly direct his team in battle, and for allowing one of his team members to vent his frustration in such a "barbaric" way, as they put it. This made Julius mad, more so because there was nothing he could say or do to defend himself or his friends. Freja had been clear on that score—no public actions were to be taken on this matter until it was resolved at a higher level.

On top of that, T'Rogon had done his best to enhance the image of a manipulative Lunar Perimeter, rife with dangerous learners and a serious lack of space protocol on the part of the Grand Masters, placing so much trust in those students. Rumour had it that Maks had been forced to apologise in person to K'Ssander and his team, before starting a month-long ban from Satras, and an even longer one from the Hologram Palace. Morgana had been particularly crushed by that news. Skye and Faith had told her over and over again that there was nothing to blame herself for, but she couldn't help feeling that she had been the cause of this whole mess.

At least the Zed Toon had kept their promise about spreading the real story as much as possible, which pleased Julius, although he knew they were preaching to the converted: every last Zed student would, of course, side with them. The real problem was back home, on Earth. How were they going to get them to realise that T'Rogon was a wolf in sheep's clothing? Freja was right: they couldn't kick and scream about it without seeming like sore losers. They would have to wait and hope for some evidence before even considering speaking out. Surely Gabriel List would manage to find something in the game log that could be used to unmask those Arneshian cheats publicly. In the meantime though, they would just have to keep a low profile and hope there would be no more surprises.

Three weeks later, Julius was in the garden, stretched out against the oak tree, reading up on the personnel that was needed on the bridge in a spaceship, while Morgana was lying with her head resting on his right thigh, as she checked her mail. Julius heard a beeping noise coming from her PIP, and looked over at it.

'It's a message,' she said, rising up and perching on one elbow. 'It says to watch the Space Channel.'

'Not again,' groaned Julius, getting worried.

Morgana tuned her PIP into the news channel and moved her hand a little so that Julius could also see it. Iryana Mielowa was sitting in the Space Channel studio, facing

T'Rogon. The first thing that was noticeable was that there was none of the recent cheeriness in her expression; even her lipstick was of a more modest shade. Julius didn't think that was a good sign at all.

'Ambassador,' she said. 'You called for this vidcon in order to make an important announcement. We are listening.'

T'Rogon smiled. He seemed confident and strong. To Julius, in that moment, he looked more like Salgoria's right hand than a simple messenger. Even Julius' old nemesis, Red Cap, had not exuded this much power.

'Thank you, Ms Mielowa. Over the past few weeks we have greatly enjoyed your hospitality. We have learned much of your recent history, both Earth's, and the Lunar Perimeter's. We have met some truly outstanding Earthlings during our visit.' He bowed his head once, towards the camera. 'My people and I have been aware for some time now that among you live quite a vast number of late generation Arneshians, or Nuarns as you call them. I have to admit, we thought that it showed remarkable qualities on your part to be so welcoming of a people who have not done particularly well by you. Up until now, that is. For this, my Queen is forever grateful.

'A powerful feeling came over my colleagues and I when we found out just how many Arneshians are currently living on Earth—50 million, if I'm not mistaken—and we felt that we couldn't really leave without extending a formal invitation to each and every one of them, to come meet us aboard our ship.'

Julius shuddered. All he could think of was Michael.

'And what exactly would be the purpose of this visit?' asked Mielowa.

'To meet their own people, naturally.'

'Their own people? I'm sorry Ambassador, but aren't they already living with their families?'

'You tell him, girl,' whispered Morgana, totally absorbed in the interview.

'Well, they are biologically related to their parents, of course. But are they really the same as them? No, they are not. Now, for the first time in their lives, they have the opportunity to fully comprehend what it means to be an Arneshian; to encounter likeminded people who appreciate the extent of their gifts.'

'Gifts?' asked Mielowa suspiciously.

'The Grey Arts of course, my dear. Our unique talent for scientific logic is something to be nurtured, not feared.'

'And what gives you the impression that the Arneshians living on Earth are so feared by us?'

'Wrong question,' muttered Julius, shaking his head.

T'Rogon looked at her with a triumphant smile. 'What about the chokers they are forced to wear, Ms Mielowa? Isn't that a sign of fear? Suppressing the natural development of their brain, just in case an individual chooses to do wrong—as if doing wrong was only possible for an Arneshian. What about the others? Shouldn't we put a choker on everyone with mind-skills then, so nobody can do harm?'

Julius caught the briefest hint of dark shadow passing over T'Rogon's face as he said that last sentence, but he quickly regained his composure. Julius wondered if anyone else had noticed it.

'Ambassador,' said Mielowa, after a brief pause, 'exactly what do you have in mind for these visits?'

'All we ask is that any Arneshians wishing to meet with us, send us their files. We would then organise their visits and, of course, pay for all their travel expenses.'

'You tricky b-'

'Shhh,' said Morgana, leaning closer to the screen.

'How long would these visits last for?'

'Why, as long as they want them to. In fact, if they so wish, they could simply decide to return to Arnesh with us.

Our ship, Taurus One, is rather large, and it can accommodate everyone quite easily.'

'That's why he brought that mammoth ship!' cried Julius, feeling completely outraged. 'He knew it all along.'

'Back to Arnesh?' asked Mielowa, sounding understandably flabbergasted.

'Why not? If they should wish to live in a world where being an Arneshian is the norm, who are you to stop them? We have made some terrible mistakes, I know, but those days are behind us now.' Seeing as Ms Mielowa had gone silent and seemingly incapable of answering back, T'Rogon continued with his recruitment pitch. He looked straight at the camera, as if he was addressing the Nuarns directly. 'If you stay here you will never be able to enjoy a career in space, nor to develop your true path. Most of all, you may never get to meet anyone who will love you as an equal. Salgoria is giving you the chance for a new life, a new career. Who can stand in your path? No one can.'

Ms Mielowa gulped and turned to the camera, looking totally shell-shocked. 'You saw it here first. Iryana Mielowa, Space Channel.'

'That was unbelievable,' said Morgana, turning her PIP off. 'Julius? Hey, where are you going?'

But he had already disappeared inside the school.

A few minutes later, Julius was sitting at his desk, talking to his family. 'What did Michael do when he heard the news?'

'Nothing, actually,' said Rory. 'He just stared at the screen, as if we weren't in the room at all, but I could tell he was upset.'

Julius breathed a little easier. As ridiculous as the thought was, he had half feared that his brother would say he wanted to go visit the Arneshians.

'So he really had nothing to say?'

Rory shook his head. 'He's been even quieter lately, like there's something on his mind. He won't talk to us though. And he's been watching the Space Channel. Regularly.'

'You're kidding,' said Julius, knowing how little interest Michael had for anything remotely factual. Mentioning the news to Michael was like mentioning Spaceology to Julius: a sure way of sending them both to sleep.

'Your mum has tried to ask him about it, but he just shrugs his shoulders and changes topic.'

Julius sighed. 'Can T'Rogon cause any *more* problems?'

'What really worries me,' said Rory, 'is the way that Paulo Trent has just laid down the red carpet for him. He's supposed to represent us and our best interests but, so far, he hasn't done much of that. If he doesn't stand his ground soon, T'Rogon could start a schism.'

'A what?'

'A separation. He's trying to bring division among us, to create a rift between Earthlings.'

'What a mess,' said Julius. 'I wish I could talk to Michael in person. I feel so bad being out of reach like this.'

'We'll all come up for the mid-winter holiday, son. You'll have your chance then. It'll be good for Michael to see you.'

'Definitely,' agreed Julius. 'Just try not to break your leg again, Dad.'

'As long as your brother stays away from stairs and socks, I'll be fine. Just book us somewhere nice this time, no junkyards please.'

Julius chuckled. Two years ago, Michael had insisted that they have their meal in a massive holographic junkyard, which didn't go down well with Jenny. 'I'll take care of it. Don't worry.'

'Good. Stay out of trouble, Julius.'

'Yeah, I'll see what I can do,' he replied. 'But apparently I'm "an irresponsible boy, lacking in leadership skills", in case you haven't read the latest news.'

'I always knew you'd make us proud,' said Rory, with a grin.

'Thanks. Bye, Dad,' said Julius.

Rory waved and the image faded to black.

'Never rains—it pours, ay?' said Faith.

'What?' said Julius, finishing off his daily entry in his logbook. 'You talking about having the Arneshians as our new friendly neighbours, or the fact that they'll soon be recruiting an army from among our very own families?'

'Well yes, there is that of course,' said Faith, who was sporting two big bags under his eyes. 'But right now I've got this assignment to finish for Beloi on synaptic junctions for tomorrow, and the deadline for Pete's competition is the day after that. I need a holiday already.'

'I thought your design was finished,' said Julius.

'It's presentable, but I feel like it'll never be done. I keep finding bits that are missing, or need to be changed.'

'I think you're worrying too much. You've been pouring over those schematics for months now.'

'But what if I've forgotten something essential and the ship blows up?'

'Faith, you don't actually have to *build* the thing. Let Pete worry about the details.'

'I can't, Julius. I'm designing it, so it's me responsibility.' And with that he hunched over his screen again and started to scan every inch of the blueprint.

'I'll leave you to it, then ...' said Julius, packing up his things. Faith was so absorbed in his work that he didn't even notice him leaving. Julius headed out of the lounge and over to the mess hall, aiming to have a little downtime with a book before dinner. He had been so busy lately that he was still on the same page he had started three weeks ago. He crossed the mess hall, passing by a small group of 4MAs huddled at one of the long tables, fully engaged in game chat. The kitchen wasn't open yet, so he walked outside into the garden. A few students were milling about here and there, but there was no trace of Skye or Morgana. Now that he thought of it, he hadn't seen either of them since the end of their Shield class but, given that all he wanted to do was chill out and read, it wasn't necessarily a bad thing. He sat down, switched on his PIP and looked through his files, until he found the book he was reading—an ancient classic about androids and electric animals. Just as he had settled down and started the new chapter, his PIP vibrated to indicate an incoming vidcall. He sighed and pressed the Onscreen button. 'What's up, Miller?'

'Jules! You wouldn't believe where I've been!'

'Erm ... Satras?'

'Yeah, yeah, but where, exactly?'

'I don't-'

'Never mind—you couldn't begin to guess, anyway. Gabriel List asked me to test the very latest sim-dating programme to hit the holo-world!'

'Wow,' said Julius, not quite sure what to make of that. 'I'm not even gonna ask why he picked you.'

'I know, right?' said Skye, obviously pleased with himself. 'Anyway, stay where you are, 'cause I've got loads to tell you!'

'All right. I'll see you soon,' he answered, closing the link. 'Honestly.' He shook his head and went back to his book. He had barely managed to read four lines, when his

PIP vibrated again. He rolled his eyes, then accepted the vidcall. 'Hi Morgana.'

'Kombanwa,' she said, greeting him in Japanese. 'I'm on my way back. Where are you? Wait, I can see the oak tree behind your head. I'll be there shortly. Got loads to tell you.'

'Where have you been?'

'Tuala, visiting Maks.'

'Why?' The question was out of his mouth, before he could stop himself.

'What do you mean, why?' asked Morgana, sounding genuinely puzzled.

'I meant, I thought he was in detention or something,' Julius responded, trying to sound casual about it.

'Yeah, he's banned from Satras, but not from his friends! Besides, it's partly my fault, so I figured he'd appreciate the gesture.'

'Oh, I bet he does,' mumbled Julius.

'You OK? You seem a bit weird,' she asked, her head cocked to one side.

'I'm good. Just tired, that's all. I'll see you at dinner, all right?'

'Soon,' she said cheerfully, and signed off.

Julius found his bookmark for the second time but, no matter how much he tried, he had lost his focus. 'She didn't need to go see him, really,' he muttered to no one in particular. 'He's only in detention. And why am I even bothered? I'm not her guardian. I just don't want her to get hurt, that's all ... and now I'm talking to myself. Great.' Shaking his head, he forced himself to concentrate, leaned back against the tree trunk, and resumed his story.

'McCoy!' shouted Skye, barely thirty seconds later, from the entrance to the mess hall. 'You've got to hear this!'

Julius sighed in resignation and closed his PIP. 'I'll never finish this blinking book.' He stood up, brushed the grass from his trousers and headed back inside.

Skye managed to entertain most of the 3MAs throughout that evening, with every last little detail of the new sim-dating programme. It wasn't going to be available until the following year but, judging by the keen interest among the students, Julius could guess how successful it was going to be.

'So, what can you do with it?' asked Leanne.

'Many things,' replied Skye, sounding as confident as a seasoned salesman. 'Not only can it create the perfect date, according to your specific requirements—it can also help build up your confidence.'

'How?' asked Barth, immediately interested.

'Let's say you've never dated before, or you don't know how to dance, or how to do small talk; the programme can teach you, using one of its own super-duper holos. Once you've downloaded the software onto your PIP, you're free to create any holo-character you like.'

'Can you make it look like someone you know?' asked Siena.

'Absolutely. You just upload the matrix and the software will do the rest. You thinking of anybody I know?' he added, mischievously.

'None of your business,' she said quickly, blushing furiously.

'Did you actually try it?' asked Lopaka, in awe.

'Oh yeah,' said Skye. 'And believe me, you can't tell the difference.'

There were several murmurs of approval at that.

'Where will it be, Skye?' asked Gustavo.

'Mr List says it's primarily been created for the crews that have to go on deep space journeys, to minimise their loneliness. On Zed, you can get it at the Palace; you just book a room and, once you're there, you download the programme onto your PIP. Easy as that.'

'Nice one. I've got to tell Yuri!' said Gustavo, and hurried off.

Excited by the news, most of the Mizkis went back to their own activities, leaving Barth with the Skirts.

'Sounds grand,' said Faith, cracking open a pistachio.

'Hmm ... I don't know,' said Morgana. 'Surely it can't replace the real thing. What if you get all flustered and bothered, and then you go—hold on, this thing is fake?'

'Well, I do wanna get flustered and bothered, if you don't mind,' said Faith, making everyone laugh.

'He's right,' added Barth, thoughtfully. 'For some of us it may well be our only chance.'

'That's not true,' answered Morgana. 'You'll find your other half, one day.'

'And when I do, I need to make sure I don't cut her hair off by accident, like I did with you!'

Even Morgana had to join in on that one, despite how upset she had been about it at the time. 'All right, you win. The programme could help you be a little less-'

'Dangerous!' finished Faith.

'And you, Julius?' asked Skye. 'Are you gonna give it a go?'

'I don't seem to have a good relationship with holos,' he said half-heartedly. 'In case you forgot, Master Isshin tried to kill us all two years ago.'

'That was different,' said Skye, dismissing his answer with a wave of his hand.

'Well, if I do I'm not going to tell you,' said Julius, grinning.

'Oh, come on!'

Julius just looked back at him and grinned.

That night, after Skye had turned off the light, Julius found his thoughts turning to the sim-date programme. As the silhouette of his perfect date began advancing towards him, he realised that maybe, just maybe, he *would* try it out.

CHAPTER 8

MID-WINTER BLUES

Julius, Skye and Morgana were standing outside Pete's shop, in Satras, waiting for Faith. It was Thursday the 1st of December, the deadline for the spaceship competition. Faith had been so eager to hand in his project that he had left Tijara right after his Martial Arts class without even stopping to take a shower. The others decided to do likewise, and boarded the Intra-Rail, trying to keep out of the other passengers' nostrils as much as possible.

'It's done,' said Faith, finally hovering out of the shop.

'When will you know?' asked Julius.

'Mid-summer, probably. It depends how many entries they get.'

'I bet you feel relieved,' said Skye, patting him on the shoulder.

'You have no idea,' he said. 'I don't think I've ever worked so hard in me life.'

'Then you deserve a prize,' said Morgana. 'How about an ice-cream?'

'I think I fancy something savoury, actually.'

'I know just the place,' said Morgana. 'It's this new deli, on the fourth tier. It's called "Hallouminati: The People of the Cheese." Kaori says it's yummy!'

'What the heck kind of a name is that?' asked Skye.

'Sounds good to me,' said Julius. 'Let's go.'

When they got there, they found a small queue of people waiting to be served, so they joined in. Intrigued by the various pungent smells, Julius peered inside. The shop had several deli counters; four of which were filled to the brim with cheeses from all over the Earth. Julius read some of the labels, Parmigiano, Camembert, Emmental, Pecorino, and a variety of blue cheeses; a fifth counter contained several different types of bread, everything from rolls, to baguettes, to large, brown crusted loaves; finally, a sixth one contained fresh fruits, cut into slices. This sight, especially after three hours of exercise, made him simply ravenous. He looked at the menus on the walls, trying to decide what to order.

'Half a baguette with Pecorino and pears, please,' asked Julius, once he reached the till. He was just about drooling by then. He handed over two Fyvers and scurried along to the counter, where two men were preparing the food with practiced care.

'There you are,' said one of them, handing him a plate.

Julius thanked him and headed for one of the small circular tables outside the shop. Soon, the others joined him.

'Come to papa,' said Skye, lifting his filled roll in both hands.

'You look like an anaconda trying to eat a sheep,' said Julius, staring at Skye's cavernous mouth.

'It's called cranial kinesis,' said Skye, pausing for a moment. 'That's why snakes can eat animals that are bigger than them. I looked it up 'cause I wanted to know if I could do it too, but no.'

'You're kidding, right?' asked Morgana.

Skye just winked at her and bit into his food.

'Hey look,' said Faith, pointing to his right, along the path. 'The GMs.'

When he turned around, Julius was surprised to see Freja, Kloister and Milson walking along the path, seemingly window shopping. Then he realised that it wasn't just the three of them; they were accompanied by a young couple and a small girl which he guessed must be their daughter.

'How odd to see them outside of school like this,' said Morgana.

Julius agreed with that but, then again, of course they must also have an actual life. 'Maybe one of them is related to the couple,' he said.

'Wow,' said Faith. 'Check her out.'

He was pointing at the girl, who was standing in front of a large flower pot, which was twice her size. Her blond curls were held back by a red hair band, highlighting the delicate features of her young face; she was wearing a white and red dress, with black, shiny shoes and short white socks. All in all, she had a doll-like look about her. She couldn't have been more than seven years old, but Julius could tell that she was Zed material: one of her little hands was stretched towards the pot and, with no apparent difficulty, she was lifting it up and spinning it in a small circle.

'Farrah!' called her mother, hurrying towards her.

As the child was scooped up, Kloister was quick to freeze the pot in midair, before it could crash back down again.

'Nice save,' said Faith, turning back to his food.

Julius watched Edwina Milson caress the little girl's cheek, before the whole group resumed their stroll, and eventually disappeared from view.

With December came the realisation that the Earth President was not going to do anything to stop T'Rogon's open invitation to the Nuarns. Whether he wouldn't, or couldn't do so, Julius didn't know but, as the weeks passed, an increasing number of them began to apply for the trip to Taurus One. The 14th was the date set for the first group of travellers to journey into Zed orbit, and Julius had been scanning the news since early that morning. The Space Channel had sent its reporters to all the Zed departure centres involved, to gather as many interviews as they could. By lunchtime, there were at least fifty of these in the archives, and Julius scanned through them eagerly on his PIP.

'Let's watch that one,' said Faith, leaning closer to him. 'It's from the centre where we took off from Earth.'

Julius obliged him, while slowly eating his lentil soup. As he pressed the button, the Prague departure centre appeared in the background, where a man carrying a suitcase was being interviewed. The first thing Julius noticed was the man's choker, which was still visible under his shirt.

'Mr Schneider,' said a man's voice from out of shot, 'you are the ten-millionth Nuarn to have booked this trip. What made you decide to visit the Taurus One?'

'Mainly curiosity, I guess,' answered the man. Although he spoke in the common speech, his accent sounded northern European to Julius. 'As it is, I would never have been allowed to leave Earth otherwise. T'Rogon is giving me that opportunity.'

'Aren't you afraid of boarding what we always believed to be an enemy ship?'

'I don't know about being afraid, but an enemy ship? I don't think so. Ambassador T'Rogon said it right: we are alike. I have nothing to fear from them.'

'How long do you plan to stay on board?'

'As long as they let me. This may well be my only chance, so I intend to take full advantage of it.'

'Why the large suitcase?'

'I might just decide to stay ... indefinitely. In any case, I would like to be prepared.'

The interviewer thanked Mr Schneider, who picked up his luggage and headed for his shuttle.

Julius closed his palm, deactivating his PIP, and shook his head. 'We should have seen this coming.'

'You heard Beloi,' said Faith. 'Diplomatic immunity. We couldn't have prevented their visit.'

'Dad said Salgoria is trying to create a schism, a division among us.'

'That sounds about right,' said Faith, finishing his breaded escalope. 'There's three billion of us and about 50 million Nuarns on Earth, and T'Rogon wants to separate us.'

'Well, he's not getting Michael, that's for sure,' Julius said bitterly.

'Has he said anything?' asked Faith, quietly.

'He won't talk about it,' answered Julius. 'I'm hoping to have a chat at our mid-winter meal. It's long overdue.'

Faith nodded. 'If there's anything I can do ...'

'Thanks, mate. I'll keep that in mind.'

The last day of term flew by quicker than Julius could have expected. By all accounts, Friday the 24th was supposed to be an exciting day from start to finish: there were only two hours of lessons in the morning—Telekinesis with Professor King and his infamous stuffed reindeer, Jeff—followed by a free afternoon to spend in the Palace before it was shut down for the mid-winter meals. Yet, Julius wasn't as thrilled as the others were, his mind preoccupied with his brother's visit.

Because of the Tijaran school's upcoming relocation to Gea One in a week's time, the Mizkis had to see their families earlier than previous years, that coming weekend, leaving Julius with less than two days to decide what to book for his meal.

'I think I'll go somewhere in Polynesia,' said Faith to the others, at lunch.

They had gone back to the Hallouminati shop which, incidentally, was the only place with a few free tables.

'I want a very Earthy place this time,' said Julius.

'Why?' asked Morgana, slicing her roll into smaller, more manageable pieces.

Julius looked at the Palace, in the distance. He was trying to voice the thoughts that had been bouncing around in his mind over the last few days. 'If Michael ... if he should decide to go to Taurus One, they would probably give him as much technology as he wants.'

'But they can't give him Earth,' Faith finished for him.

Skye and Morgana nodded in agreement.

Julius looked at them, relieved that they had understood him so quickly. 'Earth is his home, and if we go somewhere that feels like it, then maybe Michael ...'

'Makes sense,' Skye cut in. 'It'll help him see what he would be missing.'

'Anywhere special come to mind?' asked Faith.

Julius thought back to their childhood and the things they had done together. 'We used to go camping up north—I mean in the Highlands—Glen Affric.'

'Oh Julius, it's so beautiful up there!' cooed Morgana.

'Michael loved it there too,' said Julius. 'He would spend the whole day chasing red squirrels and watching out for Golden Eagles; Dad would fish for our dinner and Mum would get the barbecue going.'

'It sounds like a grand place,' said Faith. 'Go on and book it.'

Julius nodded. There were many other places that brought back good memories, but somehow Glen Affric felt right.

As soon as they had finished their food, they headed for the Palace, where they had to queue for ten minutes before they could all make their reservations. With that concern out of their minds, the Skirts treated themselves to their last Fight game of the year.

When Michael stepped out of the shuttle, Julius was caught by surprise: the person standing between Rory and Jenny wasn't the sweet little kid that Julius had seen the year before on this very same platform, but a young teenager almost as tall as he was, with a long, light brown fringe hiding his dark eyes. He had a troubled look on his face, as if some mental struggle was raging inside his head and a little crease had formed between his eyebrows, similar to the one his dad had had for years. There were no two ways about it—Michael looked older.

It was Jenny who hugged Julius first—something his brother had eagerly done in previous years—followed by an affectionate embrace from Rory. In stark contrast, Michael's arms felt almost limp around Julius' shoulders, and his smile had lost some of its natural warmth. As he stood there, holding his brother, Julius felt as if there were so many things he wanted to say, but no words were actually coming out. On second thoughts, that was probably a good thing: the Zed docks were hardly the right place for a deep and meaningful chat.

'How was the trip?' asked Julius, grabbing his mum's case.

'Great!' answered Rory, beaming. 'But I'm looking forward to getting to our hotel right now. I'm knackered.'

'I'm so happy to see you, Julius,' said Jenny, squashing him against her and kissing his cheek.

'Mu-um!' he said, blushing. 'Not here.'

Jenny laughed amiably. 'You'll never be too old for your mum's kisses, my boy!'

'He probably has a girlfriend around here, somewhere,' said Rory cheekily. 'You'll ruin his star-rep.'

'No way!' answered Julius quickly. 'That's Skye's thing. I'm busy as it is, anyway.'

'He's only fourteen, Rory,' said Jenny. 'Let him enjoy his youth without the pangs of the heart. Speaking of, how's Morgana? I saw a picture of her the other day, and she looks so beautiful.'

'Speaking of? What's she on about?' thought Julius to himself; then out loud, 'She's good. Her folks arrived early this morning.'

'You give her a big kiss from me, if I don't manage to see her.'

'A kiss? Unlikely,' he said, horrified.

'It's just an expression!' said Jenny, sounding amused.

Rory laughed. 'Don't worry dear, he'll not be so horrified at that thought soon enough.'

'Can we just change topic, please?' Julius implored.

'All right,' said his dad, grinning. 'So, what did you book for us this time?'

'I thought it would be nice to go up north,' he said.

'Are we going to Glen Affric?' said Michael suddenly.

Julius was overjoyed to see a smile light up his brother's face; he had chosen well after all. 'Aye. I got us our usual cabin and kept all the dragonflies, but completely left out the midges.'

'Nice one,' said Michael, visibly relaxing.

'Excellent choice, son,' said Rory. 'We all love that place.'

Feeling heartened by their reaction, Julius led them to their hotel with a lighter step, anticipating a really good mid-winter meal.

The midday sun was shining down on the glen, the heat intensifying the smell of the surrounding pines, birches and oaks; the grass was green and punctuated by many colourful plants, from creeping ladies' tresses to twinflowers. The cottage stood by the shore of Loch Beinn a' Mheadhain, whose still surface reflected the eagles soaring above it. Rory and his sons were standing by the water, armed with fishing rods and patience, while Jenny was getting the barbecues going and preparing the side dishes.

Julius had ensured there would be plenty of fish and meat in the fridge since, simulation or not, it wasn't guaranteed that they would actually catch anything. He felt good standing there, barefoot on the fresh grass, surrounded by his family. He had calibrated the artificial sun to give off a moderate warmth, and when both him and Michael had taken their t-shirts off, he had to work hard to convince his mum that they didn't need any sunscreen.

'It's only a programme!' he said, trying to avoid the dollop of cream that she was chasing him with.

'You're Scottish, dear,' she said, unconvinced. 'You would burn under a desk lamp.'

Eventually, Julius had to let her have her way, so that he could carry on fishing in peace.

They sat down for their meal around two in the afternoon, under the branches of an old pine tree. The air was fresh and filled with the smell of grilled meat. Julius found himself answering the usual barrage of questions in front of a kingly food spread: sausages, lamb cutlets, trout, salmon, pickles, coleslaw and fresh bread. He had even remembered to order dessert, so the family was treated to a delicious wild berry cheesecake, with plenty of coffee and fresh juice to go with it.

As the afternoon passed in a sort of peaceful haze, Julius realised that he would have to pluck up the courage to have a proper chat with Michael. He felt that the day had been relaxed enough to put his brother in the right mood for talking, or at least he hoped so.

'Hey bro,' he said, sitting up in his deck chair. 'Why don't we give those two some privacy and go for a walk?'

Michael seemed unsure.

'Come on. We can go check if the squirrel house is still there,' said Julius. 'Besides, I need to walk off all that food.'

'All right,' he said, standing up.

Julius threw a glance at his folks, and saw his dad nodding knowingly. They started off along the shore, following a small path which skirted the edge of the forest. A group of dragonflies hovered above the water while, in the forest, a Scottish crossbill sung its unique song.

Julius had been thinking all morning about an icebreaker to use with Michael, but now he was completely at loss for what to say. Eventually, it was Michael that took the lead.

'Did you tell your friends about me?' he said.

'Of course. As soon as I got back to school.'

'And what did they say?'

'They were really sorry that you couldn't join us. They were looking forward to you being on Zed.'

'It didn't bother them knowing I'm a Nuarn?'

'Why should it? You're still Michael to them,' said Julius.

'And to you? Am I still your brother, Julius?'

Julius stopped abruptly and turned to face him, putting both hands on his shoulders. 'Yes, you are. And don't you ever doubt that, you hear me? What I said last year is still true: you are a real McCoy, no more, no less.'

Michael looked at him and nodded. Then he carried on walking. Julius followed him, aware of the fact that his brother had a worried look back on his face.

'I always wanted a career in space-'

'But you still can, Michael.'

'Let me finish,' he said, a bit louder.

Julius was startled by the seriousness and hurt in his voice. No twelve-year-old should feel like that.

'I wanted to build ships and watch them fly across the galaxies. I wanted to live on the Zed space stations and teach others how to fix things. That was my dream, and it's all gone now.'

'You can still do that,' said Julius, aware of the pleading in his own voice.

'No I can't, and you know it. Nuarns aren't allowed in space. The closest I can get to it is by visiting you on Satras. And that will also end when you graduate, in three years time. All I can do on Earth is build spare parts for shuttles; end of story.'

'How do you know all this?' asked Julius, genuinely surprised.

'It was in the leaflets I got from Taurus One.'

Julius' jaw dropped an inch. 'From the Ambassador?'

'Yes. They sent them to all us Nuarns, explaining about the travelling procedures.'

'But ... but you're not really thinking of going, are you?' he said, stopping dead in his tracks. 'T'Rogon is a manipulative oaf, who's trying to take you away from us, your families, for some nasty reason of his own. They've already cheated during our game and now they're trying to trick you all!'

Michael paused, lost in thought for a moment, but it didn't last long. 'T'Rogon said that I can be an engineer if I want, or a pilot. There are no restrictions on Arnesh for what I can or can't do.'

'Arnesh ...' Julius' jaw had dropped another inch, while his eyes were widening in disbelief.

'They would get rid of this ... dog collar, for a start, and give me a circlet.'

'A circlet?'

'Yeah, like the one T'Rogon wears; that all Arneshians wear. It's like a crown that amplifies our Grey skills.'

Julius' surprise gave way to anger and he felt it slowly mounting in his body. Trying hard to keep his voice level, he asked, 'And what else is he going to give you?'

'A job, a school to go to—like Zed, but for kids like me. He can give me a future I'll never get here.'

'Michael, are you seriously telling me that you would leave all of us behind, your real family, to join a bunch of folks who have been trying to kill us for the last 230 years? Folks who can't even win a game fair and square?'

'He told us that you people would say that.'

'*You people*?' Julius was furious. He could feel hot energy surging along his arms, making his fingertips tingle. The last time that had happened, he had been facing Red Cap. But Michael was not an Arneshian, only a scared kid who had just been given a shortcut, right out of the frying pan and into the fire. He needed to calm down, before his powers messed up this situation even more. He took a deep breath and started walking again. Eventually, Michael followed him.

'I realise this must have been tough for you.'

'You do, Julius? How exactly? How can a White Child, the Solo champion of Zed, possibly know what it feels like to be a Nuarn, to be destined to a second class life, while everyone else around him has it all? How can you?'

Julius was stunned to a halt again. Where was this bitterness coming from? It was as if a dam had been broken, and all his brother's feelings from the last few months had finally been unleashed. 'Michael, bad things happen to everyone in life. Look at Faith, without the use of his legs forever, without a chance to get back the freedom he so wants, and yet he copes! Why can't you adapt too?'

'Because I have a choice!' he shouted.

Julius watched as the tears gushed out and ran down Michael's cheeks, glistening in the afternoon sun. Everything was silent around them, except for the buzzing of the dragonflies. Michael dropped to his knees and buried his face in his hands, sobbing. Julius' anger immediately dissipated and he knelt down by his brother's side, hugging him tightly, like he had done so many times over the years.

'Why?' he kept saying as he sobbed. 'All I wanted was to join Zed ... with you.'

'I wanted that too Mickey and I'm so, so sorry. You have to believe me. If there was anything I could do to change this I would.'

Julius held him until he stopped shaking, then he let him go and sat on the ground. 'Mum and Dad, do they know?'

'No!' he said, panicking. 'Please don't say anything about this.'

'I won't. Why don't you find out about other careers in the Development Bureau? There's one on George Street, by Charlotte Square.'

'I only read what the Ambassador sent. I thought it would be the same thing.'

'Somehow I doubt it. Listen Mickey, if I were in your shoes I would also be curious to visit Taurus One. That, I can understand. I'm not sure how much Mum and Dad have been telling you, but in the last two years the Arneshians have tried to kill me and everyone else on Zed, at least twice. They even kidnapped Morgana.'

Michael looked quite stunned by that, but not as much as Julius would have hoped.

'And now they're here, like nothing ever happened. Well, forgive me, but I don't believe them one bit. Most of all, I don't want you in harm's way; that's why I'd rather you didn't go meet T'Rogon.'

'Well ... I'll ask Dad to take me to the bureau,' Michael said half-heartedly.

Julius had to be content with that for the moment. 'All right. Let's go back. They'll be waiting for us.' He stood up and helped Michael back to his feet. Somehow, this didn't feel like a victory to Julius.

The rest of the day flew by and Rory decided they should go for an ice-cream at Mario's Ice-Land. Jenny wanted to pick up a few things to take back with her, so after a quick supper, they said goodbye to their cabin and Glen Affric.

Julius and his family left the Moon-Hole Inn around 10:00, the morning after, and went for breakfast at Global Brioche. By the time they reached the docks it was close to midday. As they stood by their shuttle, Jenny performed her last-minute dispensing of hugs while Rory made the usual list of recommendations. It always pained Julius watching his parents go away; he missed them very much, but there was little he could do about it.

Before seeing his brother off, Julius took him to one side. 'I know I'm not around as much as I would like,' said Julius, 'but if you ever need to talk about something—anything—you call me, all right?'

Michael nodded. He looked a bit better than yesterday, but he was still unusually quiet.

'Will you remember to check the bureau tomorrow?' asked Julius, hopefully.

'I will.'

It wasn't much, but it would have to do. 'Take care, little bro.'

'You too, Julius,' he said.

As he turned, Julius saw Ambassador T'Rogon walking along the platform, and realised with dread that he was about to walk past them, escorted by two of his men. Alarmed, Julius tried to think of a way to hide Michael from view, but couldn't, at least not without making the situation worse. A few seconds later, Julius found himself face to face with T'Rogon.

The Ambassador seemed as surprised as Julius was to be meeting him like this. Instinctively, Julius had shoved his brother behind his back, worrying that the Arneshians would see Michael's choker and try to use it as ammunition against him later on. There was an awkward moment of silence, where they all stood there, not knowing what to say. Julius knew that T'Rogon could see Michael very well, but he still hoped the choker would remain hidden from his view.

Just then, to Julius' relief, Master Cress emerged out of nowhere and stepped between them. 'Ambassador, a word if I may,' he said firmly.

Julius, who couldn't afford to forget protocol, bowed quickly. But, as he straightened up, he was certain that T'Rogon had clearly seen Michael's choker. A tiny snarl curled the corner of the Ambassador's mouth briefly, making Julius' skin crawl.

'Was that really T'Rogon?' asked Michael, once they had moved away.

'Yes,' said Julius, trying to calm his nerves.

‘He looks so normal,’ said Michael.

‘He’s not a nice guy, believe me.’

‘Why did you hide me from him? Are you ashamed of being seen with a Nuarn?’

‘No. It’s not that. I had to because-’

‘Never mind. I don’t need your explanations,’ he said.

‘Michael, please,’ said Julius, trying to grab his arm.

His brother shook him off curtly, and boarded the shuttle without turning back.

CHAPTER 9

GEA ONE

On Saturday the 31st of December, all students had to collect their uniforms for the ball from Twitch and Stitch, an operation that took up the best part of the morning. It seemed that most of the Mizkis had left this task to the very last minute. After a stop at Going Spare, so Morgana could choose her birthday present, and a quick bite at Halloumi-nati, the Skirts headed back to school.

The Tijaran Mizkis had been asked to assemble in the hangar by 14:00. When Julius arrived on the main platform overlooking the shaft, he leaned over the rail to look down. The five decks, stacked one beneath the other, opened outwards like a huge fan. The first three decks were for the Cougars, and the last two for the Storks.

'Look! The decks are moving,' said Morgana, pointing down.

Julius watched as the decks shifted to the right, exactly like a fan would fold in on itself. From the bottom of the shaft a new, long deck began to surface, coming to a stop where the first one had been just a moment before. Smoothly, six different new decks fanned out to the left, each one riddled with small shuttle pods.

'Mizkis,' called Captain Foster, from a raised ledge.

The students turned to face him and fell silent at once.

'First years to the first deck; seconds to the second deck, and so on and so forth.'

'Let's go, let's go!' chirped Morgana, visibly thrilled.

'Here we go again,' said Julius, allowing her to drag him by the arm.

The Mizkis headed for the stairs and the lifts, trying to negotiate the crowd as they went. It took a while to reach the third deck, but eventually the 3MAs were all accounted for. Eight students had been previously selected by Clavel to pilot the shuttles and, of course, Morgana was among them. She headed for the closest one and hopped on, followed by Siena, Isolde and Jiao, all looking as giddy as she was.

'Over here, guys,' shouted Lopaka, boarding another shuttle.

Faith hovered inside and sat next to Lopaka, while Julius and Skye took the back seats.

Julius was beginning to feel a bit more relaxed, allowing the excitement of the weeks ahead to sink in. The shuttle itself wasn't all that thrilling, but it was part of the journey, after all. Professor Clavel had been teaching them how to pilot these crafts since September, to the point that, after four months, Julius couldn't stand the sight of them much anymore. They were effectively smaller versions of the Storks, but not as fast; their main purpose was for carrying people to and from space stations or starships.

'3MA Liway, requesting permission to take off,' said Lopaka into his microphone.

'Permission granted,' the control tower answered.

There were plenty of runways to choose from, so Lopaka picked the closest free one and hovered over to it. Julius remembered how Morgana had managed to trigger the safety speed protocol the last time they had flown through here, but then again, the Arneshians had been hot on their heels.

This time though, Lopaka navigated the brightly lit tunnel surely and safely, flying steady behind Morgana's shuttle.

'So, Lopaka,' said Faith, trying to sound casual, 'how's your sister?'

Lopaka threw him a sideways glance. 'Nalani's good, thanks.' Then, with a grin, 'Should I tell her you're asking?'

'Mr Shanigan!' said Skye, patting his friend on the shoulder. 'Is there something you'd like to tell us?'

Faith was blushing slightly, but still managed a smile. 'So what? She's a lovely girl. Isn't that right, Lopaka?'

'That she is. And if your intentions are beyond gentlemanly, I'll cut your head off.'

Julius and Skye burst out laughing.

'I'm only kidding, Faith,' said Lopaka. 'I'd like you as a brother-in-law.'

'Thanks man, I appreciate the vote of confidence. But, uh, let's not get ahead of ourselves.'

'Siena may have some competition after all,' thought Julius with a grin.

The banter continued all the way into orbit, where the shuttle pod slowed down in the proximity of Gea One.

'Look at her,' said Faith, craning his head to take in the sight. 'She's so big.'

'She's tiny compared to my Terra 3,' said Skye. 'But she's pretty, I grant you that.'

As all of the shuttle pods reached the orbiting space station, they halted, waiting for permission to dock. Abruptly, the rotating outer rings halted, and several docking bay hatches opened simultaneously.

'3MA Liway, proceed to bay 36,' said the computer.

'Acknowledged,' answered Lopaka. He moved forward, steering gently into the opening; a large docking arm latched onto their shuttle and dragged it safely inside, while the pressure door closed behind them.

With the pod securely parked, Julius disembarked with the others, hoisting his rucksack up on his shoulder, and followed the rest of the students out of the hangar.

'Welcome aboard, Mizkis,' greeted Captain Foster over an intercom. 'There are six coloured lines flashing on the walls, each with the year group written underneath. I want you to follow yours back to the dorms on deck four. Find your rooms, drop your bags and report to the lounge, on deck three. There, you will collect the welcome pack for your PIP. It has an interactive map of Gea, your schedule for the rest of the day, the location of your classes, and the safety protocols. Read them thoroughly, and STAY OUT OF TROUBLE!'

'Will he ever tire of reminding us?' sighed Skye, shaking his head.

'As if,' added Julius.

'We're green,' said Faith. 'Me favourite colour.'

The 3MAs began to shuffle forward, their numbers swelling as more students joined in from different corridors. After a while, the green strip veered off to the right, along deck four. An archway opened onto a straight corridor, with eight doors to the left and eight to the right.

'Hey guys!' said Morgana, joining them. 'We're all on the same floor!'

'I bet that was Miller's idea,' said Julius.

'Anything to be close to the ladies,' said Skye, with a wink.

'That's us,' said Morgana, pointing at a door with her name on it. 'Jiao! Over here!'

'Catch you in a bit,' said Julius, waving goodbye before following Skye.

A minute later he was standing inside a well lit room, split into two distinct areas which mirrored each other. Julius took the bed to the right. It had a bedside table beside it and a metal chest at its feet. A door led off to the side, which he guessed must be for the bathroom, while a long rectangular window covered the length of the back wall, looking out into the vast expanses of space surrounding Gea One.

'Nice view,' said Julius peering out of it. He really did love it out here, with the calming hum of the engines, surrounded by stars, and knew that he was thoroughly addicted to life in space—it was impossible for him to now even begin to imagine his life without Zed. He felt a twinge of sadness as he tried to guess what he would have done if he had found himself denied the opportunity, like Michael had been.

'Ready Jules?' said Skye, snapping him away from his thoughts.

He nodded and together they headed out, collecting Faith and Morgana on the way. The green strips on the wall were proving to be very handy as, between the stairs, the lifts and the numerous decks, getting lost would be all too easy. They followed them to the lounge, where Julius was surprised at how large the area was. it seemed that the entire school was now assembled there, and there was still room to spare.

'Over here,' said Faith, hovering toward the left side.

Julius saw something resembling a hand-dryer attached to the wall; it had a yellow screen on its front, with the words "Welcome Packs" emblazoned on its face. Faith activated his PIP and held his hand under the scanner, until it beeped.

'That was easy,' said Julius, as soon as he had downloaded his pack.

Once they had all gathered theirs, they moved to a group of sofas at the far side of the room.

'Hey, look: they've got a Juice-Maid table!' said Morgana excitedly.

'A what?' asked Julius.

'Yeah, I've heard of them,' said Faith. 'Go on—show us how it works.'

Morgana sat up and placed her hand, palm down, on the glass top. 'Ginger Beer, Organic.' To the boys' surprise, a small hatch opened underneath her hand, and a glass filled with fizzy, opaque liquid pushed upwards into her grip. 'Cheers!' she said, curling her legs up under her.

'This is just!' said Julius, putting his hand on the machine. 'Peach tea, iced.' A glass promptly rose up from the hatch and he sipped it thirstily.

Skye quickly ordered a coconut milkshake, and Faith then ordered a lemonade.

'So, Julius,' said Morgana, 'you didn't really tell us about your mid-winter meal. How did it go with Michael?'

'I'm not too sure, actually,' he said, setting his glass down and checking that no one around them was in earshot. It was true, he still hadn't spoken to them about what had happened during, and after, their visit to the virtual Glen Affric. He had been waiting for the right moment but, for one reason or another, it had never come. 'I'm telling you guys, I've never seen Michael so bothered,' said Julius. 'It's like he's got the weight of the world on his shoulders.'

'But he didn't actually say he *was* going to join them though, did he?' asked Morgana.

'At first it was clear that he was going to,' answered Julius. 'Then, after our chat, he didn't seem quite so sure anymore. But I swear, for a moment there, I thought I was going to lose it.'

'What do you mean?' asked Skye. 'With Michael?'

'Yeah. You should've heard the stuff he was throwing at me. The bitterness in his voice. He said I couldn't possibly understand him, because of who I am, and that only T'Rogon had the solution to all his problems.'

'That's harsh,' said Skye.

'Maybe, but it's also normal,' said Faith. 'He's a twelve-year-old who's had his dreams shattered and, just when he's starting to deal with it, T'Rogon arrives and suddenly there's a way of getting those dreams back online. Wouldn't you have done the same?'

'Maybe ... if I had never left Earth, or if I hadn't been here to see the things they did to us ...' said Julius.

'Never. Not if you had been born on Terra 3 like me,' said Skye firmly.

'He received a leaflet from T'Rogon as well,' said Julius.

'The Ambassador's sure done his homework, hasn't he?' said Faith. 'With the kind of technology they've got, I bet that leaflet looks mighty appealing to a Nuarn.'

'What could they possibly have that we don't?' said Julius, throwing himself against the sofa in a huff. 'So far we've seen a psychotic V.I., a bunch of holos, and a few grey skinned folks; but what else?'

'I think it's simply that they're super-smart,' said Morgana.

'But what does that even mean?' said Julius. 'Aren't we smart too? We have Grey skills like them, and we know how to use them too. Look at Faith!'

'Thanks, buddy,' said Faith, raising his glass to him. 'But, it's more to do with faster brain processing and what they do with the knowledge. Their technology is much better than ours.'

'How so?' asked Morgana, sounding genuinely curious.

'During our engineering lessons, Professor de Boer told us a few things that ... well, if you think what we have here on Zed is cool, think again, 'cause the Arneshian stuff is way ahead.'

'Like what?' asked Julius.

'Their ships can travel twice as fast as ours can; like, they can do 10,000 light years in five years.'

'No way,' said Morgana.

'Yes way,' continued Faith. 'And they use some kind of mystery power source for their drive cores, which we still can't identify. Plus, records from Marcus Tijara's own time said that their biggest ships were protected by some sort of barrier that could easily deflect the firepower of a small fleet.'

'Have we ever taken one of them down?' asked Julius, finding himself very much captivated by the discussion.

'Apparently so, but you need to get real close.'

'I bet their destructive power is mental,' added Morgana.

'Nuclear-like,' said Faith.

'And on that note, I'm off,' said Skye, quickly standing up.

'Where are you going?' asked Morgana.

'Somewhere else, where there's no admiring talk of Arneshian technology.'

'That's not what we were doing, mate,' said Faith, looking a bit hurt.

'I'd be careful then if I were you, or people may question your allegiance.'

'Come off it, Miller,' said Faith, testily.

'I question your sanity sometimes,' added Julius, with a raised eyebrow.

Skye waved his hand in front of him. 'Forget it guys. You know me and my views. I'll go have a chat with Valentina—she's prettier than you two. But not you, darling; no one is prettier than you,' he ended off, blowing a kiss at Morgana.

'Hang on a minute: who's this Valentina, now?' asked Julius, following Skye with his eyes as he walked away.

'5MS,' replied Morgana, shaking her head.

'What's got into him?' said Faith. 'We can never talk about Arneshians when he's around.'

'Maybe he's got space station syndrome or something,' offered Morgana.

'It's his thing,' said Julius. 'Forget about it.'

'I hope Michael doesn't buy into this recruitment nonsense, anyway,' said Morgana.

'I hope so too,' agreed Julius. 'But it's done now. I told him it would be a really bad choice. He's not stupid; he'll see it for himself. Besides, my folks would never let him.'

'That's good then,' said Morgana. 'It means that you can look forward to the New Year's party without any worries; and to my birthday cake!'

'As long as it's not a Supernova,' added Faith quickly.

'No chance! I'm expecting a dance too, by the way, with both of you.'

'With pleasure, milady,' said Faith.

Julius smiled. He was trying to relax his mind as much as he could; but, as long as the Taurus One stayed in orbit, he wouldn't truly be at ease. He wanted to know that T'Rogon was far away enough to pose no threat to his family.

They spent the rest of that afternoon going over their new schedules, checking out the Gea One's facilities and chatting with their classmates. Around 18:00, they decided to return to their dorms to get ready for the ball. Julius was really looking forward to it, especially because he had missed the previous one, following Clodagh Arnesh's hologram around Satras.

The main hall on Deck six had been chosen as the venue for the New Year party. The circular room was filled with round tables, covered with silver tablecloths, leaving space for a large dance floor in the middle. Even the teachers' usual long table had been replaced with two small ones, and moved to one side.

Julius, Skye, Lopaka and Faith arrived at 19:00 sharp, looking very smart in their dark dinner jackets. Once again, Faith had blackened the panels on his skirt to match everyone else's attire.

As the Tijaran Mizkis started to pour inside the hall, Julius decided that it was time to find a table. 'Let's get this one,' he said, moving to the right hand side.

The others quickly followed him, and stood beside the table. It wasn't long before a group of 3MAs girls entered the hall. Julius caught a glimpse of lilac satin emerging from between Siena and Isolde, and knew it was Morgana, sporting her favourite colour.

'Isn't she something,' said Lopaka, sounding quite awestruck.

'Yeah,' added Julius, completely transfixed.

'Who are you talking about?' asked Faith, looking at the pair of them.

Julius was startled out of his reverie and quickly looked at Lopaka. 'Um ... they all do, right?'

Lopaka nodded happily. 'I wouldn't know who to pick, quite frankly.'

'Where are you: at the fruit market?' thundered Leanne Nord from behind them, before shouldering her way through the boys' ranks.

Julius had to quickly retrieve Faith, who had been sent drifting away as a result.

'I wouldn't pick you if you were the last apple on the Moon,' mouthed Lopaka. 'Unless I wanted a concussion, that is.'

Skye chuckled and waved to Morgana to join them. She smiled when she saw him and brought Siena and Isolde over with her.

'*Konnichiwa*,' she said.

Morgana was positively beaming, and why shouldn't she be, thought Julius: it was her fifteenth birthday, New Year's Eve, and she looked great.

'Ladies,' said Faith, with his usual flare, 'you're more beautiful every year.'

They all giggled and Siena began to blush too. Julius wondered how long it would take Faith to realise he had an admirer.

Soon, a group of waiters began to circle around the tables, serving champagne for the toast, a sign that the teachers would be arriving shortly. Five minutes later, Master Cress stepped into the hall and all Mizkis rose from their seats to face the door. Led by Grand Master Freja, the Tijaran teachers made their entrance, and headed to their tables.

'Please, be seated,' said Freja.

They all sat down and, within a few seconds, the hall was quiet.

'I welcome you all to celebrate New Year here tonight. This is the first time since I've been Tijara's Grand Master, that it will be taking place outside the walls of our school. And, I must say, the staff of Gea One have done a marvellous job, making us feel right at home.

'It has been quite the year, Mizkis. No Earthling had seen an Arneshian up close for 230 years, until now, and you have all been witnesses to this unprecedented event. We do not know how this story will unfold but, no matter the outcome, we will stay true to Tijara's code and, we shall lead our lives under the banners of honour, respect, loyalty and courage. A toast then, that the year 2858 be a peaceful and prosperous one for all mankind.'

'So let it be,' answered the students as one, before raising their glasses.

Once Freja was seated, the waiters filed in and began to serve the dinner. As always, the food was plentiful and excellent and, by the time the 6 Mizki Seniors stood up to open the dances, as per tradition, Julius was positively stuffed and content.

'Me skirt is about to burst,' said Faith grinning at Siena and patting his belly. 'I might just have to spread out, 'cause this food-baby is having a fit!'

She glanced at him, looking slightly disgusted.

'I don't think she needs to know that,' whispered Skye, leaning towards him.

'Huh?' said Faith.

'He's right, you know?' added Julius, holding his glass in front of his mouth.

'Your typical after-dinner chat with a lady should not include anything about digestion or bursting at the seams,' said Skye. 'It's not, uh, conducive.'

'Conducive to what?' asked Faith, sounding genuinely puzzled.

Skye looked at Julius, and rolled his eyes. 'McCoy, why don't you organise Morgana's cake while I explain a thing or two to this muppet about courting.'

'But I don't need-' started Faith.

'Shush,' said Skye. 'It's on the house.'

Julius grinned and left them there. Fortunately the girls were too engrossed in watching the 6MS students dancing to Strauss' waltz to notice what had been happening on the other side of the table. It took Julius a few minutes before he found a free waiter, but finally he managed to flag one down, and asked him to bring Felice Buongustaio's package to their table. Before leaving Zed, Julius had placed an order with Tijara's chef for Morgana's cake, as they did every year; only, this time, he had been too busy worrying about Michael to actually think of a specific request, so he had left it to Felice to choose. Now, as he returned to the table, he sincerely hoped they weren't going to get another Supernova. So, Julius was pleasantly surprised when the waiter arrived with a tray of chocolate cupcakes, topped with white icing in the shape of snowflakes, each one sporting a small sparkler.

'They're gorgeous!' cried Morgana, clapping her hands. 'Thank you so much!'

Once dinner was over, most of the Mizkis began to move to other tables, to visit their friends, while others took over the dance floor and began the partying.

'See you later guys,' said Skye, flattening his curls.

'And where are you off to?' asked Julius.

'Got a date with Valentina tonight,' he said. 'Don't wait up, dear.'

'Behave yourself, darling' said Julius, adjusting Skye's bow tie.

'Who's for a dance?' asked Isolde, looking in Julius' direction.

'Let's go!' said Faith, dragging Morgana and Siena to the dance floor.

'Um, I'll be right there,' said Julius vaguely. 'Gotta go see someone about something first. Bye.' And, with that, he rushed off, leaving a distinctly long-faced Isolde with the grinning Lopaka.

The evening passed by smoothly and pleasantly. As midnight arrived, Julius was engrossed in chat with a group of 4MAs who, just like him, had more interest in discussing the Zed Toon game than dancing about the place. He could hardly believe it when he checked his PIP and saw that it was past one o'clock. The party would finish at two and he was looking forward to a long lie-in the next day.

Refilling his glass at a Juice-Maid on one of the side tables, he moved over to the far wall and leaned against it, looking out at the dance floor. Faith was hover-dancing here, there and everywhere, accommodating as many requests from the girls as he could. All of them loved standing on his skirt's metallic hem and being whisked around, none more so than Siena, who was never far away. At one point in the course of the evening, Faith had even tried to see how many girls he could carry at any one time; that is, until Captain Foster threw one of his famous ice-stares in his direction, making it clear that there shouldn't be any more such experiments. Skye had spent the entire evening dancing and chatting with his new flame, Valentina, seemingly oblivious of the venomous stares that some of the other girls were throwing in her general direction. Julius hoped he wouldn't be treated to too many details over the next few days, especially because he could have sworn that the two of them had disappeared off for around an hour and a half before the bells had sounded at midnight.

All in all, it had been a good night. The Gea One had provided a smart setting for the party; Julius had chatted with loads of people, including some of the older Mizkis, and he had managed to stay away from any unnecessary dancing by starting random conversations whenever a girl came anywhere near his seat. A very good party indeed, by his standards. He was just beginning to think about bed, when Morgana emerged from the crowd and walked over to him, beaming from ear to ear.

'You've been rather popular tonight,' she said, grabbing his glass and taking a big gulp of juice. 'I heard a few girls complaining that they couldn't get you to dance at all! I wonder why that is.'

Julius smiled, 'I was bone-tired.'

'I'm afraid that doesn't work with me. And since you promised, will you give me the honour of this dance?' she said, bowing.

'Only 'cause it's your birthday,' he answered.

'Come on then,' she said, placing the glass down on the table and leading him to the dance floor by the hand.

The rest of the Mizkis were flitting around trying to find a partner for the final dances of the evening. Julius noticed Isolde on the edge of the room, whispering to another girl; judging by the cold stare she threw his way when she saw him on the dance floor with Morgana, it was clear she wasn't best pleased. He did feel a little sorry for her, but he couldn't exactly pretend to be interested in her when he wasn't.

'So,' he said, turning his attention to Morgana, 'good birthday then?'

'Cracking,' she answered.

Her head was resting on Julius' shoulder, so he couldn't see her face, but he could tell from her voice that she had had a great time.

'I love my presents, my cup cakes, and this place. I've danced and laughed a lot, plus I got such a lovely birthday card from Maks.'

Julius managed to not betray his surprise, and didn't reply.

'He wished me a great night, and said that he wanted to be here so badly,' she told him, with a giggle.

Julius became aware of a cascade of pink threads pouring out of Morgana's head as she spoke. He stretched his left hand out, behind her back, and saw that it was wrapped in the smoky wisps. He would rather have not noticed it, but there it was, plain as day: Morgana definitely had a crush on Maks.

'He's so sweet,' she continued.

'Mph ...' grunted Julius.

'Morgana lifted her head off his shoulder. 'What's wrong?'

'Nothing ...' he said, trying to sound convincing.

Morgana stopped dancing and looked Julius in the eyes. 'Are you playing big brother with me?'

'What ... No!' he said, but he could feel himself beginning to blush.

'Are you sure?' she asked again. 'Because every time I mention Maks you go all mumble-grumble on me.'

Julius saw a hint of amusement on her face and it dawned on him that his odd behaviour had been interpreted as him being protective, which was probably a good thing. Right then however, his brain was working solo, taking notice of a whole different set of things which were well and truly outside of Julius' control; and definitely not listed under the "big brother" category. Morgana's arms were still resting on his shoulders, and her face was a little too close for comfort to his own. He was also very aware now of how his hands had become glued to her back, the fingertips resting partly against the satin of her dress and, more distractingly, partly against her skin, which incidentally was the softest thing he had ever touched. And why were her eyes shining like that? Did her lips just look like juicy strawberries, or was it possible they also tasted like them?

'Julius? Hello? Anybody there?'

Her voice came out of nowhere, calling him back to reality. 'Sorry ... I ...'

'Never mind,' she said with a grin. She put her head back on his shoulder and began to dance again. 'You always were like a big brother anyway.'

'Great,' he thought. At this point he decided that it was best to finish the dance and leave the floor while he still had his dignity intact. He moved his hands so that they were resting completely against the surface of her dress, rather than her skin, and forced himself to think about Professor Gould's next checkpoint. But, try as he might, his thoughts kept creeping back to her raven black hair, tickling his face, and the alluring fragrance that wafted to meet him every time he leaned closer to her neck.

'Damn and blast!' erupted Faith, next to them.

Julius and Morgana turned to see what was going on.

'Me skirt is stuck,' he said, looking very apologetic. 'Sorry Siena, I think me dancing night is over. Julius, could you give me a hand?'

'Uh, yeah, yeah. Sure,' he answered, secretly relieved to be cutting his awkward dance short.

'Happy birthday,' he said to Morgana once more, letting her go.

She smiled at him and planted a light kiss on his cheek. 'Thank you,' she said.

A wave of shivers ran down his back. He turned away quickly, bumped into Faith, and self-consciously smoothed the creases on his shirt. Aware that he was acting a little weird at this point, he quickly wheeled the crestfallen Faith out of the room, stopping only to gather their dinner jackets under one arm. Morgana and Siena were left standing on the dance floor by themselves, not quite sure what to make of the odd couple that had just beaten a hasty retreat from the ball.

Once the two boys had reached their dorm, Faith turned to Julius. 'Sorry for interrupting you there, mate.'

'It's fine. I was done, anyway.'

'What an embarrassment. I really need to see Pete.'

'Are you gonna be all right?'

'Yeah. Thanks for the lift.'

'No worries. I'll see you tomorrow then.'

Faith nodded and entered his room. Julius, deciding that he'd had quite enough of the party and unfamiliar sensations in the pit of his belly for one night, also returned to his quarters. He stayed up to write a quick message to his family wishing them a happy new year, then watched the Zed Channel for a bit, which was showing scenes from the celebrations on Earth. It was only after he had showered and slipped under the covers that Skye walked in, and threw himself down on his own bed, smiling tiredly at the ceiling. His hair looked ruffled and there were faint traces of lipstick on his neck. Julius had his hand on the light switch, when Skye turned to face him.

'You like her, don't you?'

Julius felt his stomach contracting. 'Who?'

'You know who. I saw you on the dance floor.'

'She likes Maks.'

'That's not what I asked you.'

Julius looked at him for a few seconds, then rolled over and switched off the light. 'Good night, Skye.'

CHAPTER 10

PLAYING WITH FIRE

For the first time in his life, but most likely not the last, Julius began the new year inside a space station. The Gea One was not as large as Zed but, for some reason, it never felt like a crowded environment to him. In eight days, normal lessons would resume, so he decided to make the most of his free time by reading, sleeping and generally relaxing with the rest of the Mizkis. The lounge on deck three was large enough to accommodate most of the students easily; there were cosy booths dotted about, equipped with soft sofas, screens, music systems, snack dispensers and Juice-Maids. In fact, there were so many of these that, whenever Julius agreed to meet the Skirts in one of the booths, they had to be very specific about which one, or they risked getting lost.

Julius was finally able to finish the book he had been trying to read since December—it left him thinking that being a bounty hunter would actually be a pretty cool job—and started a new one, another old saga, all about a dark tower. Reading allowed him to stop thinking about Michael, and that was a much-needed relief. The exodus of Nuarns had gathered pace and continued throughout the festive period, with hundreds of thousands of them leaving Earth every week. Iryana Mielowa had mentioned that as many as 40 million Nuarns had already left for good. Whenever the thought of it became overwhelming, Julius remembered that at least Michael was still at home. He clung to that thread of hope with all his might.

Thinking about his new feelings for Morgana was also something he was trying to avoid but, since Maks was constantly sending messages to her PIP, making her blush and giggle every time, this was proving easier said than done. Since New Year's Eve, he had been making a fair stab at figuring out what was going on in his head—and other parts of his body too.

Girls had never really meant much in his life up until then, in that sense anyway; he preferred friends to girlfriends, as that seemed a lot less complicated than a relationship. Even knowing that Isolde was interested in him had not changed that. He could see how she looked at him whenever their paths crossed, but he didn't have any strong feelings for her, except a slight discomfort at the thought that she wasn't happy because of him. Maybe the reason why Morgana had awoken these sensations in him, was due to their long-standing friendship, and the fact that he had always been able to relax around her.

'I'm not jealous,' he thought. 'I've always taken care of her, and I don't want her to get hurt.' Julius kept repeating these words in his head, like a mantra, over and over again, until eventually he convinced himself it was true. And if Maks ever did anything stupid, well, he would just show him what a White Child could do.

'Really looking forward to our first Pyro class,' said Skye, who was stretched out on one of the sofas in the lounge. It was the last Sunday of the mid-winter break and he was determined to enjoy every last minute of it by doing precisely nothing.

Julius was sitting on the opposite sofa, his legs resting on the coffee table, with Barth and Faith on either side. Morgana and Siena were reading a magazine on her PIP, scoring all the latest Earth fashion tips.

'I'm excited too!' said Barth.

Morgana looked at him. 'Now, remember Barth, where do you go and stand when we get to Pyro class?'

'On the opposite side of wherever you are?' he said, hesitantly.

"Atta boy!' She nodded and returned to her magazine.

'Who would have thought that Chan does Pyro classes too?' said Faith.

'Yeah, but who else is nuts enough for it,' said Skye.

'Maybe Gould?' ventured Julius. 'He does sleep with his Gauntlet under his pillow, after all.'

'No, no! According to Valentina, this is a side of Chan that we haven't seen yet.'

'You expect us to believe that you two actually *talk*?' said Faith, making the others chuckle.

'Laugh all you like,' answered Skye, with a "speak-to-me-when-you-reach-my-star-rep" look, followed by another that seemed to say, "as if."

'What time is it?' asked Faith, stretching. 'Me tummy's growling.'

'Let's go to the mess hall,' said Julius. 'I'm starting to get a wee bit peckish myself.'

'Ladies?' said Faith, turning to them.

'Later, thanks,' answered Morgana, without lifting her head from her PIP.

Julius thought that Siena looked sorely tempted to join them but, seeing as Morgana wasn't going, she seemed resigned to staying behind, and shook her head.

'I'll be there in a minute,' said Skye, who was busy texting on his PIP.

Faith motioned for Barth to come with them, and he leapt up, clearly pleased at being asked—Julius saw a green wisp rising from his head, a sure sign of his happiness, and smiled, seeing how much being included in their group meant to Barth.

When they entered the mess hall on deck two, many of the Mizkis were already assembled there, looking positively agitated. The students were talking to each others in hurried, low voices. Puzzled, Julius walked towards Lopaka's table, followed by the others.

'Hey guys,' he said, 'has something happened?'

Lopaka, Gustavo and Yuri made space for them on their bench.

'Some of the Arneshians have just come aboard,' whispered Lopaka; he pointed to his left. 'Over there.'

Julius spotted them immediately, and his jaw dropped. Seated at one of the corner tables were K'Ssander, his friend A'Trid, and one of T'Rogon's colleagues. They were eating with Master Cress and Professor Clavel.

'Why on Earth are they here?' asked Julius, not caring much just then if they overheard him.

'Who knows,' answered Yuri. 'I got here earlier on and saw them. Freja and T'Rogon were just leaving.'

'It looks like they're visiting us, or something,' said Gustavo.

Faith shook his head. 'How could Freja allow those cheating traitors onboard?'

'I don't think he has a lot of choice,' said Lopaka. 'With Paulo Trent opening Earth up like that, he's probably pressured the Curia into doing the same thing.'

'Or it could be a bargaining chip, for reopening the schools,' said Julius.

'How?' asked Barth.

'A show of good faith on Zed's part,' explained Julius. 'We show Trent that we're good hosts, with nothing to hide, and maybe he'll open up recruitment again.'

'So, basically we're sucking up to Trent,' summarised Gustavo.

Julius nodded. That was it, and it would probably continue that way until T'Rogon left orbit; judging by the impressive, steady numbers of Nuarns leaving each week, that could be sooner rather than later.

By the following morning, news of the Arneshian visitors had spread around the Gea like wildfire. Kept at bay by their teachers, the Mizkis had tried hard not to show any anger at their presence, but that was as much as the students were willing to give. As the Arneshians entered the mess hall, they were greeted by a wall of quiet disdain. Julius and the Skirts decided to make breakfast a quick business, and left as soon as they had finished their food, without even a glance in the direction of the visitors.

Once out of the mess hall, Faith touched one of the wall pads and said, '3MA, Pyro class, 09:00.'

Immediately, a green cursor appeared onto the right wall and shot ahead, indicating the path to their class. All lessons were to be held on deck five, which was spacious enough to hold both White and Grey Arts classes. They hopped into the lift; three floors down, as the doors opened, the green cursor was flashing for them to follow. It led them along a corridor, first right, then left, until eventually it came to a stop outside their classroom.

They stepped inside, and found themselves in a large room with metal walls. There were scorch-marks on all sides; most of all, on the ceiling. Several fire extinguishers were placed all around the floor, obviously ready to be used in case of things going wrong. Julius walked up to one of them and had a good look: it was shaped like an old style handgun; it was red and had several settings to choose from, according to the kind of fire that needed extinguishing. This one was already prepped for 'Pyro', and Julius wondered how the fire they would be creating in this class was any different from a natural one.

'Housekeeping is slacking a bit, I say,' said Faith, sliding a fingertip over the surface of the wall, which revealed a shinier surface beneath a layer of soot. Unable to resist, he hovered upwards, all the way to the ceiling, and began to graffiti the dark surface.

'Faith,' said Morgana, 'what are you doing?'

'Just a little piece of art,' he said, the tip of his tongue sticking out as he concentrated. 'There, that's much better,' he said, admiring his work from floating-distance.

Julius looked up, and started to laugh, quickly followed by Skye and Morgana.

Faith had sketched an Arneshian boy—K'Ssander, judging by the gigantic "K" on the front of his top—being chased by a robot version of Faith, seemingly intent on zapping his backside with his Gauntlet. The boy was shielding his rear as he ran, while a speech bubble floated above the robot's head, reading, "Eat me skirt!"

'Superb!' applauded Skye, wiping a tear from his eye.

'I didn't know you could draw like that, Faith,' said Morgana. 'I'm impressed.'

Faith hovered back down to the ground, savouring the moment. 'There's more where that came from,' he added.

Just then, they heard voices and steps approaching the door and, shortly after, their classmates filed into the room. Julius was still doubled over, laughing and pointing at the ceiling, so it didn't take long for them to join in.

Mariam Richards, a quiet 3MA from Lebanon, who was standing by the door admiring the sketch, glanced over her right shoulder and suddenly became very serious. 'Psst! Chan is coming!'

Everyone assembled, facing the door. The lights had dimmed a little outside in the corridor, and everyone had quietened right down inside the room. Julius heard a faint rustling, growing louder with each passing second. He tuned in and quickly realised that it was the sound a burning fire made. He supposed that he shouldn't have been surprised by that, given that they were about to start a Pyro lesson, but he certainly hadn't expected to hear it out there in the corridor.

When Professor Chan entered the room, there was a collective gasp: he was completely enveloped by tongues of flame, dancing around him, but showing no sign of causing any harm to his skin. The Mizkis stepped back, wide eyed in admiration.

'He certainly knows how to make an entrance,' said Skye, starting to clap. 'Go, Professor!'

Chan stopped in the middle of the room and bowed, the flames still encircling him. Then, he closed his eyes and, very slowly, the fire began to diminish, until the flames fizzled out and completely vanished. The Mizkis bowed, their respect for him now swelled to a huge level.

Unexpectedly, Chan turned toward the door, and said, 'Please, step inside and take those seats along the left wall.'

Everyone looked at the entrance expectantly, and all of their enthusiasm instantly disappeared like a soap bubble popping, as K'Ssander and A'Trid strolled into the room. Julius felt a surge of anger stir beneath his skin and, as K'Ssander's eyes passed in his direction, he instinctively moved to shield Morgana from sight. The Arneshian was obviously loving his visitor privileges, as the arrogant smirk on his face clearly illustrated. Julius knew well enough that they weren't to cause any trouble but still, he decided that K'Ssander should at least get a glimpse of how the Mizkis really felt. Holding the Arneshian's attention, he motioned with his head toward the ceiling. It took K'Ssander a few seconds before he saw the sketch but, as he did, the smirk slipped off his face, and his greyish complexion was momentarily flushed with fury. Julius had a grin of his own as he returned his attention to the teacher.

'Be seated,' said Chan, kneeling in front of the students.

'What you just witnessed will be the reward for some of you, if you work hard and follow my training properly. I say some because Pyrokinesis, or the ability to create fire, is not a given. Just because you've made it into Zed, does not mean you have this ability. And if you do have it, it still may never develop beyond the creation of a mere candlelight of flame.

'Our Arneshian guests are here to observe our lesson today since, as you all know, they are gifted with Grey skills, but not White ones, and will therefore never be able to make use of their inner energies, like you can.'

Julius caught sight of a wisp of gold shooting from Chan's head: it seemed the professor was proud of this difference, which gave them a clear advantage over the Arneshians.

'Before we start, Mizkis, I must impress on your young minds that, under no circumstances, will you use this mind-skill against a fellow human being. It is strictly forbidden, and carries the heaviest of penalties. As Mizkis, you have plenty of ammunition to use against a foe, without resorting to murder.'

'Why worry?' K'Ssander's question caused all heads to turn his way. 'If your life is in danger, you should use all you have, even if it means harming a human.'

Professor Chan regarded him for a moment. 'That, Mr K'Ssander, is a major difference between our people and yours.'

'Kick-ass, Chan,' Faith whispered into Julius' ear, who nodded, deeply satisfied by the Arneshians' lack of reply.

'And now,' continued Chan, as if nothing had happened, 'I am going to split you into three working groups, according to the strength of your Pyro abilities.' He turned to one side of the room, and made a shooing motion with his hands; in response, the wall seamlessly retreated a few hundred feet, leaving the students quite astonished.

'How big *is* Gea?' asked Morgana.

'Deck five and six are massive holographic structures,' explained Faith. 'And they can expand at will.'

'I will call you up one at a time and, when I do, you will create and throw a fireball at the far end, using a basic mind-kata. Understood?'

'Sir, yes sir,' replied the Mizkis.

'Warm up for a moment then.'

Julius was beginning to feel a bit uneasy. Showing the Arneshians their powers was a bit like showing your cards to an opponent before the game was even over. Thanks to the extra treatments he was receiving each week, he was sure that his skills had developed quite a lot recently, and he feared revealing what he was capable of to them. Then again, he couldn't be entirely certain what would happen, since he had not used any Pyro skills since he had left Earth. '*Should we be doing this, in front of them?*' he asked Morgana with a mind-message.

Morgana looked up, startled, but quickly regained her composure and continued her warm-up. '*I don't see why not,*' she answered. '*The Arneshians have known about our Pyro skills for centuries now.*'

'*What about us, though? Should we be showing off what we can do so freely?*'

'They already know you're a White Child, if that's what's worrying you. Besides, it's also likely that K'Ssander knows what you did last year on Angra Mainyu.'

'But what if they're recording us?'

'Then give 'em a show they won't easily forget.'

Julius didn't know what else to say. Morgana was right, of course, but he still wasn't comfortable with this unplanned showcase they were putting on.

'Let's start from the bottom of the alphabet,' said Chan. 'Mr Yuran, if you please.'

Grigor Yuran moved to the centre of the room, looking quite nervous. Julius could understood why: after two years of sharing personal Pyro stories, they were all now going to see what everyone could really do, with the added pressure of an Arneshian audience.

Grigor took a deep breath and lifted his right hand, palm up. Slowly, a speck of light appeared above the skin and became a small flame, which steadily grew until it was the size of an apple.

'Very good, Mr Yuran,' said Chan. 'Take your time now, and focus.'

The class was completely still now; even the Arneshians were watching intently. With a quick flick of his hand, Grigor flung the fireball as far as he could. All eyes followed its luminous stream as it sailed through the air, before disappearing in a puff and being replaced by a flashing red number.

'230 feet!' said Chan, patting him on the shoulder. 'Well done. You are in group two, range of 100 to 300 feet.'

Chan activated a sign with a "2" written on it, which was hovering in midair, and pushed it back towards the left wall. The number crossed the air until it reached its destination and then hung there, suspended above the ground.

'Next: Miss Yu,' called Chan.

One after another, the Mizkis were tested and assigned to the three different groups, covering a wide range of distances. Annette Valeris was the first to be assigned to group one, for a range of 0 to 100 feet. Even the fireball she had generated had been small; no more than the size of a walnut.

The final group, in the 300+ range, was opened by Felicity Steep, who managed to throw a fireball the size of a basketball a distance of 306 feet away. By the time Julius' turn came round, Barth, Morgana, Faith and Siena had joined group one, while Skye had gone to group two.

'Mr McCoy,' called Chan.

Julius walked up beside him and lifted his right hand. Closing his eyes, he concentrated on his inner energy, focusing on the flow of it through his veins, which was slow and steady; he closed his mind to everything around him, trying to silence any thoughts of the Mizkis, and Arneshians, in the room. Maintaining his concentration, he visualised an opening on the palm of his hand, and let the heat seep out through it.

'Uh, is the flame meant to get that big?' he heard Faith ask a few seconds later. There was more than a hint of worry in his voice.

Julius opened his eyes, and instinctively recoiled backwards away from his hand when he saw what had concerned Faith so much: he was staring at a ball of fire which was easily two feet in diameter.

'Steady McCoy,' said Chan, placing a hand on Julius' shoulder.

Julius carefully bent his wrist downward, so that the burning orb was directed away from him. The air around him was beginning to heat up, to the degree where he was finding it hard to breathe.

'Control it, McCoy!' said Chan. 'Focus on the fireball and withdraw some of your energy.'

'Sir,' said Julius, now extremely agitated, 'I'm not sure how.'

'Do it McCoy, focus now!'

Julius imagined the globe as a helium balloon, with a release valve at the bottom. In his mind, he opened the valve, and allowed some of the energy to course back inside him. As soon as he did this, however, he felt as if his veins were catching fire, as if the effort of trying to draw the already unleashed energies back was entirely the wrong thing to do. Without a second thought, he opened his left hand, and rerouted the simmering energy to its empty palm, which created another fireball.

'Everyone, step back!' ordered Chan. 'Shields up, Mizkis, and make sure our guests are sheltered. That's an order.'

Julius heard the shuffling of feet behind him, followed by the sound of many shields humming into life. Chan then activated his right arm-shield, positioned himself next to Julius, and brought the shield up to rest against Julius' forearms, creating a barrier to protect them both from the heat of the fireballs.

'McCoy, you must relax now,' said Chan, calmly. 'Everyone is safe.'

'Professor, I can't reduce the flow. When I draw it back in, it burns me.'

'Then close it off completely. On the count of three, I'll shut my shield down and you will release the fireballs. I'll help you ... and don't worry about the distance please. After this stunt, you'll be in a group all of your own anyway. Here we go: one ... two ... three!'

Chan's shield deactivated on three and, as it disappeared, Julius whipped both of his hands forward with as much strength as he could muster. The fireballs zoomed away from him, their speed amplified by Chan's Telekinetic powers, and hurtled into the far wall. A red number flashed up indicating 400 feet.

'Woah!' cried Skye in astonishment.

The Mizkis erupted, hollering and whooping, so impressed were they with the distance Julius had managed. He and Chan were slumped forward, breathing hard as they recovered from their effort. Julius' t-shirt was sticking to his body, and there were pearls of sweat beaded across his brow.

'I take it the DNA enhancement treatment is working then, McCoy,' said Chan, patting him on the back. 'You singed my eyebrows.'

Julius nodded, still too tired to reply. He turned to look at his classmates, who were still enthusiastically cheering for him, and couldn't restrain a grin. The smile quickly disappeared though, as he spotted K'Ssander and A'Trid deep in quiet conversation.

The Skirts quickly grew used to life on the Gea One, and soon it felt like a second home to them. The only things they truly missed were Satras and the Hologram Palace. Deck six did have several holodecks for private use, but they tended to be occupied by the Mizki Seniors most of the time, which Julius thought was highly unfair.

Unfortunately, K'Ssander and A'Trid were still onboard, although the teachers saw to it that they were moved around as much as possible, so as not to unsettle any one class for too long. All in all, the 3MAs had three visits from them and, on reflection, Julius thought that it could have been worse. With help from Faith and Skye, he made sure that Morgana was never left alone when the Arneshians were in the same room, not even for a second. No one liked having them there, but Freja had given his orders and, as such, the guests were to be treated with courtesy, so they just kept their chins up and waited for their visit to be over.

All of their lessons restarted in full during January, sometimes in a classroom, and other times in a holoroom. Julius' extra treatments with Walliser continued as normal, although the changes he was experiencing in his ability levels were getting weirder by the day. It was like his skills had suddenly skipped a stage of their evolution, as he was now able to perform to a level exceeding even the seniors. All of his teachers and classmates were, of course, aware of his treatment, so the fact that in his Draw lessons, he could now successfully gather energy from a rhino, rather than the koala he had been drawing from before, didn't much surprise anyone; they were becoming accustomed to having a White Child in their class. Catering for this, Professor King started to train Julius' telekinetic skills in the cargo bay, where he would practice moving crates from one side of the bay, and stacking them on the other. Sometimes, if King was in the mood, he would get Julius' classmates to sit on top of the crates, and throw small objects for him to deflect, while he was levitating them.

The really bizarre stuff however, first began during one of Beloi's classes, when the Mizkis had been split into small groups, placed in a room and instructed to have conversations with one another, using only their minds. Julius had asked a series of questions, and received replies, not only from his own team, but also from about twenty other Mizkis, who all thought that the questions were being directed at them. It took a few minutes for Beloi to understand what was happening and move Julius, and his group, into an isolated section of deck five.

After that, these surges of power cropped up at random moments. Once, Professor Farshid had sent her students to explore Gea One's command centre. Julius had soon returned to her, complaining of a splitting headache, which had been caused by him being able to hear the constant chatter of various conversations across the six decks; he was picking them up like a radio.

Eventually, Dr Walliser and Freja decided that it would be best to suspend his treatment for a while, to give his DNA more of a chance to adapt to the enhancements, which made Julius happy, not least because he was starting to lose sleep. It was also agreed that Professor Lao-tzu would work on some specialised meditation techniques to help him find a way of shielding himself from this bombardment of "white noise." It took until the beginning of February before Julius started to feel that he was once again back in control of his own head.

It was Tuesday the 8th of February, and Julius was having a long, hot shower. Professors Morales and Chan, had put the class through yet another intense Shield lesson, and all his muscles were aching. He was just beginning to drift off, savouring the feel of the refreshing water against his skin, when the sound of the doorbell echoed in the bathroom. He threw a towel around his waist and went to answer the door.

Faith was hovering there. 'I'm starving,' he said.

'Come in,' said Julius. 'I'm almost done.'

Faith zoomed inside and waited by the window, while Julius went to finish up. 'Are you still hearing voices, W.C.?'

'No,' shouted Julius from the bathroom. 'At least, not as much.' He emerged a couple of minutes later, now fully dressed, a towel draped around his neck. He sat down on the chair, slipped his boots on, and began to dry his hair. Suddenly remembering, he stopped and looked at Faith. 'And don't call me-'

'W.C.,' Faith finished for him. 'Just because I'm in a good mood tonight, I'll do what you ask.'

'And what's the occasion?' asked Julius, throwing the wet towel into the laundry chute.

Just then, the terminal beeped, signalling an incoming vidcall. 'Hold that thought,' said Julius. 'On screen.'

His mother's face popped into view, her cheeks strewn with tears. 'Oh Julius,' she sniffed.

'Mum! What's happened?' cried Julius, moving towards the terminal.

'It's ... Michael,' she sobbed.

'Is he all right?' he asked, startled by the fear in his own voice.

'He's applied to visit the ... the Taurus One and ... and a letter of acceptance has arrived this morning.' With that, she burst into a fit of tears.

Faith made as if to leave the room, but Julius indicated for him to stay. The possibility he had been secretly dreading, but which he had forced himself to believe would never happen, was suddenly becoming a reality. He waited for his mum to calm down, while his stomach tightened into a knot. He could see black, wispy threads pouring from her head which left him in no doubt that she was feeling quite terrified.

'Mum, where are Dad and Michael now?'

'They had a fight this morning, as soon as that damn letter arrived. Michael left in a huff and went off to the Nuarn office, while your dad went to file a complaint with the City Chambers,' she said, dabbing her face with a handkerchief.

'What did they say at the Chambers? Can they do something to stop him?'

Jenny shook her head. 'Rory called me at lunchtime. They told him they will try, but the chances are slim.'

'But he's only twelve; how can he decide for himself?'

'It's because he's a Nuarn, Julius. Different laws apply now.'

Julius was stunned and quite unable to believe what he was hearing. 'What can we do, then?'

Jenny shrugged her shoulders, looking very tired. 'I don't know what there is to do, honey. Your dad has gone to pick him up now. Maybe I'll have more to tell you when they get home.'

Julius felt thoroughly miserable now. 'Ask Dad to call me as soon as they're back. We'll sort something out, you'll see. Please don't cry, Mum.'

Jenny took a deep breath, kissed her fingers and touched them against the screen. Julius placed his on hers, and closed the link.

'I'm so sorry, mate,' said Faith, from the corner of the room.

Julius sighed, and shook his head. 'You know, I really thought our mid-winter chat had made a difference.'

'He may still change his mind,' offered Faith. 'And if he does end up going, maybe that'll be enough. He'll see what it's like and then go home again.'

'Maybe,' said Julius, not convinced.

'I do have an idea though.'

Julius looked up at him. 'What is it?'

'I figure if we, the Skirts and Siena I mean, each write a letter to Michael telling him about our own personal encounters with the Arneshians, maybe it'll help him understand what they're really like.'

'You could be right, you know,' said Julius, suddenly hopeful.

'Let's go find the others then,' said Faith, heading for the door.

Sure enough, Skye, Morgana and Siena were more than happy to help and, to Julius' delight, they started writing their letters on the spot, so they could all send them before dinner. It took the best part of an hour, but eventually they were all done.

'I hope you don't mind a few swearwords here and there, McCoy,' said Skye, transferring his file over to Julius' PIP.

'No worries. I know how you feel about the Arneshians, and hopefully he'll feel it too. Thanks, guys,' he said, turning to them. 'I'll put them all together and send them as one. By the way Faith, what did you want to tell me before?'

'The spaceship model I designed has been shortlisted,' he said, shyly.

'That's amazing!' said Morgana.

'Congrats, mate,' added Julius. 'We knew you could do it.'

Siena looked like she was about ready to cry from her excitement, which pleased Faith immensely. 'Thank you, guys,' he said, turning a little red.

'See, Julius,' said Morgana. 'This is a good omen for us. Send the letters now, with our good vibes. We'll wait for you in the mess hall.'

Julius nodded and started to write his own little introduction to the messages. When he was satisfied with it—he wanted it to sound fair and logical—he attached all of the other files to his own, and sent it directly to Michael. With that done, all he could do was wait and see.

When Julius stood up and headed to the mess hall, he failed to notice the two visitors in the next booth. K'Ssander and A'Trid had been sitting there for nearly two hours, quietly unobserved and patiently waiting.

As soon as Julius had sent his message, K'Ssander's own portable device had glowed red, instantly redirecting it to him. He placed a trace on Julius' mail system, so that all future messages to Michael's address would be intercepted, and skimmed through the message, the smirk on his face growing larger as he read. 'Little brother doesn't need any help,' he said coldly. 'He's already decided his path.' He quickly made a copy of the message, and sent it to T'Rogon.

Every day of that second week of February Julius called home, and every day Michael refused to talk to him. This obstinate silence on his brother's part hurt him far more than his decision to visit the Taurus, because he had shut him out of his life. Rory had explained several times already why they could do nothing to prevent the visit; in fact, the Nuarn office had told him that, if he did, he could be prosecuted for breaching Nuarn rights. To add to the frustration, Jenny and Rory hadn't been able to check if Julius' letter had arrived, as Michael flat out refused to talk about his brother.

'When is his visit scheduled for?' Julius asked his parents one night.

'We don't know yet,' answered Jenny.

'After February probably,' said Rory.

Julius nodded. The possibility of losing Michael to the Arneshians was causing a sense of unease in him like he had never experienced before.

'I'm sorry, darling,' said Jenny, after a long pause. 'We've been so worried about Michael that I haven't even asked how you're doing.'

'You don't have to worry about me, Mum,' said Julius. 'I'm fine, really.'

'My gorgeous White Child,' she said, smiling tenderly. 'You work so hard to keep us safe ... How could Michael do this to you, after all you've been through? It makes me so mad.'

Julius wouldn't admit it out loud but, now that his mum had said it for him, he realised just how upset he too was at his brother's lack of appreciation for Zed. It was a cold comfort hearing her say that.

'I hear you have some Arneshians onboard, son,' said Rory.

'You do? Really?' asked Jenny anxiously.

'Aye, they've been here since January,' replied Julius. 'Sorry, I should've mentioned it, but with all the rest going on ...' he opened his hands, '... it's not a big deal right now.'

'Be that as it may,' said Rory, 'keep an eye on them, you hear?'

'I will, Dad.'

It was the last Tuesday of the month, and the Mizkis were in the mess hall finishing their breakfast.

'3MAs, please report to the lounge, at 09:00,' announced a voice over the intercom.

'Let's hope it's not another augmentation,' said Faith, wiping his mouth and standing up.

Julius, Skye and Morgana followed him out of the room and to the lift, curious about the change of program. When they got to deck three, Professor Farshid and Clavel were sitting in the centre of the room, waiting for the students to arrive.

'Mizkis!' called Farshid. 'Over here. Take a seat,' she said, gesturing to the tables surrounding her.

Morgana chose the table closest to Clavel, where she sat, beaming at her favourite teacher.

'I can see your wisdom teeth, woman,' said Julius, nudging her in the ribs.

'I can't help it if he's so charming and magnificent,' she answered, dreamily.

'Is she going the Miller route?' asked Faith, joining the table. 'Having one teacher-stalker in our team is quite enough, I say.'

'At least she's not wearing that awful, stinky perfume Skye wore for Morales last year,' added Julius.

'I heard that,' said Skye, sitting down next to him. 'I'll have you know that was the latest love fragrance from Earth, that was.'

'Sure, if you were looking to attract a warthog,' said Faith.

'Shush,' said Morgana. 'They're starting.'

'Good morning, Mizkis,' said Clavel, standing up. 'Professor Farshid and I have a surprise for you. We have decided to take advantage of our present location and start the Spring Mission a month early.'

The Mizkis reacted with excited murmurs, making Clavel and Farshid nod with satisfaction.

'Given the course choices you have made, back in September,' continued Clavel, 'we have decided to combine this year's Spring Mission with a test of your progress so far.'

At the word "test", the air of excitement faded a little. Missions were supposed to be fun, but tests certainly weren't.

Professor Clavel seemed to sense the change in atmosphere, and proceeded to reassure the Mizkis. 'As you recall, Mr Patel told you that you would be able to change your career path if you were unhappy with your courses. Consider this test just such an opportunity.' He turned to his colleague. 'Professor Farshid, if you please.'

Amira Farshid stood up, and Clavel took his seat again. 'Next Monday, you will board the Heron for 12 days of simulated training, during which each of you will be assigned a role in line with your course choice and the abilities you have demonstrated so far.'

'Yes!' said Julius, slapping his thigh. Looking around, he could see that his classmates were thinking the same thing: the Heron model wasn't perhaps as cool a spaceship as the likes of the Ahura Mazda, but it was still a real ship, which could take a crew of up to 100 members.

'Over the next few days, Professor Clavel and I, together with your other teachers, will review your achievements in class so far and decide your individual roles for the mission, of which you will be notified at the weekend.' She pointed at Leanne as the girl raised her hand. 'Yes, Miss Nord.'

'Will we be able to break orbit, Professor?'

'You will be allowed to roam freely within our solar system of course, but no further than that.'

Julius grinned at the group. 'This is just!'

'I'm so excited I'm going to faint,' said Morgana, breathing deeply.

'Wait until they finish,' said Faith, hushing her.

'With all of you occupied in central roles, the rest of the crew will be made up by the ship's V.I. system, which will see that all basic necessities are taken care of. I'm talking about chefs, cleaners and the like. Believe me, you will feel just like real crew members.'

'It will be a great experience,' said Clavel, standing up. 'So make the most of it. Dismissed!'

The Mizkis stood and bowed to their teachers, before heading to their lessons in high spirits.

The Spring Mission was all the Mizkis could talk about that week. Yuri and Gustavo had set up a PIP app which allowed students to place bets on the Mizkis and the roles they were likely to get, and sent it to all of the 3MAs.

'Julius,' said Skye, one evening, 'you're represented in every category, you know?'

And so he was, although not necessarily as first choice for all of them. Still, it was a nice feeling knowing that the others thought him capable of doing pretty much everything. As good news as that was, he was still worried about the fact that it appeared his letter had still not been delivered to Michael yet, according to his dad, so he sent it again, hoping to reach his brother before it was too late.

Finally, that Sunday morning, the Mizkis received their duty-slips. Julius opened his in his room, and his heart literally skipped a beat when he saw Captain written next to his name. He was, naturally, overjoyed and headed out into the corridor, where he saw Faith hovering towards him, with a massive grin on his face.

'I'm Chief-Engineer!' he cried, giving Julius a high-five.

'That's cracking, mate!'

'Captain?' Faith asked him, nodding, as if he already knew the answer.

'Captain,' confirmed Julius ecstatically.

'Guys!' cried Morgana, from the opposite end of the corridor. Siena was with her, and they were running excitedly down the corridor towards them, arms opened wide.

Julius and Faith stood there, watching as the girls pelted down the corridor. Julius could see emerald green wisps of happiness spreading all around them as they ran, unceremoniously knocking any passing Mizkis out of their way. Faith, who was slightly to the side and behind Julius, spread his arms, ready to catch at least one of them, still grinning madly. Julius, however, was suddenly overcome by a sense of pure panic. In his mind, he saw Morgana's wild run ending in his arms, and her soft body slamming against him. So, as she leapt at him, he did the only reasonable thing he could think of in that moment: he stepped out of the way. Morgana and Siena shot through the air, both now aimed at Faith. Julius turned around just in time to see the Irish boy's grin turn into an O, as the girls crashed into him, projecting them all out of the door at the far end of the dorm, holding on to his skirt. Julius heard a crash and a second later Faith shouted, 'McCoooooooy!'

He decided it would be best not to wait around, and hastily retreated back into his room.

CHAPTER 11

THE HERON

On Monday the 5th of March, the 3MAs were instructed to assemble in the docking bay by 09:00 to board the Heron. As captain, Julius was required to be aboard an hour earlier than the rest of his crew, together with his first officer, Yuri Slovich.

'Aren't you excited, McCoy?' asked Yuri, as they entered the hangar.

'Scared, more like,' said Julius. 'Aren't you?'

Yuri looked at him sideways, 'If you promise to keep it to yourself, I'll admit that I'm petrified.'

'It's wild, isn't it? After two and a half years of training, here we are, about to man our first spaceship.' He walked quietly down the gangway for a minute, then spoke again. 'The truth is that I'm not bothered about commanding the Heron. I think that's the easy part. It's T'Rogon that worries me.'

'How so?'

'I feel like I can't make even the tiniest mistake for fear of getting Zed into more trouble. I mean, on Earth they already think I'm a liability as it is, thanks to T'Rogon, imagine if-' Julius stopped abruptly where he stood, and grabbed Yuri by the arm.

'Wha-' started Yuri, swinging around to face him.

Julius motioned for him to look ahead.

'What are *they* doing here?' asked Yuri.

K'Ssander and A'Trid were stepping out of one of the Heron's hatches, their visitor passes in clear view on their chests. Julius felt a pang of anger spreading through his body as he watched them strolling freely, in and out of Zed's facilities. They had no right to be here and he decided that, pass or no pass, he was going challenge their presence. 'Yuri, call security. Hurry,' he said without taking his eyes off the Arneshians.

Yuri didn't need to be told twice, and darted back the way they had come from.

'Well, well,' said K'Ssander, attracted by the noise. 'If it isn't Captain McCoy,' he said, walking slowly forward. He squared up in front of Julius, while A'Trid leaned against the wall, hands in pockets, enjoying the scene.

Julius didn't give any ground, and dropped his bag on the floor. 'You have no business here.'

K'Ssander smirked at him. 'Says who?'

'I do and I don't give a damn about that piece of plastic around your neck. You are not welcome here.'

The serious tone in Julius' voice obviously made K'Ssander think twice and drop his cocky attitude, but still he stayed where he was. Julius was aware of a tingling sensation spreading down his arms. He knew all too well what it meant, and didn't need to look down to know that tiny sparks were now spurting from his fingertips. He was mad, all right.

A'Trid must have noticed it too, because he stopped smiling and began to move away from Julius. 'Don't be stupid, McCoy,' he said.

Julius was breathing deeply, trying to keep the build-up of energy at bay. His intention was to scare, not hurt them, but they didn't need to know that.

'Does it bother you that we can come and go as we please?' asked K'Ssander, unconcerned by A'Trid's apprehension. 'Your boss says we can.'

Julius moved closer. 'My boss isn't here now, is he? And neither is yours.'

'Come McCoy, we are your guests.'

'You may fool Trent and a bunch of civilians, but you can't fool Zed. We know why you're here, like we both know you cheated your way through that game.'

'Still dwelling on it, I see,' he said, squaring up to Julius. 'You need to prove it, don't you?'

'Oh, I will,' said Julius steadily.

Only a few inches separated their faces, but neither of them were prepared to budge. Suddenly K'Ssander's hand jerked up, and grabbed Julius' t-shirt.

It took only a fraction of a second for Julius to do the same thing. The knuckles on his hand were just starting to turn white, he was pushing them so hard into K'Ssander's chest, when they heard Foster's booming voice behind them.

'What's going on here?'

Startled, they let go of each other, and turned in his direction.

'Miss Petri!' thundered Foster. 'Mr Miller, put your hands where I can see them!'

'It's not what you think, sir,' said a muffled voice.

Julius couldn't understand what was going on, and stood there baffled, watching Foster as he glowered at a niche in the wall to his right.

Just then, Yuri came running along the corridor towards them. 'Captain Foster, you got them!'

'Oh yes, I did,' he answered. He stretched his arms forward and, when he pulled them back, he had Skye by his left ear and Valentina by her right. She looked utterly embarrassed.

Julius couldn't believe his eyes.

'And what exactly were you up to?' asked Foster, menacingly.

'Sir, we ... uh ... we were just checking that panel over there … ow!' said Skye, trying unsuccessfully to weasel his way out of the pickle he was in.

'Impossible, Mr Miller,' thundered Foster. 'You didn't have any free hands for that.' Then he headed toward Julius, dragging the two young lovers behind him. 'Mr McCoy, is this element one of your crew?'

'Yes, sir. He's my tactical officer.'

'Since you are his captain, McCoy, you shouldn't be needing to call me for breaches of good conduct. You must learn to deal with indiscipline yourself. A day in the brig should do it.'

'That's not why we called you, sir,' said Julius. He turned to point at the Arneshians, and saw that they had disappeared. Frustrated, he looked around him, scanning the corridors for any sign of them, but to no avail. 'Damn it,' he thought, wondering where they had gone. He looked back at Foster, aware of the inquisitive gaze, and to Skye, who looked particularly dejected. 'We ... uh ... called you because she's not one of ours, and I'm too busy to escort her back to her quarters.'

'Very well,' answered Foster. 'I'll see to it.' And with that, he pushed Skye at Julius unceremoniously, and headed back, still grasping Valentina by her ear.

'Call me … ouch!' she said over her shoulder.

Skye blew her a kiss, looking theatrically sad, while massaging his bright red, sore ear. Once Foster was out of sight, he spun around and glared at Julius in disbelief. 'What did you do that for? Are you so heartless that I can't even spend my last few free moments in the arms of my beloved?'

Julius crossed his arms and looked at his friend, trying to remain calm. 'First off, she's not your *beloved*, but just one of the many girls with a seasonal ticket to your pants. And secondly, we didn't call Foster to break up your lip-wrestling session, but to come fetch that pain in the backside K'Ssander, and his pal, A'Trid.'

Skye look suitably astounded. 'What?'

'We saw them coming out of the Heron,' explained Yuri. 'That's why I called Foster.'

'How could they just board our ship like that?' asked Skye.

Julius shook his head. He was tempted to say that, had it not been for Skye and Valentina, they could have found out from Foster, but decided instead to let it go. 'I'll ask Faith to check our security cameras when he gets here. Come on now, it's getting late.' He grabbed his bag and walked up to the hatch of the Heron. The day hadn't even started yet and he was already stressed out. That just wouldn't cut it though: it was his first day as captain, and he needed all his wits about him. Like Professor Farshid had told them at the beginning of the year, no matter what happened, a captain had to be larger than life. So Julius forced himself to focus on the day ahead. He drew a couple of deep breaths and stepped inside the ship.

By mid-morning all 3MAs had boarded, and the V.I. crew of the Heron had been activated. Julius watched his holographic chefs at work in the galley with slight apprehension, wondering if any of them would turn sour and lead a rebellion. It was silly, of course, but the memory of Master Isshin's betrayal two years before, was still vivid in his mind.

The Heron was not meant to break orbit until midday, so Julius walked throughout the ship all morning making sure that everyone was fine, as he supposed a good captain should do. He visited Faith in engineering, drawing some amusement from the Mizkis calling him Chief and allowing him to direct them at will; then popped his head in at the War-deck, where Skye and Isolde were discussing security and checking the catalysts' upkeep. Finally, he arrived at the bridge, where he jumped a little as someone shouted, 'Attention on deck!', followed by a standing salute from all present.

'At ease,' he said, once he realised they were addressing him. It looked like everyone was taking their roles very seriously, so he decided it was only proper to play his part too.

Morgana, beaming like it was her birthday, was doing a great job as first pilot, checking her station, and guiding Barth and Siena through their duties as navigation support officers.

Julius nodded in satisfaction and strolled over to Yuri, who was carefully examining an electronic log. 'Commander Slovich, what's our status?'

'We are on schedule, Captain. All supplies are onboard, the Mizkis are at their stations, and our Chief has confirmed that all V.I. systems have been activated.'

'What about sickbay?'

'All in order. Doctor Flox has given us the all-clear.'

'Flox, is he a human or …'

'V.I.'

'Thank you, Commander. Order the crew to change into fleet uniform. Then report our progress to Master Cress and confirm our departure time as midday.'

'Aye, Captain. And don't forget your log,' he added quietly.

Julius had indeed forgotten his log, but he wasn't about to mention that to Yuri. Now that everything was ready, he moved off to examine his own quarters, which were just off the bridge. He grabbed his bag, which he had left outside his door that morning, and let the security sensor scan his eyes. The door slid open silently, revealing a large, luminous room. To his left was a desk, fitted with a monitor, and a comfy leather chair; to his right was an L-shaped sofa, with a glass top coffee table in front of it. A huge window ran along the length of the back wall, with tea lights dotted along its windowsill. There were pictures on the walls, one showing the Lunar Perimeter under construction, another Marcus Tijara standing outside the Hologram Palace, and an evocative one of Earth, taken from space.

Julius knelt next to his bag, and opened it. He rummaged in it for a minute, until he had retrieved an electronic picture frame, which he placed on his new desk. Sitting down in his chair, he touched a pressure pad on the side of the frame and a series of images began to scroll slowly across the glass. He smiled as he saw one of Michael hanging from Julius' neck like a small monkey. He remembered the occasion well: they had been in the Meadows, in Edinburgh, having a picnic for his brother's seventh birthday. 'Computer,' he said, leaning back. 'Activate 3MA McCoy.'

'Online. Welcome aboard, Captain,' answered the ship computer.

Julius coughed a little, to clear his voice. 'Captain's log. Stardate 5-3-58. Err ... so ... we are all aboard and ... hmm ... engine looks good, according to Faith—Chief Engineer, I mean—and ... computer pause!' he said, shaking his head. As far as first logs went, that was pretty rubbish, he thought. He would need to work on it, especially since Farshid could very well choose to broadcast it to the whole of Zed, just to teach him a lesson. He stood up and paced to the far right corner, where another door led on to a conjoining bedroom. Being the captain had its perks, judging by the size of his bed, and the fact that he didn't have to share a room with anyone. The latest Zed fleet uniform had been laid out on the bed: a fitted, navy blue jumpsuit, with his name and rank on the left sleeve, and a com-link on the chest. Feeling more and more like a real captain, he grabbed it and got changed.

At 11:50, Julius entered the bridge; this time he was prepared for the formal salute, and took his place at the large chair in the centre of the room. Skye and Isolde occupied the control panels to his left; Yuri was at his right, along with Barth and Siena; Morgana sat at the front of the ship, where her pilot chair was set between a kaleidoscope of holographic panels of varying sizes.

The front end of the bridge was transparent, giving a breathtaking view of space. The large window wasn't strictly necessary, in the way that a windscreen was on a fly-car, but it did add to the experience.

As the clock ticked down to midday, Julius felt the excitement mounting and knew he wasn't the only one, judging by the large grins on various faces on deck; there was perhaps a little apprehension too, as Barth's white knuckles proved. Julius pressed the Heron's intercom button. 'Heron One, this is the captain speaking.' He paused for a moment, trying to steady his voice. 'Prepare for departure.' Finally, he turned to Morgana. 'Lieutenant Ruthier, take her out.'

'Aye, Captain,' she answered.

Julius watched as she pushed and slid various levers and buttons on the holopanels surrounding her. With her left hand, she grabbed the shift handle, and pushed it forward with slow, controlled speed; her right hand continued tapping away speedily on the screen in front of her, adjusting the trajectory as she went, until the Heron broke orbit.

It took no more than a couple of minutes, but to Julius it seemed longer. He knew that Farshid and Clavel were watching, and probably so too were Freja and Cress—by now, he knew that very little escaped the Grand Master. From the point of view of the Spring Mission, he needed to prove to Farshid that he had what he took to be a leader. It didn't matter to him that Zed would need more than one captain for its fleet; Julius wanted to be the best.

'Straight and steady she goes,' called Morgana, proudly. 'Heron's docking has been cleared. Where to, Captain?'

Julius realised that he hadn't actually thought about that, so he looked over at Barth, hoping for his navigational skills. 'Ensign Smit,' he called.

Barth looked up quickly, looking guilty.

'What would you recommend as a first stop?' asked Julius.

Barth's face lit up with relief. 'Venus is supposed to be beautiful at this time of the year, sir. I would suggest we start there, and then visit the rest of our planets ... sir.'

'Ensign Migliori,' said Julius.

'Aye, Captain?' answered Siena.

'What speed would you recommend for that?'

'Light speed, sir. It will be two light minutes to Venus, four to Mars, thirty to Jupiter; then it's one light hour to Saturn and four to Neptune. By the end of the week, we will have seen all our planets, with time to spare. And, if we're in a hurry, there's always the hyperjump option.'

'Very well. Set a course for Venus.'

'Aye, Captain,' she said, visibly pleased at having been asked for her input.

'*That was nicely done, Julius,*' Morgana told him with her mind. '*You're doing a grand job.*'

Julius grinned a little, grateful for the show of support and, he had to admit, for the private moment she had just shared with him.

The next few days passed by smoothly, and all the Mizkis seemed to be having a great time. Barth's itinerary had worked out well, and they had managed to visit all of the planets, moons, and satellites in their solar system. They gathered samples from the rings of Saturn, practiced shooting at small asteroid fields, and watched Morgana taking hundreds of pictures for her latest project: creating her very own Vbook on the most scenic routes between planets.

Every evening, for an hour, Julius would report to Professor Farshid, and study the data she had gathered during the day from each student. She would advise Julius on the best ways of improving an individual's performance, and how to teach them the right way to complete a task, in a professional manner. Afterwards, she would comment on Julius' own actions, what he had done well, and what he needed to improve on. Lastly, she would go over the list of requests made by Commander Slovich, from daily supplies to crew requests, approving the ones she saw fit and explaining to Julius why she had selected some over others. That time spent with Farshid was really important to Julius, and he came to look forward to it every day. He really wanted to impress her, so he strove to do his best in all his actions and decisions. By the end of the second week, he had the feeling that he had aced the Spring Mission, and was looking forward to seeing his final report.

On Thursday the 15th of March, they re-entered Zed's orbit, and stopped within range of the Gea One. That evening, after his usual meeting with Professor Farshid, Julius was up on the deck, scanning their checklist for the following day, which would also be their last. Morgana had told him she would wait for him to finish, so she kept herself busy at the helm, showing Faith a few minor adjustments that she wanted for the shift handle. Julius was almost done when he received a message on his PIP, so he quickly finished his work, and checked it. The message was short, but as he saw who it was from, his eyes grew bigger. It read: "Check the Space Channel. K'Ssander."

Julius looked up, 'Faith. Is there a screen for the Space Channel in here?'

'Yeah,' he replied, hovering over to the captain's chair. There, he pressed a couple of buttons and the front window of the deck turned into a large screen.

Morgana looked up and took a few steps back so she could see properly as well. 'What's the matter?'

Julius didn't answer, but sat up straight in his chair as the Space Channel's evening edition began. A sense of anxiety was creeping up on him, making the hair on his arms stand up. Why would K'Ssander be messaging him for this?

Faith and Morgana must have noticed his odd expression, because they moved and quietly stood to either side of him, watching the screen intently. The view was that of the Prague Departure Centre for Zed, and it looked like another busy evening.

'We are here in Prague to follow the latest wave of departures for the Taurus One.' Julius recognised the speaker's voice as belonging to the man who had interviewed the Nuarns before. His heartbeat sped up.

'More than 45 million Nuarns have already left Earth,' continued the man, 'and many are wondering if this exodus will continue until the very last one has joined Ambassador T'Rogon. So far, only a few thousand have returned to Earth. I'm going to try and talk with some of the travellers who are here tonight,' he said.

Julius watched as the camera swung to the right, and headed straight for a group of people standing at the back of a long queue.

'Excuse me,' called the reporter. 'May I have a word, for the Space Channel?'

The two people standing at the back turned around at the same time, and faced the camera. Julius felt all the air escaping his lungs, and a cold grip closing around his heart; Faith let out a sharp intake of breath, while Morgana's hand tightened on Julius' shoulder.

Seeing Michael's face on camera was the last thing that Julius had expected, and even less so the boy standing to his brother's side: it was none other than Billy Somers, looking as full of himself as ever. He was taller, but his square face and large shoulders were the same; a puffed up version of the bully they had met two years before. In comparison, Michael looked rather slender, although it seemed to Julius that he was a few inches taller than when he had last seen him. But, what was Somers doing there, with his brother?

'What is your name, young man?' asked the speaker, out of shot.

'Billy Somers, and this here is Michael McCoy,' he said, smugly.

'May I see your t-shirt?'

'Yeah,' he replied, stretching the bottom corners of it so it was clearly visible for the camera. 'And in case you can't read it, it says, "Zed Sucks."'

'The cheek,' whispered Faith.

'Why the animosity toward Zed, Mr Somers?' asked the reporter.

'Because they're a bunch of losers, with second class technology and staff so inept that it took them almost a year before they realised I was a Nuarn!'

'What?' cried Morgana to the screen.

'What do you mean?' asked the speaker.

'They tested me, enrolled me, and shipped me off to Sield school. They wasted nine months of my precious life—which I will never get back—before they realised that I wasn't gifted enough for them. So they booted me back to Earth.'

'You must have been devastated,' commented the reporter.

'Quite the contrary. Who would want to be with that Mizki trash when I can be with the Arneshians, my own people? They will give us back our freedom and our dignity. See this boy here?' he said, grabbing Michael by the shoulder and pulling him close. 'This boy is Julius McCoy's brother, and you know what Zed's precious White Child did when he found out? He got him collared like a dog, like everyone else does on Earth, when they have a Nuarn in the family. If his brother doesn't care for his own blood, and if my parents don't care for me, why should we stay here? Answer me that!'

'How can you do that ...' Morgana's voice was trembling.

'Mr Somers, what are your plans now?' asked the speaker.

'To leave this dump you call home. For good.'

'Are you joining the Arneshians in their journey back home?'

'Damn right I am. We both are. We're boarding that shuttle tonight, all the way to Pit-Stop Pete, and tomorrow morning we'll be on the Taurus One, on our way to Arnesh.'

'And what about you, young man?'

Michael looked up, looking quite unconcerned. 'I believe the Ambassador can give me a better future.'

Julius had remained quiet during the interview. Now, he stood up, walked past his friends and headed to his quarters without saying a word. Soon after, the interview ended.

'Faith, what should we do?' asked Morgana, wiping a tear from her cheek.

'Leave him be, for now. I'll tell Yuri to take charge for tonight.'

In silence, they left the bridge and headed to the canteen.

'Julius, it's me,' said Morgana, knocking at his door.

Julius was startled out of sleep, and heaved himself up on his elbows.

'Julius?'

He stretched his hand towards the control on the wall and unlocked his door, before slumping back on the covers. He heard steps out in the front room, then something being placed down on the glass table.

'Have a shower and come out, please. I need to talk to you.'

He checked his PIP and saw that it was 06:40. He had slept the whole night through, without eating or even undressing. Slowly, he rolled out of bed and headed to the bathroom. Fifteen minutes later he emerged into the lounge, wearing a clean uniform. Morgana was sitting on one side of the sofa, legs gathered under her; she had brought him a latte and a couple of pastries. He sat down next to her and grabbed the coffee.

'Rough night, huh?' she said.

Julius took a long sip, then put the cup down. 'I really believed he wouldn't go,' he said, looking at a point on the floor, between his feet. 'Have the others ...'

'Yes, they saw it,' she answered. 'Most of them were pretty astonished about Somers' revelation, to tell the truth.'

Julius nodded absently. Of course, to see Somers there had been a surprise, but in the face of Michael leaving, he couldn't care less if Billy had claimed to be the reincarnation of Marcus Tijara.

'As for Michael,' she said, 'our lot knew he was a Nuarn. Even my roommate Jiao has a Nuarn cousin who left last month. I guess they thought it could happen. They've all been thinking of you, Julius.'

He buried his face in his hands and rubbed his eyes, tiredly. Then he looked up at her. 'How could he do that, Morgana? How could he leave his own family like that?'

She shook her head. 'He's only a child-'

'Don't give me that! We were his age when we destroyed Kratos and saved Zed, or have you forgotten?'

'People are different, Jules. Situations are different. He'll never have our chances, and he really believes that T'Rogon is going to give him what he wants. Can you blame him?'

Julius had gone over that argument a thousand times the night before. What didn't sit right with him wasn't so much that Michael had made the life-changing choice he had, but more the fact that he may never see him again and, knowing this, his brother had made no effort to see him one last time. That, more than anything, had really shaken Julius quite badly. He hadn't felt up to actually speaking to his parents after the interview, so he had messaged them instead. Judging by his dad's short reply, that had probably been for the best: they were both still in shock, and needed time to try process the pain of Michael leaving.

'He's safe at least,' added Morgana.

Julius looked at her, not knowing what she meant.

'He's one of them, Julius. They won't harm him.'

Part of him knew she was right. At least that was one positive thing out of this whole mess. But still, his heart felt like it was being weighed down by a brick.

'Right now though, we need you, Captain McCoy,' she said, standing up. 'You have one last job to finish and a crew to take home. I know this may seem like a joke in the light of last night, but it isn't. If you really care about your future in Zed, you better rise to this challenge.'

Julius knew all too well what his duties were, but he was grateful to Morgana for being there for him, to remind him. She had always been his voice of reason. He grabbed one of the pastries and took a bite, and realised he was absolutely famished.

'That's better,' she said. She ruffled his hair as she stepped past him, and left the room.

At 08:00, Julius was standing on the bridge, waiting for his officers. Skye walked in first and momentarily put a hand on his shoulder. He didn't say anything, just gave a light squeeze, and resumed his post. Shortly after, all the deck's crew had reported for duty. When Julius' PIP beeped to indicate an incoming call, he was fearful that it would be more bad news. But it was only Isolde, offering her ear, should he need to talk to someone. It was a kind offer, but he would rather talk to the Skirts if he really needed to. Besides, he thought it best not to give her the wrong impression, just in case she took it as a sign that he was letting her into his private space. He looked at her and nodded his thanks, which caused all sorts of pink and green wisps to shoot out of her head. No, he definitely couldn't talk to her. A few minutes later, Yuri confirmed that all sectors had checked in, including engineering. Julius hailed the Gea One, and requested permission to dock.

'Heron, you may dock in bay 15.'

'Copy that, Gea. We'll be there in ten minutes.' He turned to Morgana. 'Take us home, Lieutenant.'

'Aye, Captain.'

Julius was holding on to the fact that very soon he would have three full days of rest, in which he didn't need to be responsible for anybody and could just be by himself if he wanted to. This Spring Mission had really spelled out what Farshid had meant when she said that a captain must be larger than life: come hell or high water, his crew would always rely on him to keep them safe and take them home in the end. He wondered if Captain Kelly had ever felt that way before, and made a mental note to ask him the next time they met.

He looked past Morgana's station, into space. It was some view from the bridge. He could see a slice of Earth beyond the Moon and Pit-Stop Pete, with its busy docks. Further away, to the right, was the Taurus One, lurking like a silent, evil giant. It was even bigger out here than it had looked on video; by now it was carrying almost 50 million Nuarns. 'And soon, my brother too,' thought Julius glumly. Why would T'Rogon need a ship that size though, wondered Julius. Even with all the Nuarns on board, it was simply massive. There was also its uncanny ability to morph.

Suddenly, he noticed that the image in front of him was shifting slightly to the right, like when a camera pans sideways in a movie. 'Lieutenant?' he said to Morgana.

'Ensigns,' called Morgana to her officers, 'check our course.'

'It's not us,' said Siena, looking worried.

Morgana pressed a few buttons, scanned the sensors, and turned to Julius. 'The Heron has changed course, Captain.'

Julius saw grey wisps surrounding her aura, and knew it wasn't a good sign. He looked at Skye and Isolde, but they only shook their heads in dismay.

'Do we have *any* control over the ship?' asked Julius.

'None,' said Morgana.

'And where are we heading?'

'Pit-Stop Pete,' said Barth, turning rather white. 'If we can't change course, we'll cut right through it in less than five minutes.'

'McCoy to engineering,' said Julius.

'Go ahead, Captain,' said Faith. 'What's happening?'

'Right now,' answered Julius calmly, 'it looks like a repeat of the Zed Toon game. Do you know what I mean?'

There was a brief pause. 'It's not us steering, is it?'

'Correct. You need to shut down the engines from there, before your beloved Pete Kingston gets blown to smithereens.'

'What?' cried Faith, suddenly fully alert. 'I'll take care of it, Captain!'

Julius kept his eyes on their route. The Heron had now completely shifted and Pete's docking station was perfectly centred in the middle of the window. 'Morgana, anything?'

'No. I'm still locked out of the controls.'

'Damn it,' said Julius, slamming his fist on the armrest of his chair.

'Oh no,' said Barth, feebly.

'What is it?' asked Julius.

'We're shifting again,' he answered.

Julius looked out and saw Pete's station moving to the left, while an Arneshian spaceship was detaching from it at the same time. The Heron was unmistakably heading for a new target. 'Faith!' cried Julius. 'Why aren't we stopping?'

'Because I wasn't in charge of designing this piece of junk, that's why! If I had, we wouldn't be having this conversation.'

'Yes but, can you stop it?'

'I'm trying McCoy, trust me.'

'Julius,' called Morgana, 'that shuttle ... our new target ...'

'What about it?'

'I've just checked; according to the dock logs there's only one shuttle due out today. '

'So?' urged Julius.

'It … it's the one carrying Michael!'

Suddenly, everything made sense: K'Ssander and A'Trid's visit to the Heron had had a very specific reason. Somehow, they had managed to rig his ship, just like they had during the game, to their robots. Zed was no longer in control of the helm; Arnesh was, and if Julius didn't do something quickly he was going to lose his brother, and cause a diplomatic incident. Dismayed, he also realised that, in the excitement of the mission, he had completely forgotten to ask Faith to check their internal security cameras when they first boarded the ship, and mentally cursed himself for it. If only he had performed his duties as captain properly, none of this would be happening. He felt like he had failed them all. Still, he couldn't allow himself to dwell on it; if ever there was a time to get his act together, it was then. He needed to stop the Heron. 'Morgana, how much time to impact?'

'Less than two minutes.'

'Heron,' called Julius over the ship's intercom, 'I want every single Mizki on War-deck, right now. Faith, stay where you are and work on the engine—keep whatever help you need. Morgana, go to tactical alert and contact Master Cress immediately. Everyone else, move!' He headed for the door, motioning for Skye, Isolde, Siena and Barth to follow him.

'War-deck?' asked Skye, catching up with him. 'What are you thinking of doing?'

'We're going to give the shuttle a little push,' he said, tapping his head.

A smile spread over Skye's face. 'Professor King would be proud!'

The Mizkis were filing in from the different decks and corridors. Julius hoped that linking the telekinetic skills of more than 25 students would give them a better chance of clearing their path, before it was too late. The War-deck was positioned above the bridge, and was where all the Heron's catalysts were fitted. The walls and ceilings were made of unique transparent panelling, to give a perfect view of outside.

'Are we using the catalysts?' asked Lopaka.

'Not unless you want to blow that shuttle up,' answered Julius.

'We are going to push it away,' explained Skye, 'using our powers, and *Julius* as a catalyst.'

'What?' gasped Lopaka, wide-eyed.

'Face the shuttle and hold each other's hands,' said Julius. 'You're going to focus on me. When I tell you, start pushing and I'll channel our energies towards the shuttle's port. Clear?'

'Are you sure we're not going to just end up blasting your brains out?' asked Gustavo.

'Trust me, you won't.'

'All right, let's do it,' called Leanne Nord, pushing her way to the front of the room. She took Julius' left hand in her right, and gave her other hand to Skye.

The rest of the Mizkis grabbed each others' hands, and silence fell on the room. Julius closed his eyes and began to breathe deeply. He was aware of the clock ticking and the sound of the impact alarm blaring throughout the Heron; he pushed the noise to the back of his mind, until it became soft, and faraway. As had happened before, they were creating a human conduit, the energies of his classmates filling his mind, making his hair stand on end. He could feel a greater control over his body this time though, probably as a result of his latest augmentations, and he was glad because he would need all his strength to avert the crash. Slowly, he opened his eyes, and saw the Arneshian shuttle drawing closer and closer. He stretched his right hand forward, toward the port of the shuttle, holding Leanne's hand tight in his left. This was the moment. 'Push!' he urged the Mizkis.

The energy streamed out of Julius' hand with all the strength of a cork popping out of a bottle of champagne, making him stagger backwards a little. The Heron stuttered and, although it didn't completely stop, Julius could feel that it had slowed down. He focused on the small vessel in front of him, and pushed as hard as he could. It was almost as if a cushion of air had formed between the Heron and the shuttle, stopping them from coming any closer. For one fleeting moment, Julius believed they had managed it. Then he saw that they were still moving towards the target.

'Faith, report!' said Morgana over the intercom.

'I'm almost done!' he answered.

'Come on guys,' thought Julius.

'30 seconds to impact!' shouted Morgana.

'Keep pushing, Mizkis!' called Faith over the intercom. 'We can do it together, but we're cutting it real fine!'

The Mizkis all pushed with renewed vigour. Julius felt an incredible surge of energy leaving his body, and wondered how long they could maintain this for.

'Done!' cried a victorious Faith. 'Morgana, steer us away!'

No answer came from the helm, but Julius felt the ship veering right. The engine had stopped now, but they were still travelling toward the shuttle.

'It's too late,' whispered Julius.

The Heron had stopped, but it was still drifting and Julius realised that Morgana wouldn't make the turn in time.

'Captain to all hands,' he cried. 'Hold on!'

The impact shook the whole ship, sending the Mizkis sprawling to the floor. They had thankfully slowed down enough to avoid an explosion, but not to prevent a head-on collision. Julius scrambled to his feet and realised just how close he was to the Arneshian shuttle: he could now read the serial number on one of its portholes.

'Skye,' called Faith, 'seal off the lower decks. We're losing oxygen.'

'Breached hulls, sealed.'

'Everyone, back to stations,' ordered Julius. He rushed to the bridge, feeling very light headed, but knowing he couldn't stop now.

'Isolde, report,' he said, once he was back in his chair.

'Decks one to four are breached, but contained. We're fine, Julius. And so is the Arneshian shuttle.'

'Captain, the Grand Master is hailing us,' said Siena.

'Put him through,' said Julius.

Freja appeared on the front screen of the ship, looking worried. 'McCoy, is the crew all right?'

'Yes, sir. I'll have Flox check us out in a minute. Sir, it wasn't our fault. The ship's engine and helm were out of our control.'

'What are you saying?'

'I'm saying that this is a repeat of the game.'

Freja looked flustered. He turned around and began to talk quietly to the Master. Eventually, they saw Cress leave in a hurry. 'McCoy, there will be an enquiry.'

'An enquiry? It is clearly not our fault!' said Julius angrily.

'Be that as it may, it is protocol. The 3MAs are forbidden to leave the Heron, or to attempt to remove the ship from the Arneshian shuttle's port until the end of proceedings. We will make sure that you have all the supplies you need for your extended stay.'

'But, sir-'

'You have your orders, Captain,' cut in Freja.

'Sir,' answered Julius, realising there was nothing else he could do. At least Michael's shuttle was still there too. Maybe, just maybe, he would at least get a chance to try change his brother's mind.

CHAPTER 12

REALITY BITES

In the following hours, all of the news channels were ablaze with vicious verbal attacks from the Arneshians against Julius and his crew. Not one hour passed without a flurry of new, spiteful words from T'Rogon. Even though Earth knew full well that the Curia was examining all the recordings from the collision and that there was a full enquiry on the go, Paulo Trent and the Voices of the Earth seemed to have added weight to the Ambassador's opinion that Zed's incompetence, and Freja's recklessness, were ultimately responsible for this diplomatic incident.

'And we cannot excuse the White Child,' said T'Rogon during an on-air face to face with the Curio Maximus, Roversi, the morning after the incident. 'McCoy may still be in training, but the fact that he is so gifted should make him even more accountable for what has happened. If you can't control him, then you are guilty too.'

Julius and the Skirts were seated on the sofa in the captain's quarters, watching all of this. Iryana Mielowa was hosting the meeting in the Space Channel studio.

'Ambassador,' began Roversi, clearly straining to keep control of his temper, though his nostrils were still twitching, 'surely you can't be serious. Accidents can happen on a training mission. You have students too; you should know.'

'You have said it, Curio. We have students, but you seem to be training bitter children, and McCoy is a classic example of that. Or have you forgotten about the fight after the game? In fact, let us remind the people of Earth about that ignominious moment; let's show them what *really* happened.'

'We don't actually have any footage of that event, Ambassador,' said Mielowa, curtly.

'No matter,' answered T'Rogon. 'I do.'

To everyone's astonishment, T'Rogon placed two fingers against his left temple and pressed: the circular Arneshian symbol lit up on the back of his hand, and a holographic screen appeared in front of him, large enough to be seen clearly by all present.

'What kind of bio-technology is that?' muttered Faith, awestruck.

'I don't care if that screen comes out of his rear-end,' said Skye, growing livid. 'He's going to show that stupid fight again. Why don't they stop him?'

It looked like Mielowa was wondering the same thing, because she was looking imploringly behind her, possibly for her station aids, to see why they weren't intervening.

As was to be expected, the fight was shown very much from an Arneshian perspective: it started, in fact, with Maks storming in and punching K'Ssander, and then being joined by Julius and Skye.

'That's not fair!' cried Morgana, indignantly.

'See there?' continued T'Rogon. 'Your pupils are out of control. That boy just stormed in and hit one of my students for no reason; well, for no other apparent reason than they had just lost a very important game.'

Roversi seemed at loss for what to say. It was as if he had never been briefed about the full story of what had really happened, and was now being confronted with something he didn't know how to handle diplomatically. 'Boys will be boys, Ambassador,' he said, trying to shift the focus onto something else.

'Really?' he said, sitting up in his chair like he was preparing to take off at a sprint. 'Let me tell you something more, Curio, that may finally open your eyes and change the lax attitude with which you run this Lunar Perimeter of yours. You should really get to know your Mizkis better than this. That McCoy, as well as being a sore loser and a lousy leader, will stop at nothing to get his way.'

Julius bristled with anger, and sat up in his seat. What was T'Rogon on about this time?

'When he found out that his brother was a Nuarn, instead of encouraging him to strive for something better in life, he tried to stop him any way he could from fulfilling his dreams. To begin with, he threatened him with false letters written with the help of his friends.' As he said this, he touched his temple again, and a series of emails began to scroll down on his personal holoscreen, which was still sitting open before him.

'How did he get those?' cried Julius, standing up. He knew full well that T'Rogon had seen Michael's choker that day at the docks, during the mid-winter break, but how could he have known about those letters?

'No wonder Michael never got them,' said Faith.

'Then,' continued T'Rogon, looking quite pleased with the effect he was having on Mielowa and Roversi, who both seemed spellbound by his words, 'when the letters didn't work, he attacked the very shuttle his brother Michael was using to travel to the Taurus One.'

Julius slammed his fist on his thigh, 'How dare you?' he yelled in frustration, throwing a kick at the holoscreen, right at T'Rogon's face. Yellow sparks of energy were falling from his fingertips onto the floor, where they fizzed out.

Morgana switched off the feed and stood up. 'We've wasted enough time. I think we need to make a little enquiry of our own.'

'She's right,' added Faith. 'We're probably the only ones who actually believe that this was foul play. Julius, you said K'Ssander and A'Trid came out of the Heron before we left; I'm going to put a team together and start examining all communication channels in, and out, of this ship.'

'Good idea,' said Skye. 'Isolde and I will check the cameras, from two hours before we saw the Arneshians. I think we can safely assume they didn't sleep in here, but if I can't find something, I'll search back further.'

'Do that,' said Faith, 'and get the Mizkis to search the entire ship for anything out of place. Morgana, I need you to map the exact trajectory of the Heron in the ten minutes before the collision; I want to see if I can match it with my findings.'

'All right,' she said, turning to Julius, 'And you, glowing boy, need to calm down and resume your captain's duties. There's a long list of people waiting to talk to you, starting with Professor Farshid. Help them help us out of this mess.'

Julius nodded. He really wanted to lend a hand onboard, but that was not how a captain helped. 'Sure thing. I'm on it.'

They left him in his quarters, eager to start their duties. Julius sat at his desk, pushing his anger about T'Rogon's accusations out of his mind. It wasn't easy, but he couldn't afford to let the Arneshian get the upper hand at a time like this. 'I am the root of this tree,' he said to himself. 'They depend on me, and I will not fail them again.'

Faith had spent the best part of two days inside engineering. He had instructed Lopaka to direct their classmates Annette, Femi and Barbel to scour the security channel, while he himself had started by thoroughly examining Julius' PIP chip, thanks to Dr Flox, in sick bay, who had removed the chip from Julius' hand for a while. It hadn't taken him long to isolate the tracing code which K'Ssander had tacked on to Julius' bio-software. Julius had been quite gobsmacked when he saw it flashing up on the screen. Faith had then returned to engineering, to ensure he found a way of recording the code so it could be processed as evidence.

It was towards the end of the second day, around 22:00 hours, when Femi called her team to her. 'I think I've found something,' she said.

'Don't play it yet,' said Faith, on a hunch. 'Patch it through our earpieces, channel one.'

Lopaka looked at him, puzzled, but quickly complied. He sat down on the floor, next to the girls, while Faith hovered back and forth anxiously. Then Femi pressed play.

'It is done, Ambassador,' said K'Ssander's voice.

'Very well,' answered T'Rogon. 'Salgoria is extremely pleased with your efforts. And you know how forthcoming she can be towards her faithful.'

'It was an honour to serve her.'

'Don't be modest, Mr K'Ssander. It took skill to plant those devices on their robots in the middle of a game. They didn't even notice. As they will also not notice us steering the Heron.'

'They're not as advanced as I thought they'd be, Ambassador,' K'Ssander scoffed contemptuously. 'It was like stealing candy from a child.'

Faith stopped his pacing, and clenched his fists.

'Yes, quite,' continued T'Rogon. 'Our mission is almost complete. We have enough Nuarns to last us a lifetime of experiments.'

'When can we break orbit?'

'As soon as the minefield is in place and activated, which will not be long now. We will be ready in time for the last shuttle delivery; the shuttle which I'm standing in now.'

'You mean, the one that will be carrying the McCoy boy?'

'The very one.'

'Will the field be enough to ...'

'Enough to blow them to the four corners of the galaxy? Why yes, I believe it will.'

The recording stopped there, leaving the Mizkis staring at each other in silent fear.

'Femi,' said Faith, after a couple of minutes, 'show me the matrix for this dialogue.'

Femi stood up, her legs shaking a little. She pressed a few buttons and a long code streamed onto the screen in front of her. Faith moved closer, activated his PIP, and displayed the tracing code he had found inside Julius' PIP chip, alongside this new one. 'I want you to look for this inside the dialogue code.'

'Isn't that the tr-' started Lopaka.

Quickly, Faith placed his hand on Lopaka's mouth, gesturing for everyone to be quite. Lopaka looked at him, mystified, but nodded. The girls did likewise. Faith pointed at the air above him, then at his ear and chest, and mouthed the words, 'They are listening to us.'

Everyone's eyes grew large with understanding, and they began the search. Eventually, Barbel pointed at the screen, a satisfied grin on her face. The code was there all right, embedded in the Arneshian dialogue. Faith needed to warn the others immediately. 'Come with me,' he said, before heading for the bridge.

When Julius saw Faith and his team rushing onto the bridge all flushed and flustered, he leapt up from his chair in alarm, only to be shushed by the waving of Faith's hand. Morgana, Skye, and everyone else on deck looked at them, dying to know what was going on. Faith went straight to the security panel, shoving Skye hastily out of his way, and pressed several buttons in quick succession.

In the meantime, Lopaka casually plonked himself down in the captain's high chair and flicked on the intercom. 'Aloha folks! This is Mr Liway from the deck,' he said, winking once at Julius. 'The Captain has a surprise for you all, and is cordially inviting you up on the bridge right now!'

Morgana stared blankly at Julius, hoping for answers, but he could only shrug and shake his head in reply. Annette Valeris and Barbel Frank stood at either side of the entry door, motioning for the Mizkis to be quiet as they stepped inside. Soon, the deck was packed with 25 very perplexed students.

'Done,' said Faith finally, letting out a sigh of relief. 'You can talk now.'

'What was that all about?' asked Julius.

'The Heron is bugged,' replied Lopaka.

'What?' cried Skye.

'And there's more,' said Faith, preparing his PIP. 'You all need to hear this.' The 3MAs listened to the recording of the dialogue in silence, until Faith stopped it. 'K'Ssander and A'Trid have bugged the entire ship,' he explained. 'Right now, only the deck is safe.'

'Wait,' said Julius. 'Does that mean they know you've heard their dialogue in engineering?'

'No,' answered Faith. 'I had a hunch and got my team to put on headsets the first time we listened to it. They also don't know we've found out about the bugs on the Heron. I've just patched a virus through the deck relay. We have about twenty minutes before they can listen in on us again in this room, so we need to be quick.'

'How did you find out, Faith?' asked Siena.

'Julius' PIP chip was bugged. I just had a feeling that they could have done the same to the Heron.'

Siena looked at him proudly.

'This is the proof we need against the Arneshians,' cried Leanne Nord. 'We must broadcast this dialogue through the Space Channel.'

'Not without a confirmed signature on their voices, we can't,' said Faith.

'He's right,' added Julius. 'We must link this recording to the Taurus One shuttle, or they'll think we made it up.'

'And how do you propose we do that, Chief?' asked Skye.

'We can get K'Ssander easily, since he was standing right here on the Heron. For the shuttle though, that's a different story; we can only get T'Rogon's signature directly from the relay he used.'

Julius fell silent for a minute, lost in his thoughts. This was the chance he had been waiting for—an opportunity to board the shuttle and see his brother again. But it wouldn't be easy. 'We need a way to avoid being seen once onboard. Judging by the shuttle's size, there could be about 50 people standing between us and the relay.'

'We could use the Exoskin suits,' said Skye. 'We have a couple on board.'

Julius nodded, he looked at the rest of his classmates. 'As captain, I have decided to board the shuttle; not just because my brother is on it, but also, if I had done my duty properly, this accident may never have happened.'

The Mizkis looked at him, listening intently as he carried on.

'The day we departed from Gea, I saw two of the Arneshians stepping out of the Heron. I should have requested a full scan, but ... in the confusion beforehand, I didn't. I'm sorry.'

'Actually,' added Yuri, sounding a little sheepish, 'I was standing right by your side and I forgot too. It's also my fault.'

'Ahem,' coughed Skye. 'I believe the biggest blame lies with me actually, since I ... distracted you all.'

'I am the captain,' said Julius. 'It was my responsibility.'

Skye and Yuri seemed set to disagree, when Morgana put an end to it. 'And now that you've done your confessions guys, we need to vote for who goes on this mission; I vote for Julius and Skye—and if I have to explain the reasons why it should be them, then you've chosen the wrong career path,' she ended, crossing her arms and tapping her foot rapidly on the floor.

'I agree,' said Manuel Valdez, quickly followed by a general nodding of heads from the rest of the Mizkis.

'Bossy lady is right,' said Leanne, seriously. 'What do you want us to do in the meantime? And let's decide quickly. If the Arneshians are really listening, they'll be wondering where the heck we all went.'

'Faith?' said Julius, indicating for him to carry on. He had done a great job up until now, and he had a better overview of the technical situation.

Faith seemed very pleased to be given the lead on the mission, and moved to the centre of the deck. 'Right, those of you with bridge duties, stay here. Lopaka, take a team to engineering, and start repairing the engine. Leanne, you're in charge of fixing the breached hulls—we may need to make a hasty retreat. Everyone else is on security detail. Keep scanning every nook and cranny of this ship for anything out of the ordinary—we can't afford to miss anything else.'

'Watch what you say everyone, and watch what you send through your PIPs,' added Julius. 'Use your mind-skills for private stuff. This is our last chance to prove what the Arneshians are really up to.'

As the crew filed quietly away, Jiao Yu stopped by Julius' side. 'Is it true what they said about experimenting on the Nuarns?'

Julius looked at her and saw that she had been crying. Then he remembered that her cousin had boarded the Taurus One already. 'Don't worry, Jiao; we won't let them get away with it.'

Jiao looked at him for a few seconds, until she seemed convinced that he could really do something, then nodded and walked away.

When the other Mizkis had all left, the meeting continued.

'Once you two access the relay,' explained Faith, 'they'll find out pretty soon.'

'What kind of equipment are we dealing with?' asked Isolde.

'I don't know; which leads to another issue: our comlinks may not work inside an Arneshian vessel.'

'And the PIP?' asked Morgana.

'Same thing.'

'What about telepathy?' asked Skye.

'Possibly,' said Faith.

'What, from *another ship*?' asked Isolde.

'I think I could,' said Julius. 'At least I can try.'

'Good, because right now it's the only option we have,' said Faith.

'What about those mines T'Rogon was talking about?' asked Morgana. 'We need to tell Freja.'

'Faith, are you sure there's no video surveillance on the deck?' said Julius.

'Positive. I've checked the room and it's clean.'

'All right. Get Cress on the line, and keep him talking.'

'What should I say?'

'Improvise, but be careful, the 20 minutes are up in a few seconds.'

Faith hailed the Gea One, requesting permission to talk to Cress, who came on screen shortly after.

'Chief Shanigan, what can I do for you at this late hour?'

'Master Cress! What a pleasure to see you again!'

'Cut to the chase, please. In case you haven't noticed, we are rather busy trying to get you out of there.'

'But of course. I'll be brief,' he said, starting to hover randomly across the deck. 'Tonight, I couldn't sleep. Me tummy was really upset, and I was wondering what in the name of...'

Julius saw that Cress was about to interrupt, so he jumped in front of the screen and waved to get the Master's attention. Just for good measure, he shushed him too. The expression on Cress' face in response to this disrespectful behaviour was a frightening cross between shock and bewilderment.

'...me great-great-great uncle Phil who, bless his soul, had an unnatural likeness to a mountain troll...' said Faith, unperturbed.

Julius began to type quickly on his PIP, his screen facing Master Cress, so it served as a notice board to transmit his message: "Cannot send. Heron bugged. Call Freja."

Cress read the screen carefully, then activated his own PIP, and nodded to Julius.

'... In fact, not just any mountain troll, but a mountain troll with a very ugly mother, and possibly a gorilla for a father ...'

'Mr Miller,' said Cress, trying his best to play along with the farce, 'I believe that your chief engineer is having problems. Could it be something he ate?'

'Possibly, sir. I should go fetch Captain McCoy, perhaps.'

'Yes, maybe you should.'

'Surely it couldn't have been that leftover mutton leg I found floating in the plasma core the other day ...' Faith rambled.

When Grand Master Freja joined Cress, he caught the last bit of Faith's monologue and his left eyebrow shot upwards. Cress pressed a button to close the audio channel between them and the Heron, and briefed Freja. Julius saw comprehension dawning on the Grand Master's face and leaned close as Freja typed something quickly on his own PIP and held it up for Julius to read.

"Explain."

Julius quickly typed his response: "Found chat between T and K. It proves Heron/Game compromised. Nuarns wanted for experiments. Faith can retrieve signature from relay on shuttle."

"Do it. How can we help?"

"No need. You find the minefield around Zed!" Freja's face grew dark at that, and Julius added, "T said mines all linked and set to go off."

"When?"

"When Michael's shuttle reaches Taurus One."

'... but then I say, how can it be? Me stomach can digest cement and spiders, surely the mutton ...'

'That's enough, Mr Shanigan,' said Cress. 'Mr Miller, I order you to lock your engineer in the brig until next year.'

Morgana and Siena had their hands clamped over their mouths, trying to stifle their laughter.

'Yes, sir!' said Skye, staying exactly where he was.

"Be careful," wrote Freja. "We'll take care of the minefield."

Julius nodded, relieved. Finally, they had a chance to set the record straight once and for all. He bowed to Freja and Cress, and motioned for Faith to stop acting.

'I have no more time to waste,' said Cress. 'Tell McCoy I want an official apology for this insult.' He looked at them, with a hint of a smile. The show had definitely amused him.

When the screen went dark Skye stepped closer to Julius and sent him a mind-message, '*I've noticed you didn't mention to Freja that we need to be onboard the shuttle to fetch that signature.*'

'*It must have escaped my mind,*' answered Julius vaguely.

CHAPTER 13

DECEPTION

In the early hours of the 19th of March, Julius and Skye had fixed the Exoskin devices onto their uniforms, and were standing on deck two, where a portion of the Heron was lodged firmly inside the Arneshian shuttle. Annette Valeris had just cut into the metal, creating an opening big enough to let the boys pass through it. With the aid of a handheld sonar device, she had been able to locate a passage that would open into one of the service conduits, allowing the team a safe entry point.

'*I've downloaded the layout for the shuttle onto your PIP, based on my best guess, plus details of all the Arneshian relay schematics known to Zed,*' explained Faith telepathically. '*Just bear in mind, I don't know exactly what you'll find over there. It would be easier if you took me with you.*'

'*We need you here,*' said Julius. '*You're the only one that can safely retrieve the signature once we access it, and patch it straight through to Zed.*'

'*I know. It's hard being a genius.*'

Julius smiled, then said aloud, 'Annette! Skye and I are going to have a game of chess. Leave us alone for awhile, will you?'

'I think I'll go for a nap,' said Faith.

'Of course. I'll make sure no one bothers you,' said Annette, with a wink.

Julius and Skye pressed their Exoskin buttons once, to activate the suits. Instantly, their bodies were wrapped in energy fields, which transformed into dark, solid armour.

Morgana was standing to the side, looking anxiously at him. Julius wanted to hold her right then, just to soothe her, and put her mind at ease, but he settled instead for a brief smile.

He looked at Faith. '*I want you to seal this port once we're in.*'

'*What if you need to make a hasty retreat?*'

'*You could be needing to do that yourself, and you're now responsible for the lives of 28 Mizkis.*'

Faith considered that for a moment. '*All right, but if you need to, I want you to breach the lower decks. We'll depressurise after you. Clear?*'

'*Clear,*' he replied. Without further word, he tapped Skye on the shoulder, prompting him forward, and through the hole. As they crouched inside the service conduit on the other side, Julius stopped to watch Annette seal the gap shut behind them. She was quickly done, and they were shrouded in darkness. He flipped the safety off on his Gauntlet, waiting as his eyes adjusted. It took a few moments, but eventually a light began to filter through grids into the shaft.

'Which way?' whispered Skye, activating the light on his Gauntlet, and shining it first in one direction, then the other.

'The closest relay station which can give us access to the bridge should be south of here,' answered Julius. 'Let's go.'

Stooping, they cautiously made their way along the conduit, lightly testing the panels ahead of them with their feet, trying to keep to the edges and avoid stepping on the lighter centre areas which might give off telltale noises under their weight. The light from Skye's Gauntlet wasn't particularly strong, but they avoided using anything brighter, for fear of it being spotted through the hairline cracks in the duct; for all they knew, this service conduit could have been passing over the middle of a restroom.

As they went, Julius intermittently paused to check the map on his PIP, whenever they came to a fork in the path. 'We're almost there,' he said. 'about 30 feet.' They carried on, but there was now a sense of unease steadily growing in Julius' mind. It felt as if some important piece of information was trying to get to the forefront of his thoughts but, as much as he tried, he couldn't quite put his finger on it. He was still dwelling on this when they reached the relay panel. Skye moved closer, and pulled out a small, rectangular handheld tool from his pocket.

'What is that?' whispered quietly Julius. He had never seen anything like it before.

'It's an Omni-gizmo,' answered Skye, pushing a lever on its surface, which caused a small blade to pop out. 'Valentina got it from Pete's shop, in Satras.'

He watched as Skye wedged the blade into the side of the relay, and popped the cover off it. There was a circuit board beneath it, with all manner of tiny bright lights blinking away busily. Julius activated his PIP, and selected the file with the schematics that Faith had given him, tilting his screen towards Skye, so they could both examine it. They scanned the various blueprints, comparing them with the board in front of them, but with no joy. Desperately, they checked it again, but still couldn't find one that would match the shuttle's relay.

'Jules, I think you need to contact Faith,' said Skye. 'Morgana told me she would be helping him meditate, so he would hear you better.'

'Let's hope it works,' Julius replied. He took a deep breath. This was going to be another first for him and, as far as he knew, a first for any Mizki. He had certainly never heard of anyone ever successfully communicating telepathically from ship to ship; the vast reaches of space had proven just too big an obstacle to be conquered in that way. However, he knew that his skills had been seriously boosted of late and, if what he had accomplished in the first Pyro lesson was anything to go by, he believed he could truly pull this off.

He focused his mind on Faith, visualising his friend's green eyes staring into his own. He zoomed his mind's eye in on the pupils of Faith's eyes, until the blackness of them was filling his entire vision. Then he began to call to him. It wasn't strong at first, but rather soft, and probing; it was as if Julius was trying to tune a radio, and every time he called his friend, he got a little closer to the right frequency. He didn't try to rush this, knowing that it would take time for Faith to hear him, and do his own tuning-in.

'*... ius,*' a voice whispered at the back of his mind. It was faint, but definitely Faith's.

Julius twitched, a little surprised that he had actually managed it. He reached out for the voice and found it. '*I'm here,*' he said. There was a hint of pain in his head at first, like a pulse, then it was gone.

'*... lius ... Julius,*' repeated Faith.

'*Can you hear me?*' asked Julius.

'*Now I can,*' answered Faith.

'*I need your help with the relay station. I don't know how to access it.*'

'*Describe it to me, or maybe ... Remember three years ago, when we landed on the Moon? You saw through my eyes. Can you make me see through yours?*'

Julius wasn't sure if it was possible, but just then it seemed like the only solution left. '*I'll try, but Faith, you have to focus.*' He took a deep breath and examined the relay station, exploring its angles and lines with his eyes; every one of its lights and patterns, until it was all firmly embedded in his mind.

'*I see it, Julius!*' cried Faith. '*One moment.*'

Julius hoped this would work and, especially, that Faith would be quick about it. The pulsing pain in his head had returned, and this time it was staying put. Still, he didn't dare let his concentration falter.

'*Press the second light from the bottom,*' said Faith.

Julius focused and did what he was told, as Faith continued to issue instructions for the next few minutes while, all the time, the throbbing pain in his head grew relentlessly.

'*The last part now,*' said Faith. '*The amber button: press it. It will send T'Rogon's signature to the Heron.*'

Julius did so, and relaxed; his headache subsided just a touch. '*Done.*'

'*Great. Now get the heck outta there. You've no doubt set off all the alarms in their network.*'

'*On our way,*' said Julius, shaking his head and massaging his temples.

Skye placed the cover over the panel, and turned back the way they had come. Julius put a hand on his shoulder, and stopped him.

'What's wrong?' asked Skye, quietly.

'I'm not coming yet. I need to find Michael.'

Skye stared at him, as if he was set to argue, but stopped himself, obviously realising that he wouldn't have been able to change Julius' mind, no matter how hard he tried. 'Right. Over there,' he said, eventually. 'There's a grid we can use.'

Julius looked along the duct leading off to their left, to where Skye was pointing. According to their map, it led right onto the bridge. They inched forward and, a minute later, Skye stopped. He crouched down, motioning for Julius to do the same. There was a meshed grille under their noses which looked down onto the floor below them.

'I think the coast is clear,' said Skye.

It certainly appeared that way, but that same nagging doubt of earlier had crept back over Julius' mind. Skye was right: there was no one in sight below, but why was that? Faith had seemed certain that, by accessing the relay station, they had blown their cover. So then, where was everybody?

However, there wasn't much choice in the matter, as far as he was concerned—he had to get to his brother.

Gingerly, he lifted the grille and propped it against the side of the conduit to his right. Next, he activated his helmet and tapped the Exoskin button on his chest twice, triggering the cloaking mechanism, making him instantly invisible. Cautiously, he stuck his head through the hole and scanned the room; it was empty. He grabbed the edge of the opening in front of him, rolled head-over-heels through the gap and landed agilely below it. A couple of seconds later, he heard Skye drop down next to him.

He quickly lifted his Gauntlet, and inspected around him, double-checking that they really were alone. '*Scan the shuttle,*' he said to Skye's mind.

'*The bridge is clear,*' said Skye, a few moments later, moving the scanner in his PIP from side to side. '*There are no bio-signs.*'

'*What about holos?*'

'*No electromagnetic interferences, either.*'

'*What's the radius on that scan?*'

'*About 500 feet, I'd s-*'

'It's empty,' interrupted Julius, out loud.

'Shhh!' urged Skye.

'The shuttle is empty,' repeated Julius, not caring. Now he knew why he had felt so odd. Even though they had been careful, and the shuttle was moderately big, there was surely no way the sound of their passage could have gone completely undetected. When Faith had checked with Cress earlier, it had been confirmed that the transport had left Pit-Stop Pete with a full cargo. 'There should be 50 people in here.'

'Well, we should first make sure we definitely are alone,' whispered Skye.

'That won't be necessary!' They jumped as T'Rogon's voice filled the air suddenly.

Julius and Skye spun around quickly, Gauntlets at the ready. Behind the main control panel was a platform, with the holographic image of the Arneshian ambassador staring contemptuously at them.

'Now Mizkis, where are your manners?' said T'Rogon. 'I like to look my enemies in the eyes. Is that too much to ask?'

Julius pressed the Exoskin button on his chest, deactivating his helmet and camouflage. 'Glad you know that we are enemies,' he said, gesturing for Skye to reveal himself. 'Where is everybody? Where's Michael?'

'Why? Were you expecting to find him here?' taunted the ambassador.

'You said he would be. We have a recording of the discussion between you and K'Ssander, and very soon, the whole world will hear it too.'

T'Rogon laughed heartily, as if he had just been told a particularly funny joke. Julius bristled; the throbbing pain in his head had returned and, to make things worse, T'Rogon was now laughing at him.

'What's so funny?' growled Skye.

'I'm sorry,' said T'Rogon, recomposing himself. 'How very rude of me. There is a big difference, you know, between what you heard, and what actually is.'

'Is this some kind of a joke?' said Julius but, by now, he was getting a pretty clear idea of what the ambassador meant. Not only was the shuttle really empty, but Julius was now sure that there had never been any Nuarns, or Arneshians, on it. 'Why lead us to believe there were people onboard? Why the set up?'

'My Queen said this to me: "This White Child has been a thorn in our side twice already, T'Rogon; that is twice too many. Make sure he is out of the way when you do what you are really there to accomplish." And so, you are here. Does that answer your question?'

'You mean, your conversation with K'Ssander ...'

'Was a diversion? Yes. Of course, what we said about the game being fixed is true. The same goes for the Heron's sabotage. But you knew that already, didn't you? Alas, these things won't matter, soon enough. Our mission is almost complete.'

'What mission?' said Julius, fists clenched tightly at his sides.

'I'd rather not say, except that, you should keep an eye on Earth: it will be the show of the century. By the way, did you tell Freja about the mines? Of course you did. Thank you, dear boy. Now even the Grand Master of Tijara is busy elsewhere, on a fool's errand.'

'Fool's errand?' repeated Skye.

'Yes, chasing the imaginary minefield.'

Julius looked at Skye, astonished. Surely this couldn't possibly be true.

'*Tempus fugit*,' said T'Rogon. 'I'll leave you with a piece of good news, and some bad news. The good news is that some friends of yours didn't want to leave without saying goodbye: K'Ssander, A'Trid, B'Nold, step out if you please.'

From a darkened corner of the bridge, the three Arneshians walked forward.

'But the scanner; it didn't-' began Skye.

'Earth technology really isn't that great, you know,' said K'Ssander, with a smirk.

'I'm dying to hear the bad news,' said Julius drily.

'Oh, you will. This shuttle will self-destruct in ten minutes, starting now. Goodbye,' said T'Rogon, before his hologram vanished.

'*I have to warn Faith*,' Julius mind-messaged to Skye.

'*I'll keep them busy. Do it now!*' he replied.

Julius touched his Exoskin twice, selecting the full helmet and camouflage. There were two exits, one to each side of him; he sprinted for the one on the left, and leapt between A'Trid and B'Nold. To make sure that they would follow him, he stretched out his Gauntlet behind him and shot out a single, small fireball.

'Damn it!' Julius heard A'Trid cry out behind him, and hoped that he had slowed him down.

Julius ran through the exit and veered right, trying desperately to clear his mind of all T'Rogon's words. He was feeling far too much anger, and he needed to get rid of it if he hoped to use his skills properly. He focused on Faith and began to mentally reach out to him. '*Faith! Can you hear me?*' he cried. In his mind, he saw his words smashing against rocks. '*Faith!*' he tried again, more urgent this time. Again, nothing.

Suddenly, he saw a shadow advancing on him; he skidded to a stop and hurtled down a corridor leading off to his left, shooting a fireball behind him. Reaching the end of the corridor, he realised that it was a dead end, and started to turn back, but stopped as he saw A'Trid closing in on him. If he shot a fireball now, in such close quarters, he could seriously wound the Arneshian, so instead, he activated his shields and created a barrier between them.

'That's not fair,' shouted A'Trid in frustration, as he struck the shields with a flurry of powerful kicks and punches.

Julius ignored him, breathed deeply, and called out again with his mind to Faith.

'*You almost blew me head off!*' said Faith.

'*Get the Heron clear. Now! ... tell Freja ... minefield is ... ake!*'

'*Is what? I can't understand! I'll come and get you.*'

'*NO! Get them out!*' shouted Julius. His head flared with searing pain. He lost his focus, and the channel with Faith. At that moment, he knew that he had also lost his last chance of getting away: if he couldn't find an escape pod, he and Skye would both surely die on the shuttle.

A'Trid abruptly stopped his physical attack, opened his right hand and pointed it at Julius' shield; the symbol of

Arnesh lit up in the middle of his palm, making the skin look almost transparent. He waved his hand and a stream of electricity surged outwards, striking the magnetic field in front of Julius.

Julius felt the shields quivering, as if the combination of the two energies had created something quite unstable. He knew he couldn't remain like that much longer, so he mustered as much strength as he could manage and shoved forward with his mind. It was too much for A'Trid to resist; he flew backwards, and smashed against the far wall, before landing on the floor unconscious.

Julius closed his shields, and rushed back to the bridge, trying to ignore the bright pain filling his head. When he got there, he saw B'Nold holding Skye by his arms, with K'Ssander standing in front of him, his right palm pointed menacingly. Julius caught a glimpse of the disk embedded in K'Ssander's hand. The Arneshian raised the disk to Skye's head, who began to twitch, as if a current of electricity was suddenly passing through him. Skye's cries of agony drove Julius into action. He stretched his right hand forward and mind-pushed K'Ssander away, then rushed at the Arneshian, springing onto him and dragging him to the floor.

That gave Skye the chance he needed. He wriggled free of B'Nold, spun around, and pushed him backwards with several short, powerful bursts of energy. The Arneshian jerked wildly, as Skye advanced forward, pummelling him out of the room and knocking him out cold. Julius, meanwhile, was feeling completely drained, and was struggling in vain to hold onto K'Ssander. The Arneshian broke away from his grip, and rushed at Skye.

'Watch it!' shouted Julius.

Skye heard the shout too late; as he stepped back inside the room, a strong arm wrapped itself around his neck.

'Let him go!' cried Julius. Slowly, he lifted his Gauntlet, and aimed it at the Arneshian's head.

Skye was tearing at K'Ssander's arm, trying desperately to prise it away from his windpipe.

'What do you care if he dies, McCoy?' he replied coldly. 'I thought you were here to save your little brother. Shame you won't get to see him one last time because, once they start the experiments on him, he'll never be the same ever again. Then he'll really be like us.'

'Leave Michael out of this,' warned Julius, through gritted teeth.

K'Ssander tightened his grip and moved his head behind Skye. He lifted his right hand and placed it against Skye's head; the disk in his palm glowing to show that it was active.

Julius could see that Skye was in agony, while his face was turning purple. He wasn't sure how much more his friend could take, but he was certain he wouldn't last much longer. Julius felt anger surging through his veins, and made no effort to restrain it this time; it was washing away the pain in his head and lending him some much-needed strength. As happened so often when he was that furious, the energy was dripping from his hands now, circling his arms like golden wisps.

'The ship is about to explode,' said Julius, steadying himself. 'We can finish this elsewhere.'

'I'm not afraid to die, McCoy. That's the difference between you and me.'

Julius saw Skye's eyes roll upwards and knew there was no time left. He didn't think twice about what to do next. 'So be it then,' he said, opening his left hand and beginning to draw from the Arneshian.

K'Ssander, who was clearly expecting a direct attack of some sort, was taken completely by surprise. Not knowing what was happening to him, his eyes grew large, like he had just realised something very important. His mouth fell open, but still he wouldn't let go of Skye. His skin, which was already greyish in colour, turned a good shade darker as he gasped for air.

Skye was still clawing at the Arneshian's arm, but weakly now; he didn't have much fight left in him.

'Let him go!' cried Julius again.

Whether or not K'Ssander could actually hear him was hard to tell, but he continued gripping Skye tightly. It was as if time itself had frozen in that one horrible moment: Skye's hands fell down by his sides and his head slumped forward. K'Ssander wheezed one last intake of air, before finally letting go, and crumpling onto the floor.

As that happened, a hand grabbed Julius' wrist from the side, immediately stopping the Draw. 'Enough,' a familiar voice said, gently.

Julius turned, wide-eyed, and saw Kelly standing next to him. A spark of hope lit up his heart, and he realised that he wasn't going to die on that shuttle after all.

'Skye!' he said, launching himself forward. But an officer appeared from behind him, grabbed him by the shoulders, and started to walk him away from the bridge. Julius, however, refused to leave without knowing whether Skye was alive or not, so he turned and held his ground, as Kelly knelt beside his friend.

'Is he all right?' asked Julius, his voice wavering.

Kelly scanned the boy quickly with a portable medical scanner. Then he placed a strange mask over his face. 'He's ok.'

Julius exhaled in relief. Then his eyes grew wide. 'T'Rogon rigged the shuttle to blow; we'd better get out of here!'

'Well, come on then; let's go!' said Kelly, scooping Skye up and running toward the exit. Three more officers quickly followed, each carrying one of the Arneshian boys.

'How did you know we were here?' asked Julius, as they ran.

'Freja told me to keep an eye on you,' he replied. 'And I figured, if you want to take my place some day, I better keep you alive.'

Julius looked at K'Ssander, who was dangling limply in the arms of one of Kelly's men, his skin still abnormally dark. A shiver ran through Julius; certainly, he had meant to severely hurt the Arneshian, and he would have finished him off to save Skye, but what would Freja think of him when he found out that he had used his Draw powers against a human being? All those lessons about being responsible with his skills had been flung out the window in a matter of seconds. Most of all, just then, Professor Chan's words echoed in his mind, like ghosts in a haunted house: "That, Mr K'Ssander, is the difference between our people and yours." Julius felt he had surely just proven that they were no different, or better than the Arneshians. The only thing he could be sure of right at that moment though, was that, when he had been given a choice between Skye's life or K'Ssander's, his heart had made the decision for him.

'Move it everybody!' urged Kelly. 'This joint is about to blow!'

They rushed toward the shuttle port, and through it into the Ahura Mazda, which was attached like a limpet. An officer sealed the port shut behind them, and the ship pulled away from the shuttle.

'Hold on, kid!' shouted Kelly to Julius.

Julius grabbed hold of the nearest railing, just in time. The blast of the shuttle explosion shoved the Ahura forward, like a stone from a slingshot. Julius turned to Kelly. 'Captain, we have to warn Freja!'

'He knows about the mines, Julius. Don't worry, the whole of Zed is mobilised, looking for them.'

'It's a trick, a decoy!'

'What do you mean?'

'T'Rogon told us that it was all a diversion, to get us out of the way. There's never been a minefield.'

Kelly stared at Julius, weighing the situation. 'Stay here.'

Julius nodded, and went over to Skye. The doctor was wrapping a Heal-O Collar around his neck, but not before Julius caught sight of the large dark bruises beginning to appear on his skin. 'He could have killed him,' he thought. Julius stood up, looking for the Arneshians, but couldn't see them anywhere. It was probably for the best though, given that he had almost regained his full strength now, thanks to the Draw he had done, and he was still feeling pretty angry.

'McCoy,' called Kelly. 'Come over to the bridge.'

Julius sprinted up the steps and joined the captain.

'The Grand Master is onscreen. Tell him what you know.'

Julius bowed quickly to Freja, trying not to think about the fact that he hadn't really been given permission to board the shuttle like he had. 'Sir, T'Rogon tricked us. The shuttle was empty and he said that there was never a minefield; it was just a way of keeping us busy. He said to keep our eyes on Earth, because the real show would be there.'

Freja stared back at Julius thoughtfully, then switched his gaze to Kelly. 'I want the Taurus One o-'

Before he could finish, the Ahura Mazda began to tremble like a frightened animal. Julius saw Freja grab hold of the arm of his chair, inside his own ship.

'What's happening?' said Julius.

'Lieutenant, report!' ordered Kelly.

Elian Flywheel, from the pilot's seat near the front of the ship, was trying unsuccessfully to steer the Ahura Mazda on a straight course. 'We're stuck, Captain. I can't move her an inch.'

'It's the Arneshians,' said Julius. 'They did the same thing to the Heron.'

'It looks like the entire Zed fleet is immobilised,' said Elian.

Suddenly, all the lights in the ship flickered and went out, leaving them in darkness.

'Sir, whatever's keeping us still seems to have drained all the power out of our ship,' said an officer to Kelly's right.

The trembling slowly subsided, allowing Julius to stand without having to hold onto something. The only light filtering in was from beyond the front window of the ship where, in the distance, the near side of the Earth was bathed in sunlight.

'S-sir,' said Elian, almost in a whisper. 'You've got to see this.'

Julius followed as Kelly moved over beside her. What he saw, out in space beyond the Ahura, froze him to the spot. He gripped the left arm of Elian's seat, a clawing sense of dread spreading over him.

Silent and lethal, the Taurus One had left its moorings, and was moving through space like a jellyfish through water. Every ship in its path was being pushed gently aside, as if carried by the crest of a small wave. For the previous few months, it had maintained its spherical shape, making Starfleet quite forget about its ability to morph. Now, as it glided past the Moon toward Earth, it began to seamlessly transform and stretch, until it had become a vast, flat disk, its surface so great that it obscured the sun. Not one of the Zed ships was intervening, trapped by the invisible energy field that was holding them all at bay.

The Arneshian disk continued on its relentless course, until it was directly above Earth, where it stopped, and hovered like a giant hat, blocking the planet from the rays of the sun. Oceans, mountains, plains and deserts had all turned a sickly grey hue, swathed in the shadow of the disk; they seemed to have lost their vitality and life. The disk sat there, silent and ominous for a moment, then began to morph again. Like a silk scarf covering a ball, it melted over the surface of the Earth, until it had completely enveloped it, creating a perfect, gigantic cocoon.

Julius' knees gave in and he slumped to the ground. Thinking of his parents, witnessing all this from within it, was too much to handle, and his brain shut down.

The Taurus One began to glow, dimly at first, then brighter, until it was so fierce that the bridge of the Ahura Mazda was flooded in light, forcing everyone onboard to shield their eyes behind their arms. Then, just as it seemed it couldn't get any brighter, the light dimmed again. The cocoon gently opened, and began to rise up, until Earth was freed once more from its grasp. The Taurus floated there for a brief moment, and then continued to rise, up and up into space. Its task completed, it entered into warp and, in a flash, it was gone.

The lights on the bridge flickered back to life a second later, and the crew stood blinking at each other in stunned silence.

'The power is back online, Captain,' said Elian, snapping out of it.

'Take us closer to Earth, Lieutenant. Run a scan,' ordered Kelly.

The Ahura Mazda moved within range, and Kelly strode over to his tactical officer. 'Report. Have they hurt our people?'

'Sir,' gulped the officer, turning white. 'There are no people. Sir ... all the humans are gone!'

CHAPTER 14

NO MAN'S LAND

Julius' footsteps echoed in the abandoned street. The sky was clear, the kind of blue he hadn't seen in three whole years. There were no clouds to be seen, and no gulls or birds of any sort. Edinburgh Castle was sitting proudly atop its rock, unconcerned by the lack of tourists and the eerie absence of the one o'clock gun, a memory of centuries past.

The air here seemed fresher to Julius than on Zed; the smell of the trees, the grass and the sea mingled together, filling his lungs. He could see his house halfway down the lane, his dad's Bumble Bee fly-car parked out front, its little wings reflecting the July sun. Julius stopped beside it and looked at the garden. The weeds had grown significantly in the last three months, suffocating some of the flowers that Jenny McCoy loved to grow along the edges of the stone path. If he had had more time, he could have cut the weeds back a little, but then, what was the point really? He stepped forward, toward the front door, looked into the retina scanner to its left, and pressed the entry button.

The buzzing noise of the door opening startled Julius. It almost seemed inappropriate in that silence, like talking loudly at someone's wake. He stepped inside and was immediately hit by the smell of rotten food and stale air. He stopped breathing through his nose and said, 'Computer, activate ventilation system.'

A jet of fresh air streamed into the living room, confirming that at least the house computer was still working. A thick layer of dust had settled over all the furniture and pictures, giving the place a horribly abandoned feeling. In the absence of its normal occupants, it appeared that a family of little spiders had moved in, and Julius had to duck to avoid a clutch of cobwebs as he climbed the stairs.

He pushed his bedroom door open and walked in. It had been a long time since he had last seen it, but everything was just the way he had left it. Sunlight streamed in through the window, illuminating his bed. He noticed something sticking out from under his pillow, and he grabbed it; it was a sealed envelope, labeled, "To Julius. M."

Julius stood there for a moment, staring at the familiar handwriting. Michael could have chosen to send him a message over the net, but hadn't. Instead, he had chosen something a lot more personal, which was why this, more than anything, was hurting him the most. He pocketed the envelope without opening it, knowing that he couldn't really cope with it just then.

Before going back downstairs, he checked the other bedrooms. His brother's bed was made, which didn't surprise him, and so too was his parents' bed. He wondered how much sleep they had managed since Michael's departure, and gently closed their door.

When he arrived in the kitchen and saw the dining table, his heart skipped a beat. At the moment in which the Taurus One had closed over Earth, Jenny and Rory must have been sitting down for breakfast. The table was set for two; a couple of slices of old mouldy toast were on a separate plate in the middle of it, and there were dead flies in the marmalade jar, which had been left open. There was also a spoon on the floor beside one of the chairs, with bits of what looked like dried food stuck to it. It was as if his dad—because Julius knew that that was his seat—was moving the spoon towards his mouth when it had happened.

Julius activated his PIP and selected the bio-particle detector. All of the Mizkis had been given one before they left Zed to come down here, so they could scan their homes for human traces. He passed the chip in his hand over the chairs, table and floor, without noticing anything out of the ordinary. When he finally sent the readings back to Tijara, he let out a sigh of relief; the Arneshians had not vapourised them.

'Julius? Are you in here?' called Morgana from the front door.

He gave a last look around before leaving the kitchen. Morgana was standing by the door, looking tired. Julius saw that her eyes were red from crying, and guessed that the emotion of seeing her empty house must have proved too much.

'How did they do it?' she asked.

Julius shook his head. He had been wondering the same thing. 'I take it you didn't find any traces either.'

'None, thankfully. Let's walk back, please. I don't want to stay here a minute longer.'

Julius stepped outside and locked the door, knowing that the house computer would also shut down. 'Kaori?'

'She's gone to check her roommate's place, near Tollcross. She'll make her own way back.'

They walked in silence, side by side. Julius was so overwhelmed by the emptiness that he didn't even flinch when Morgana hooked her arm in his. Right then, the gesture felt like the most normal thing in the world. He unhooked his arm and placed it over her shoulders—it felt good when she leaned her head against his shoulder, and wrapped an arm around his waist.

'It's too late,' she said. 'Now that the truth is out, it's too late.'

Julius knew she was right. The recording of T'Rogon had been broadcast to all the Earth, and Zed, colonies, and Mr List had been able to prove that the game had been compromised. But the people who really needed to hear this, people like Paulo Trent and his brother, weren't around anymore. So it didn't matter.

'What's Freja going to do?' she asked.

'They'll shield the planet at the end of June. It'll give it a chance to take a break ... from us, I guess. They think that by the time we return, it will have renewed the land.'

'Can we really get them back?'

Julius could hear a hint of tears in her voice, and held her tighter. 'We'll get them *all* back.'

'How are we going to do that, Julius?'

'We're going after them.'

Morgana stopped, looked up at him and, after a few seconds, nodded once, her gaze sure and confident.

They began to walk again, heading towards the shuttle. Julius had no idea how they were going to accomplish the rescue, but he felt sure that Freja would find a way.

Still, for now, the Arneshians had won.

About the Author

Francesca Tristan Barbini was born and raised in Rome, Italy, in 1976. After years of volunteer work around the world, she completed a MA Honour in Religious Studies at New College, Edinburgh, focusing on the Ancient Near East and the Dead Sea Scrolls.

Her free time is divided between family, painting RPG miniatures and writing books for children and adults. An active member of the Tolkien Society, she also runs a kinship on Lord of the Rings Online. Barbini is currently working on the fourth instalment of her Tijaran Tales series.

For more information please see **www.ftbarbini.com**.

THE ADVENTURE CONTINUES...

BOOK 1

WHITE CHILD: When 12 year old Julius McCoy is told that he has been selected to join the elite Zed Lunar Academy, he is over the moon...literally. It promises to be a year of neck-breaking races in The Hologram Palace, spaceship-pilot training and of course, developing his own very special mind-skills.

Yet even as he begins to get a grip on his fantastic abilities, strange things start to happen around him. Who are the three mysterious men hanging about in Satras, the moon capital - particularly their sinister leader in the red cap, who seems to know a lot more than he should about Julius?

And what of the growing threat of the evil Queen Salgoria, head of the technologically-gifted Arneshian outcasts, who are making ominous advances again? It's all a lot more than a young boy should be expected to deal with. Yet, little does Julius realise exactly how critical he will be to the fate of Zed, and ultimately, Earth itself.

BOOK 2

TIJARAN TALES

The Oracle of Life

F T Barbini

THE ORACLE OF LIFE: 13 year old Julius McCoy is about to start his second year at Tijara Academy, in the Zed Lunar Perimeter. With the threat of the Arneshians averted for the moment, he can get on with the important part of his school life: developing his rare mind-skills.

Of course, what any student on Zed looks forward to most, is gaming in the Hologram Palace. But who is the mysterious lady hidden in one of the games? This encounter will set in motion an exciting and dangerous treasure hunt, that will give him a whole new perspective on the real history of Zed, and ultimately beyond, to a shocking truth that could jeopardise the safety of everyone he holds dear.

When an old enemy returns, it becomes clear that the Arneshians are back with a new plan for taking over Zed and seizing control of Earth. As the pieces of the puzzle fall into place, and he is drawn towards a climactic showdown, it will take all of Julius' mind-skills as he is forced into a deadly final duel.

BOOK 4

TIJARA'S HEART: Defeated by the technological superiority of the Arneshians, the Zed Academy is left to deal with a desolate planet Earth. In spite of their fears, they must abandon the safety of the Lunar Perimeter and venture out into the farthest reaches of space, in the biggest rescue mission ever attempted by mankind.

Julius McCoy is desperate to find his own family and bring them back home, but the Curia, it seems, has other plans for him. If he refuses, he risks jeopardising Zed's one great hope of peace, and a possible victory over the Arneshians. But, if he accepts, he will lose everything he has, and become Tijara's ultimate sacrifice.

High space adventure abounds in this fourth instalment of FT Barbini's Tijaran Tales series.

COMING SOON!